Isaac Asimov's
Halloween

Edited by

Gardner Dozois

AND

Sheila Williams

ACE BOOKS, NEW YORK

This is a work of fiction. Names, characters, places, and incidents
either are the product of the author's imagination or are used
fictitiously, and any resemblance to actual persons, living or dead,
business establishments, events, or locales is entirely coincidental.

ISAAC ASIMOV'S HALLOWEEN

An Ace Book / published by arrangement with
Dell Magazines

PRINTING HISTORY
Ace mass-market edition / September 2001

All rights reserved.
Copyright © 2001 by Dell Magazines, Inc.
Cover art by Walter Velez.
Copyright information for individual stories
can be found on page 249.

This book, or parts thereof, may not be reproduced
in any form without permission.
For information address: The Berkley Publishing Group,
a division of Penguin Putnam Inc.,
375 Hudson Street, New York, New York 10014.

Visit our website at
www.penguinputnam.com

Check out the ACE Science Fiction & Fantasy newsletter
and much more on the Internet at Club PPI!

ISBN: 0-441-00854-2

ACE®
Ace Books are published by The Berkley Publishing Group,
a division of Penguin Putnam Inc.,
375 Hudson Street, New York, New York 10014.
ACE and the "A" design
are trademarks belonging to Penguin Putnam Inc.

PRINTED IN THE UNITED STATES OF AMERICA

10 9 8 7 6 5 4 3 2 1

"Aw, now, *Ma*—!" The same voice which earlier had declared my waking state now sounded again in my ear. The thin mattress beside me sagged as a second being, marginally nearer the human form than Ma, plopped himself down beside me on the bed. "Don't you mind her none. She always gets kinda brassy to guests when it's our turn to host the sabbat prayer meet."

"*Brassy*, am I?" Ma's tone hit somewhere between a first alto and a blender full of cockatiels. She boxed her offspring's ear smartly and snapped, "That's how I learned you manners? You keep a civil tongue in your head, boy, or I swear I'll—!"

"Shoot, Ma, where else *would* I keep it?" he replied, and with that an unimaginable stretch of flabby blue-black flesh shot out of his mouth and flew the length of the trailer, returning with terrible alacrity and a copy of *TV Guide* stuck to the tip. "Thee?" he concluded as he wrestled with the tongue-tying periodical . . .

—From Esther M. Friesner's
"The Shunned Trailer"

Also available . . .
Isaac Asimov's Father's Day

Featuring stories by
HARRY TURTLEDOVE, PAMELA SARGENT, JONATHAN LETHEM,
and others

CONTENTS

WORDS AND MUSIC

William Sanders

"Words and Music" appeared in the July 1997 issue of Asimov's, *one of only a handful of sales William Sanders has made here, each one acclaimed and memorable. Here he offers us an evocative, colorful, and downright frightening look at what can happen when the words and music are wrong . . .*

William Sanders lives in Tahlequah, Oklahoma. A former pow-wow dancer and sometime Cherokee gospel singer, he appeared on the SF scene back around the turn of the last decade with a couple of alternate-history comedies, Journey to Fusang *(a finalist for the John W. Campbell Award) and* The Wild Blue and Gray. *Sanders then turned to mystery and suspense, producing a number of critically acclaimed titles. He credits his old friend Roger Zelazny with persuading him to return to SF, this time via the short story form, and has made sales to* Asimov's Science Fiction, The Magazine of Fantasy and Science Fiction, Tales of the Great Turtle, Alternate Generals, Wheel of Fortune, *and* Lord of the Fantastic; *one of his stories, the acclaimed "The Undiscovered," was on the final Nebula and Hugo ballots a couple of years back. His most recent books are a reissue of* Journey to Fusang, *and a new novel,* The Ballad of Billy Badass and the Rose of Turkestan; *both books can be ordered through the author's website,* www.sff.net/people/sanders/bbrt.htm, *or through Xlibris Press.*

Jimmy Hominy was fifty-four years old and had been a *didahnvwisgi*—what the whites called a shaman or medicine man; a lot of Cherokees said *adanisgi*, wizard, and some said plainly *'sgili*, witch, though not to his face—for most of his adult life. He had also done a hitch in Nam, played guitar for Buck Owens on two national tours, and been married to a Kiowa woman, so all in all he figured he'd been around and not much could surprise him. But when the preacher from Limestone showed up at Jimmy's trailer out on Stick Ross Mountain Road and said his church house was being witched, Jimmy's chin dropped so far it nearly hit his chest.

"Doyu?" he said, rubbing a big callused hand over a face the color and texture of an old saddle. "Somebody's witching a church?"

"So they say," the preacher said. "You hadn't heard?"

"Hey," Jimmy Hominy said. "I stay clear of that end of the county. You go listening to those Indians down around Limestone, you're liable to hear anything."

He grinned at the preacher. "But then that's your job, right? Got to love all God's children. Even the ones he probably wishes he'd drowned, like the Sparrowhawk brothers. Better you than me, *chooch.*"

The preacher didn't return the grin. He was a bony-faced man somewhere in his forties, with a big nose and dark brown eyes. His thin straight black hair was combed forward in a failed effort to hide a hairline in full retreat, the inheritance of a white grandfather. He had on a really bad black suit.

His name was Eli Blackbird, but Jimmy Hominy usually thought of him simply as the preacher, because he was the only preacher Jimmy knew personally. Oh, every now and then some local Bible wrangler would come calling with the missionary light in his eyes—it would be a big coup to talk a notorious character like Jimmy Hominy into taking the Jesus road—but they didn't stay long enough to get acquainted.

But this one never got on Jimmy's case about following the old ways, or accused him of worshipping the Devil, and Jimmy had finally decided he was all right. Now here he was sitting at Jimmy's kitchen table with a story about the Sparrowhawk boys witching his church, and Jimmy didn't know *what* to think.

The preacher let out a long sigh and began fumbling in the pockets of his suit jacket. "I admit the Sparrowhawks aren't easy to love—"

He pulled out a black briar pipe and a plastic pouch and began cramming tobacco into the bowl, spilling a little blizzard of Prince Albert flakes in the process. Jimmy didn't say anything about it. The place was already in a mess anyway. Had been for a couple of years, ever since his wife had died.

Jimmy said, "Yeah, Luther and Bobby Sparrowhawk been nothing but bullies and sneak thieves since they were kids. And yet their mama was a real fine lady."

The preacher nodded. "Oh, yes. Old Annie Sparrowhawk." He was fishing around in his pockets again. Jimmy pushed a box of wooden matches across the table. "Thanks . . . as a matter of fact, that's where the trouble began. Annie left that property to the church when she died, and her sons have been trying to get it back ever since."

He struck a match and applied it to his pipe. "Which," he said, puffing, "they can't do. Annie paid a lawyer to draw up a will, legal and airtight."

"What do they want with it? That rocky old land around Limestone's not worth anything. So damn poor the whites never even bothered to steal it."

"It is now," the preacher told him through a cloud of bluish smoke. "Word is some developer from Tulsa has plans for the area."

Jimmy thought about it. While he thought he held out his hand. "Uh, you think you could spare—"

The preacher handed over the tobacco pouch. Jimmy got his own pipe from his shirt pocket and loaded it and lit up. The preacher didn't notice that Jimmy didn't bother to use a match. Or if he did notice he pretended not to.

"Surprised they don't just burn you out," Jimmy said at last.

"They've made threats. But they're both on probation for assault as it is. Any rough stuff, they go to the pen. The sheriff already warned them."

"So now they're trying to witch you out. Wonder who they got to do it."

The preacher looked disappointed. He must have been hoping Jimmy would know who was doing the witching, or could find out. Probably thought people like Jimmy stayed in touch some way, like those white kids Jimmy's grandson was always talking with on his computer.

Jimmy said, "Could be they're trying to do it themselves. That's crazy, but then *they're* crazy."

"It's possible," the preacher agreed. "They do have a reputation for dabbling in, uh, the occult. And yet they both got religion last year. Bobby married a white girl from one of those holy-roller churches and now he and Luther are in there at every revival, shouting and speaking in tongues, even handling snakes."

"The snakes got my sympathy," Jimmy said sincerely.

He knew what the preacher was getting at. The boondock holiness outfits were even stricter than other Indian churches when it came to "heathen" ways; some would kick you out just for going to stomp dances, let alone anything heavy.

But there was nothing so unusual about Cherokees trying to work both sides of that particular street. Almost all the people who came to Jimmy seeking cures for illness or protection against witchcraft or interpretations of dreams—he didn't do love charms—were solid members of Bible churches that officially condemned such things as the Devil's work. It was just something people didn't talk about.

Jimmy said, "I didn't think you preachers believed in these superstitions."

This time the preacher did grin. "That's the white half of me. The Indian half—" He spread his hands. "It doesn't really matter what I think. If the people believe the place is being witched, they'll stay away. You know that. Last Sunday we had half the usual turnout."

"So you thought if they heard you were bringing in your own *didahnvwisgi*—" Jimmy had to laugh. "Boy," he said, "now I've heard everything. The church asking a medicine man for help."

If the preacher minded being redassed he didn't let it show. He said, "Actually, I came to invite you to an all-night gospel singing. We're having one this Friday night."

Jimmy quit laughing. The preacher had hit one of his weak spots. He might be a long way outside the church, but he dearly loved Cherokee gospel music. Both his parents had been noted singers on the Oklahoma gospel scene; his older brother Clyde had sung with them, before running off to become a honky-tonk musician. Some of Jimmy's earliest memories were of all-night singings, and of falling asleep in the back of the family pickup to the sound of gospel music coming through the trees.

He said, "Real old-fashioned Indian gospel? Not that fancy new crap, sounds like they're planning to go to Heaven in an elevator?"

The preacher nodded. "Should be a lot of good singers there."

"I thought you said people were staying away."

"They won't if they know you're going to be there."

Jimmy didn't know what to say to that.

"And," the preacher added, "the women are baking pies."

Jimmy groaned softly. Pie was his other weakness. "You got me," he said. "What time do you want me there?"

The preacher stood up. "Come by the house about seven." He was obviously trying hard not to look too pleased with himself. "We may as well go together."

"*Howa,*" Jimmy agreed, getting up too. "You can tell them I'll be there."

Friday evening at almost exactly seven Jimmy Hominy stopped his old Mercury in front of Eli Blackbird's house near the tiny crossroads community of Limestone. The preacher came to the door as Jimmy stepped up on the porch. " *'Siyo, Jimi.*"

" *'Siyo, chooch.*" Jimmy nodded in the direction of the Mercury. "Let's take my car." He didn't want to ride in the preacher's little Japanese car, which was cramped and uncomfortable for a man his size and had screwy door latches besides.

"Sure." The preacher followed Jimmy out to the road and bent to open the Mercury's door. The dome light came on and he stopped, staring at the oversized guitar case lying in the back seat. "Bringing that thing?" he said. "Going to play, are you?"

"Could be," Jimmy said, going around to his side. "You never know."

The church was a small, low concrete-block building with no steeple or other identifying features except a four-by-eight plywood sign that read LIMESTONE INDEPENDENT INDIAN CHURCH. The words were repeated underneath in the curling black letters of the Cherokee alphabet.

Right now the building was dark except for a single bulb burning above the front door. The big grassy clearing beside the church, however, was lit by several floodlights rigged on poles or in the trees. A flatbed truck had been parked at the edge of the woods to serve as a stage, and two men were crouched on its bed doing something to a set of amplifiers, while a tall kid in a Seminole jacket fooled with the tuning knobs of an electric bass. Teenage boys were setting out rows of folding chairs. Other people stood or moved about the area, mostly near the long wooden tables where women served food on paper plates.

"I thought we'd have the singing outdoors," the preacher remarked as they got out of the Mercury. The dusty parking area was already half full of pickup trucks and heavy old cars. "Looks like a nice night for it."

It did. The sky was clear and full of fat white stars; a light warm breeze was coming through the woods, bringing various pleasant smells. It also carried the scent of blackberry pie from the tables. Jimmy's nose began to twitch.

"Well," the preacher said, "I better get up there." He gestured in the direction of the flatbed truck, where one of the men was now adjusting a floor-stand microphone. A brief horrible squeal came from the speakers. "Almost time."

When the preacher was gone Jimmy stood still for a moment, getting the feel of the scene. So far he couldn't detect anything wrong; at least the hair on his arms wasn't standing up, or his fingers tingling, or any of the other warning signs. If this place had been witched, it had been done very badly.

Or else, of course, it had been done very well.

He began to walk, staying in the shadows and avoiding people, making himself ignore the pie smell. As he neared the darkened church he started to pick up a certain vague sourness, like a single out-of-tune string. More curious than worried—whatever it was, it didn't feel dangerous—he moved closer.

He found it easily, under the front steps of the church: a little buckskin bundle, tied with rawhide. Dry things crunched and crackled as he rolled it in his hand. He didn't untie it; he knew pretty much what it contained. He walked back to his car and tossed the little bundle onto the front seat. Later, maybe, he would tie the bundle to a rock and drop it into a moving stream, and then whoever had made it would come down with severe chills for a week or so.

If this was the worst the Sparrowhawks could do, the

preacher was worrying about nothing. Still, he was here now and he might as well do the job right.

He dug in his pockets and got out his short-stemmed pipe and the little bag of prepared tobacco, while up on the improvised stage Eli Blackbird commenced speaking into the microphone, welcoming the people who were now starting to drift over and take seats. The men behind him quit messing with the amps and began opening cases and getting out guitars.

Jimmy packed the tobacco carefully into the pipe, making sure not to spill a single flake. He did not sing or speak over the tobacco; there was no need. He had doctored the tobacco that morning, down by the banks of the little creek that ran behind his place, holding it up to the rising sun and stirring it with his forefinger, singing the appropriate *igawesdi* words, four times over. Now the tobacco was programmed, needing only to be burned to release its power.

He lit the tobacco and began walking, puffing. The preacher was now leading the crowd in "Amazing Grace":

> *"U-ne-hla-nv-hi U-we-ji*
> *I-ga-gu-yv-he-i—"*

Blowing smoke, Jimmy Hominy circled the church grounds counterclockwise, taking in the building and the singing area and even the two outhouses. The preacher began a prayer in Cherokee: *"Agidoda, galvladi ehi, ga-lvquodiyu gesesdi dejado'a'i—"* He was still at it when Jimmy started around for the second time.

He circled the grounds four times, following carefully in his own tracks. He was aware of people looking at him—mostly sideways or behind his back—but nobody spoke to him, and the few people in his path suddenly found reasons to go stand somewhere else when they saw him coming.

At the end he knocked the ash out of the pipe and stood

leaning on the Mercury's fender, listening to the music. The first group of the evening, the Gospel Travelers from Adair County, were hammering down hard on "I Will Not Live Always":

> *"U-tli-na-qua-du-li-hv ga-lv-la-di jo-sv-i,*
> *Ga-lo-ne-dv Ji-sa, u-wo-du-hi-yu,*
> *Da-ni-no-gi-sdi-sgv-i."*

—with skinny little Grover Fourkiller singing bass like a son of a bitch and Louise Soap hitting the highs clean as an Arkansas mockingbird.

Jimmy decided it was time to check out that blackberry pie.

It had been a good season for blackberries and two different women had just set out fresh pies as Jimmy came up to the table. Naturally he had to have a piece of each, so as not to hurt anybody's feelings. He was finishing the second piece when a voice behind him said, " *'Siyo, Jimi. Jiyosihas'?"*

Jimmy jumped and turned around. Idabel Grasshopper stood there, holding a big steaming pot. She said, "Want to try some of my chili, big boy?"

Jimmy had never considered that Idabel Grasshopper might show up. A lifelong member of Hogshooter Indian Baptist Church, she was a long way from home. But maybe she'd heard he was coming. Damn that preacher.

He said, "I think maybe your chili's too hot for me."

Idabel Grasshopper giggled and Jimmy made a note to kick himself in the ass, next time he felt limber enough, for encouraging her. As far back as he could remember, her two big goals in life had been to get Jimmy Hominy into the church and into her bed—preferably, but not necessarily, in that order. Change of life hadn't helped; in the last few years she'd just gotten holier and hornier. She'd also picked up about forty pounds and a Don Ameche mustache.

"And here you are at a gospel singing," she said. "Praise the Lord!"

"I just came to listen to the music," Jimmy mumbled. *Damn* that preacher.

"The music," she said severely, "doesn't mean a thing without the spirit. Now in Philippians two-ten it says—"

But Jimmy was no longer even pretending to listen. Over the top of her Brillo-pad perm, he had spotted the Sparrowhawk brothers coming across the parking area.

He hadn't seen either of them in years but they hadn't improved any in the ugly department. Luther, the older brother, seemed to have a few more facial scars, but otherwise there wasn't much difference between them; just a couple of lumpy, overgrown Indians, nearly as big as Jimmy, with hooky noses and eyes set way too close together.

All of a sudden, right at the edge of the grass, they stopped so hard they practically bounced.

Jimmy Hominy watched, ignoring Idabel, as they looked at each other and then tried again to cross the medicine line he had laid down. It was like watching a pair of big stupid birds flying into a plate-glass window.

Finally, looking pissed off, they turned and stomped back across the parking lot and got into a big pickup truck. A minute later they blasted out of the church grounds, throwing gravel. The crash of bad gear changes drifted back on the breeze as their lights disappeared up the road.

The preacher was standing over by the edge of the trees, smoking his pipe. "Did you see that?" he said as Jimmy came up. "Whatever you did, thanks—"

"Never mind that," Jimmy told him. "I'm going to kill you. That hooting sound you hear is the owl calling your name."

The preacher laughed softly. "Idabel's still after you?"

" 'Big boy,' " Jimmy said, shuddering. "Nobody's called me that since Saigon."

Up on stage the Kingfisher Family were getting down with "Orphan Child":

*"Ja-ga-wi-yu-hi hna-quu ta-ti-hnu-ga di-je-na-sv
Ju-no-ye-ni-quu de-hi-ni-yv-se-sdi ni-go-hi-lv."*

"Come on," the preacher said. "Let's get some coffee. Going to be a long night."

The night did take its time passing. Singers took their turns on stage, alone or by duets and trios and quartets, and most were at least reasonably good. Even the ones that weren't came off sounding fairly decent, thanks to the backup. Homer Ninekiller and Dwight Badwater had been playing at gospel singings for twenty or thirty years, Homer with his old Les Paul Gibson electric and Dwight with his even older Martin D-28 Dreadnought flattop, and they were good enough to fill in the holes for the most raggedy-assed group. The kid on bass wasn't in their class but he was okay, keeping up a steady boom-boom and not trying to show off.

The audience applauded and occasionally shouted *amen* or *praise the Lord* and now and then wandered off to the tables for pie and coffee. Little kids ran here and there chasing lightning bugs or just grabassing around, till at last the night got too long for them and they fell asleep in their mothers' laps or in the back seats of cars.

Jimmy got himself a folding chair and found a place under a big oak tree where he could keep an eye on everything. He still wasn't convinced it was over with the Sparrowhawks. It had been too easy and those two were known for their blind-mule stubbornness. But the hours rolled by and there was no further sign of them. When Jimmy's watch showed midnight he felt sure this would be the time something would happen, but nothing did.

The preacher appeared out of the shadows. "Having a good time, Jimmy? I am, now I don't have to worry about the Sparrowhawks."

Jimmy grunted. It was now well after twelve by his watch and he was starting to think nothing was going to happen after all, but he still wasn't ready to admit it.

On stage the musicians were into an instrumental break while the next singing group was called. Homer Ninekiller was doing amazing things to "He Will Set Your Fields On Fire" and Dwight Badwater and the kid in the Seminole jacket were loping right along with him. *"Asv,"* the preacher said as they finished.

"Picked that one and sent it home naked," Jimmy agreed. "Who's on next?"

"The Heaven-Bound Disciples."

"Shit."

"Please," the preacher said reprovingly. "This *is* the Lord's service."

"Sorry," Jimmy said. "But I bet that's pretty much the Lord's opinion too."

The Heaven-Bound Disciples consisted of a loud-mouthed preacher named Mason Littlebird, his incredibly fat wife, and their big-knockered teenage daughter. None of them could sing worth a damn and Mason Littlebird had a habit of preaching windy sermons, "witnessing" he called it, between songs. Watching Mavis Littlebird clambering up the ladder to the stage—the truck was already tilted over on its shocks from her mother's weight—Jimmy decided this was a good time to take care of some increasingly urgent business.

"See you," he told the preacher. "Got to visit the BIA office."

There was somebody already inside the outhouse when Jimmy got there. He shrugged and stepped off into the trees. Fine Indian he'd be if he couldn't even take a pee in the woods.

He gave a post-oak a good soaking down, hearing Mason Littlebird's voice blaring through the trees: "And I used to be a sinner, a-men, I drank and gambled, praise the Lord, yes and I sinned with women, thank you Jesus—"

Zipping up, he walked back out of the woods and managed to get himself a foam cup of black coffee without being spotted by Idabel Grasshopper, who was gazing toward the stage with a look of holy joy. Maybe, Jimmy thought hopefully, she's getting the hots for Mason instead of me. Amen, praise the Lord, *and* thank you Jesus if she does.

He was finishing his coffee when it all began to happen.

The Heaven-Bound Disciples were into a long depressing song about sinners going to Hell—the words in English, of course, none of them spoke Cherokee even though Mason claimed to be a full-blood—when all at once there was a Godawful racket from the speakers and then silence except for the voices of the Disciples, trailing off uncertainly as they turned to stare.

Homer Ninekiller and the bass player bent over the silent amplifiers. From the look on their faces Jimmy guessed the breakdown was a major one. He could smell the kind of smoke you got when electric things died.

He felt no serious concern. This sort of thing was always happening at these affairs; the cheap amplifier systems, that were all most Indians could afford, broke down all the time. And, as far as he was concerned, this time was as good as any. Anything that shut the Littlebirds up was okay with him.

Dwight Badwater, though, was speaking to the Disciples, who were still staring at the dead speakers. After a minute they turned back around, while Dwight went into a flatpicking introduction, and began again to sing. Their voices were thin and weak without amplification, but they tried, while Dwight Badwater's big flattop boomed behind them. There was a burst of applause.

Then, with a sickening cracking sound, the bridge tore clear off Dwight Badwater's guitar. It happened too fast to see; one second Dwight was sitting there playing big mellow acoustic chords and the next he was grabbing his right wrist, bloody where the lashing strings had cut it, and looking down in disbelief at the splintered top of that beautiful old Martin.

Jimmy Hominy felt as if he'd been kicked in the stomach. Yet something made him turn his head, just at that moment, and when he did he forgot all about old friends and ruined guitars.

Half a dozen men in white suits were coming across the parking area. Behind them, two more men were getting out of a big white van that practically glowed in the dim light. It was too far and too dark to make out faces or details, except for the man in the lead, but that was okay because he was the only one Jimmy was really looking at.

Not that he was anything special to look at; he was just an average-sized man—maybe a little on the short and slender side—in a fancy white suit. But Jimmy Hominy took one look at him, checked his watch again, and shook his head in disgust. "Son of a bitch," he muttered. "Forgot about daylight saving time."

The stranger crossed the parking ground with a quick sure step that was almost a swagger. When he came to the edge of the grassy area he stopped. The others coming up behind him stopped too.

He stood for a moment studying the ground at his feet. Then his head came up and turned, slowly, until he was looking straight in Jimmy Hominy's direction; and he smiled, a wide flash of very white teeth, and stepped forward again. Along the ground on either side of him was a bright blue flash, too fast and too small to see unless you were looking for it, where the medicine line had been.

Jimmy Hominy felt something with cold feet walking up his backbone. As far as he knew there was only one person in all Creation who could do that. Well, okay, two, but he was fairly certain this wasn't the other one.

The other suits followed their leader through the break in the medicine circle, walking single file, none of them looking down or around. Behind them, shuffling along with hunched shoulders, came Luther and Bobby Spar-rowhawk.

Jimmy started to move, to head the strangers off—to tell the truth he didn't know what the hell he meant to do—but Idabel Grasshopper came up beside him and grabbed his arm. "There you are," she said in the way of somebody finding a missing possession. "Look, who's that? Don't they look handsome."

The strangers were standing beside the stage now, while the leader spoke to Eli Blackbird, who nodded and then climbed up on the truck, raising his hands for atten-tion. "Good news," the preacher shouted over the growing noise of the crowd. "We've got a new group here, and they've brought their own equipment. Soon as they get set up, we'll go on with the singing."

The white suits were already trooping back to their van. With amazing speed and efficiency they began carrying things from the van—speakers, amplifiers, cased instru-ments—and setting them up on stage. Meanwhile the Sparrowhawk brothers took seats on the front row and sat there side by side like a couple of mean toads, staring straight ahead and not speaking to anybody.

"See, Jimmy?" Idabel Grasshopper sighed. "Just when everything was going wrong, the Lord sent us help. That's how it is, if you have faith—"

By the time Jimmy got loose the strangers were all set up and standing ready on stage. The preacher stepped up to one of the shiny new microphones they had brought. "All right." His voice boomed out through the big speak-ers and rumbled off through the woods. "Let's all give a big welcome to—" He checked a piece of paper in his hand. "Brother Seth Abadon, and a group called Maran-atha!"

The crowd applauded and amenned. The preacher got off the stage, the strangers took a step forward—all to-gether and on the same foot, like a half-time drill team—and the music began:

> *"Oh people, get ready,*
> *Oh people, get ready,*
> *Oh people, get ready,*
> *He's coming to take*
> *you away."*

Jimmy Hominy had worked his way up to the front now, and he put his hand to his back pocket, to the little pouch of extra-special tobacco he had brought along in case things got rough. But then, remembering how the stranger had broken that power circle without so much as a song or a word, he changed his mind. That tobacco was strong enough to knock seven witches on their asses at a range of seven miles, on the far side of seven mountains, with one good puff; but he had a feeling that using it against this well-dressed joker would be like trying to stop a buffalo with a blowgun.

So he let his hand fall empty to his side, and went over and stood under the big tree again, where he could study the men in the white suits. He'd never seen anything like them.

And yet there was nothing weird or shocking in their appearance. In fact the peculiar thing about them was that there *wasn't* anything peculiar about any of them. Even the most ordinary-looking people had various little details—a crooked nose, a big chin, a mole—that marked them as who they were; even white people, who did tend to look pretty much alike to Jimmy Hominy, had their own faces if you really looked. But these gents, except for their leader, might have come off some kind of assembly line. They were so exactly the same size and build that they could have swapped their snazzy Western-cut white suits around at random and all ended up with just as neat a fit, and Jimmy wouldn't have been a bit surprised to find out they were able to switch arms and legs and heads as well.

That was speaking of the five regular members of Maranatha. The leader—Seth Abadon, if that was his name;

Jimmy figured he was also known by many other names—
was something else. And that was screwy, too, because
he didn't look all that different from the others, in any way
you could put your finger on. He was a little shorter and
more lightly built, and his suit fit him just a little better, but
that was all . . . but he stood out on that stage like a timber
wolf in a pack of stray mutts. Something in the way he
stood, in the way he held his head; whatever it was, nobody
in the world would have needed more than a single glance
to know which of the strangers was The Man.

At Jimmy's side the preacher said, "Isn't it great? A
real professional group showing up at a little country singing like this, we really lucked out tonight."

Jimmy snorted. "What's a bunch of *yonegs* doing
here?"

"You think they're white?" The preacher sounded surprised. "They look Indian to me."

Actually, you couldn't tell. The strangers' faces seemed
to shift somehow in the yellowish light; it was like looking through a car windshield in a rainstorm, or trying to
read with a pair of those cheap glasses off the rack at
Family Dollar Store. They wouldn't come into focus; they
looked sort of Indian, and then they looked sort of white,
and now and then Jimmy caught flickering glimpses of
other things he didn't even want to identify.

"Anyway," the preacher said, "who cares? Just listen to
that music!"

Jimmy was listening; it wasn't exactly something you
could ignore. Whoever these people were, they had
brought some serious equipment: gleaming high-tech-
looking amplifiers with lots of knobs and switches and
colored lights, black studio-grade microphones, and great
big speakers like the ones at the rock concert Jimmy had
once attended with his grandson. One, standing right behind Brother Seth Abadon up by the truck cab, was easily
the biggest speaker Jimmy had ever seen; the damn thing
looked to be bigger than his trailer's front door.

The music surged and rolled from the speakers, not

blasting nose-bleed-loud like at the rock concert, but in a
soft pulsing flood that soaked right through your skin and
blended with your breathing and your heartbeat. There
was no rejecting it; it got to you, like it or not, and Jimmy
kept catching himself tapping a foot or nodding his head
with the rhythm. Though why this was so he couldn't
understand; it certainly wasn't the words of the song,
which were simple-headed to the point of childishness:

> *"People, have you heard the call,*
> *Going out to one and all?*
> *Listen and you'll know it's true*
> *He is coming after you."*

—they sang, in intricate high-rising harmonies, so tight
it was impossible to tell who was singing which part.
They had fine voices, too, clear and strong and dead true,
never the faintest sourness or roughness to mar that amazing flow. If anything they were too perfect; the effect was
that of drinking distilled water—so pure there was no flavor, nothing really *there*.

But the singing was only a part, and maybe the lesser
part, of Maranatha's sound. The vocals rode along atop
an elaborate structure of complex chords and driving runs
laid down by the instruments: two rhythm guitars, bass,
keyboard—the kind that hung around the player's neck
rather than standing on legs—a sort of tambourine, and
Brother Seth Abadon himself on lead guitar. None of the
instruments were of any familiar make; the shapes, in fact,
were a little disturbing if you looked closely.

The rhythm guitars chonged and whopped, the bass
thudded, the keyboard wheeped and tootled, the tambourine jingle-jangled, and Brother Seth's white solid-body
guitar threaded in and out with graceful ease; and over it
all sang the voices of Maranatha:

> *"Oh brother, get ready,*
> *Oh sister, get ready,*

Oh children, get ready,
He's come to take you away."

"Who's taking who where?" Jimmy wondered under his breath. To the preacher he said, "Where are these guys from, anyway?"

There was no answer. Jimmy turned and saw that the preacher was staring wide-eyed and slack-faced in the direction of the stage. His head was nodding, his shoulders moved rhythmically, and he shifted his weight from foot to foot in time with the music. He didn't respond when Jimmy spoke his name; he didn't even appear to notice when Jimmy jabbed an elbow into his short ribs.

"The hell," Jimmy said, out loud and not caring who heard him.

Doing some staring of his own, he looked out over the crowd. Sure enough, all the faces he could see were looking toward the stage with the same glazed-and-dazed expression, and a lot of people had begun to sway from side to side in their seats or where they stood. More were standing now, he noticed, than had been before. As he watched, others rose slowly to their feet.

The music swelled and rose, and there was something new, a hungry triumphant note such as you might hear in the voices of a dog pack about to tree a coon. Jimmy turned back around and saw Brother Seth Abadon was looking at him.

—Who are you?

The words sounded in Jimmy's mind, not his ears. On stage, Brother Seth's mouth had not stopped singing, or smiling, but Jimmy had no doubt who had spoken. He wasn't particularly startled; he had known several old medicine men who could do that trick of talking to you inside your head.

He said, "I'm that tall Indian you always hear about things being ass-high to. Who wants to know?"

Still singing and smiling, still playing his white guitar,

Brother Seth tipped his head to one side.—*Interesting*, said the voice in Jimmy's head. *I didn't expect to find one of your kind here.*

Down front, where he had been standing ever since the amplifier breakdown, Mason Littlebird took an unsteady step toward the stage.

—*This is not your place*, the voice said. *This does not concern you. Go away.*

"Up yours," Jimmy said, and folded his arms.

Brother Seth shrugged.—*Then stay out of the way. I won't answer for your safety.*

The white guitar's neck swung down past horizontal as Brother Seth began a long riff, up through the scale and slipping in and out of the minors. Dense chords crashed from the speakers as the others followed, modulating to a higher key.

Jimmy saw that something strange was happening to the front of the huge speaker that stood behind Brother Seth. The black rectangular surface no longer looked solid; it looked more like a hole, an opening into some place of absolute darkness.

"Come to take you away, come to take you away,
Come along, come along, he's come to take you away—"

Jimmy felt a rush of dizziness, and something tugging him forward. He shut his eyes and clutched at the little leather bag, no bigger than his thumb, that hung around his neck. Almost immediately he felt the four things inside begin to move against his palm, and a moment later the dizzy feeling fell away. He opened his eyes and looked up at the smiling face of Brother Seth Abadon.

"All right, you son of a bitch," Jimmy Hominy said. "*All* right."

Both the Mercury's rear doors were jammed shut and he had to crawl in and reach over the back of the front seat to get the oversized guitar case out of the back. He dragged it out of the car and laid it carefully on the fender and undid the snaps and lifted the lid, saying certain words in a language older than Cherokee.

Inside the case was a guitar that was like no other guitar in the world.

For one thing, there was the sheer outrageous size of it. Back in the fifties, when Jimmy's brother Clyde had first begun to play roadhouse gigs with it, people said that that crazy Indian Clyde Hominy had built himself a guitar as big as a doghouse bass. That was a little bit of an exaggeration, but it was at least as big as one of those Mexican walking basses, that mariachi players call *guitarron*.

For another thing, the body wasn't wood, but steel. In fact, it looked a little like a giant version of the old steel-bodied National that the black bluesmen used to favor so highly. And then there was that neck, wide as Route 66, and that extra string. . . .

But those were merely the things anybody could see at a glance. What made the big guitar truly unique was known to no living man but Jimmy Hominy: the steel of its body had been cut from the car Hank Williams was riding in when he died.

Oh, there was a car somewhere in Tennessee that was supposed to be the Hank Williams death car, but it was a fake. Clyde Hominy had been home from Korea only a couple of months when they broadcast the news that Hank was dead, and he had taken off immediately eastward, hopping freights and riding boxcars in the freezing January nights, till he got to Oak Hill, West Virginia. He had stolen the big white Cadillac right out of the county impound yard, where it was waiting for the legalities to be settled, and had driven it all the way back to Oklahoma without once being stopped or spotted, protected by the special medicine given him by a great-uncle who had in his day been the top horse thief in the Indian Territory.

He had hidden the car in the woods, unsure what to do with it, until one night Hank had appeared to him in a dream and told him. Then he had boosted a welding rig from a bridge construction site, and cut and welded the huge box and its resonator from the heavy steel of the Cadillac's doors and fenders, carving the neck from wood from a lightning-struck walnut tree that stood in a hundred-year-old Indian graveyard near Lost City; and when he was done he had run the remains of the car off a cliff above the deepest hole in the Arkansas River, and had taken the guitar and hit the road.

Nobody but Clyde had ever been allowed to play it— that hadn't been hard to enforce, since few men even cared to try and lift it—until that night in '58 when Clyde, gunned down on a Tulsa street by a drunken and Indian-hating white cop, had passed the guitar and its secret on to his little brother as he lay dying in the hospital.

Jimmy stood for a minute looking down at the guitar, running his fingers over a roughly welded seam; Clyde had been after sound, not looks. Then he picked the guitar up, slung the buffalo-hide strap over his neck and shoulder, fitted the slide—not the usual glass bottleneck, but a four-inch section of twelve-gauge barrel cut from a sawed-off shotgun that had once belonged to Pretty Boy Floyd, and never mind *that* story—to his ring finger, stuck his pipe between his teeth and lit it, and headed back toward the stage.

When he got there he saw right away that there was no time left to screw around. Half the people were on their feet now and all of them were swaying in unison from side to side, their faces absolutely blank and their eyes huge. Mason Littlebird was at the foot of the metal ladder that went up to the stage, and a long line of men and women had formed behind him—Jimmy saw Idabel Grasshopper in there, and Eli Blackbird, and the Sparrow-hawk brothers—all moving with the same strange slow step, as if wading in knee-deep water. The music had grown higher and the beat stronger, and the blackness within the enormous speaker was now lit by a faint red glow.

Jimmy shoved Mason Littlebird aside and went up the ladder fast, no hands. As his feet hit the truck bed he slammed a horny thumb across the strings of Clyde's guitar, making an ugly dissonant crash. He slashed out a wailing slide chord like a jail full of busted whores, walked down through the basses with first and second finger, and screamed back up on the high strings with the slide clear on top of the box. It was as crude and violent as an attack with a broken bottle.

And as effective. The wild riff cut through Maranatha's slick sound—it shouldn't have been able to do that, not even this guitar, not against amplified instruments, but a lot of impossible things were going down tonight—and disrupted the seamless harmony, wrenched the progression just the least bit off track, tangled itself around the pretty melody and turned it into something slightly but definitely nasty. Down front, Mason Littlebird paused with one foot on the ladder, and the people behind him stopped their slow-motion march. The rest of the audience continued their rhythmic swaying, but the motion had become a little uneven.

Brother Seth kept playing. He kept smiling, too, as he turned to look at Jimmy Hominy, but it wasn't the same smile as before.

—*So? You challenge me?*

"You got it," Jimmy said without taking the pipe from his mouth.

—*You have no idea what you're doing. Look!*

The nearest microphone turned suddenly into a giant rattlesnake, standing on its tail. It rushed at Jimmy, striking at his face, yellow venom dripping from long curving fangs.

And Jimmy laughed, thinking maybe this was going to work after all. Brother Seth Abadon might be—well, who he was—but obviously he didn't know everything. He didn't even know what half the Indians present could have told him: that *inada* was Jimmy Hominy's personal power animal and spirit guide. Jimmy said a couple of words and the rattlesnake slithered up his arm and wrapped itself companionably around his neck and went to sleep. He blew a long stream of smoke that condensed itself into a great monster of a rattlesnake, twice the size of the first, that reared up in front of Brother Seth.

"Mine's longer than yours," Jimmy pointed out.

Brother Seth looked from one rattlesnake to another.— *Interesting.* He made a gesture with his little finger and both snakes vanished. *Very well, then*—

He nodded to the other suits. Immediately Maranatha began laying down a quick-stepping two-four rhythm: no tune, just a steady repetition of a single major chord by rhythm guitars and keyboard, while the bass looped again and again through the same three-notes-and-rest phrase. It was a monotonous but compelling sound, holding the ear like the drone of a bagpipe.

Jimmy glanced out over the crowd and saw that the swaying had stopped. Everything, in fact, had stopped; people sat or stood in place, even those in obviously uncomfortable or off-balance positions—half out of their seats, or about to step off on one foot—and nobody, nothing, moved. They could have been a collection of window dummies.

—*Forget them.* The voice had an impatient edge. *They will keep for as long as this takes.*

Without warning Brother Seth took off on a long spectacular guitar solo, picking out shower after shower of high brilliant notes, then dropping down to the bass strings to turn the showers into thunderstorms, and back up to the little frets for a display of lightning. It was a fantastic performance, and when it seemed the elaborate structure couldn't carry any more, Brother Seth spun a dazzling ribbon of sixteenth notes to wrap it all up like a Christmas package.

Whereupon Jimmy Hominy proceeded to play the whole thing back to him, note for note, but adding all sorts of extra little ornamental figures and grace notes, playing it all with just the first two fingers of his left hand. At the end, just for prickishness, he tacked on the opening bars of the theme from *Gilligan's Island*.

"Not bad," he said. "Know any more like that? I could sure use the practice."

And that was how it went for a long time, while the stars wheeled overhead and a small-hours ground mist crept out of the woods and wetted the grass. Brother Seth would build something marvelous, only to have Jimmy Hominy knock it to pieces and then kick the pieces off the stage. Very soon there was no smile at all on Brother Seth's face and what there was instead was not a good thing to see.

He played a moaning dirgelike blues, so mournful and lonesome and crying-about-your-mama sad that several owls in the trees nearby committed suicide by diving headfirst into the ground. Jimmy shut that down by interrupting with mocking puppy whines and hound-dog howls that he made with the slide. Brother Seth switched to a weird hypnotic modal number, like those ragas from India you heard in the Sixties. Jimmy picked up the basic line and turned it into a toe-tapping stinky-finger rag, ending up with a deliberately corny *dew-dew-dewdy-yew-dew* straight off Hee Haw.

All this time the audience remained frozen where they were, as they were, with never a twitch or blink. Jimmy wondered if they were all right, and whether they could see or hear what was going on. But he didn't wonder much, because the battle with Brother Seth was taking everything he had and it was starting to look as if even that might not be enough.

The sound from the speakers changed suddenly to a vicious shriek, hard-edged and merciless as a straight razor, as Brother Seth began a series of string-bending riffs evil enough to make the nastiest heavy-metal player sound like Lawrence Welk. Things without shapes appeared in the air and hung there gibbering at Jimmy Hominy.

Flames broke out around him and the guitar in his hand started to smoke. The strings burned his fingers.

Well, he hadn't really expected a fair fight from Brother Seth Abadon. He took care of the immediate problems by puffing at his pipe—it was still burning, hadn't gone out all this while even though he hadn't had a chance to reload it; there were only two other men alive who knew that trick—and calling up a little rain to cool things down. He noticed Brother Seth didn't get wet.

But making rain took energy he didn't have to spare. The truth was, Jimmy Hominy was getting tired. His arms and shoulders ached, his hands were cramping, and his back hurt from the weight of the heavy guitar. Worse, his head was going numb; he was running out of ideas. He could still keep in there awhile longer, but he felt very doubtful about the final outcome.

At his side, a voice he hadn't heard in over forty years said, "In trouble, *chooch?*"

Clyde was standing there, grinning at him; a wispy, shadowy Clyde—Jimmy could see right through him— even more wasted-looking than when he was alive. Jimmy said, "*Din'dahnvtli!* What, uh, how—"

"No time." Clyde's voice was thin and scratchy, barely audible through the racket Brother Seth was making. "Here."

Clyde's hand came out and touched the guitar's tuning knobs. Jimmy couldn't see how such an insubstantial figure could hope to move material objects, but Clyde still had power over that guitar. Whang boing chong, he retuned the top three strings to a strange straight sixth, like nothing Jimmy had ever heard before. "Try it now."

It took Jimmy only a few seconds to get the hang of the new tuning and an idea of its possibilities. By then Clyde was looking even more washed-out.

"So that's what you do with that seventh string," Jimmy said. "I never did know."

"I'd of told you," Clyde said, "but I was sort of leaky at the time. Listen, you got to quit counterpunching and go after him. Way you're going at this, he's wearing you down. Before long you'll start to lose it." Clyde shook his head. "You don't want to know what happens then, *chooch*. Get him now, while you still got a chance."

He started to drift away. His feet didn't quite touch the stage. Jimmy said, "Don't go, Clyde. Stay with me."

"Can't, *chooch*. I'm already gonna catch hell for this." He glanced at Brother Seth, who was watching him with a bad expression. "And I do mean catch hell. . . ."

He drifted over to the enormous black speaker. There he stopped and looked back. "Oh, yeah. He can't play augmented chords. They make him crazy."

"How do you know so much about him?"

"Shit, *chooch*." Clyde's laugh had been spooky enough in life and it hadn't been improved by death. "Who do you think taught him to play?"

He stepped into the black rectangle and vanished. Just like that.

—Your brother. I should have known. Brother Seth was looking at Jimmy in a new way. *You know, I could use a man like you. You'd be worth an infinite number of—*he flicked a contemptuous look down at the Sparrowhawk brothers, still rigid like everybody else. *I would make it worth your while.*

"Full benefit package?" Jimmy said dryly.

—Among other things, you could talk with your brother whenever you wished.

"Yeah," Jimmy said, "but if I went to work for you he wouldn't talk to me."

More words sounded inside his head, but Jimmy Hominy was no longer listening. He was playing guitar.

He had no name for what he was playing. He had never played anything like it before, even in his imagination; and he knew as he played that he would never be able to do it again. It was a thing only of that moment, as one-time and singular as a snowflake or a murder.

It began with a few bars of almost aimless riffing up and down the frets, exploring the new tuning, staking out scales. It burst suddenly into a chopped-and-lowered version of "Blackberry Rag"—that was for Clyde, it had been his signature tune—and then slid sideways into a wailing "Third Stone From the Sun." That turned somehow into a peyote-ceremony song learned from a brother-in-law who was in the Native American Church; while he was visiting six-tone country, Jimmy threw in part of a tune the locals used to sing in Vietnam. He came back nearer home with a sobbing ay-ay-ay-ay *ranchera* heard one night on the radio, floating up from Mexico, and then stepped off into a quick "Billy In The Low Ground," using the slide to make the big guitar sound like a dobro. That gave way to something that sounded vaguely Cajun and could have been, Jimmy having briefly driven a truck out of Bossier City, but might have been French Canadian since he had also spent a long-ago summer playing at a club in Montreal and trying to get into a certain Mohawk waitress's pants.

Needless to say, he put in lots of augmented chords.

There was Django and Blind Lemon and Charlie in there, and Les and Merle and Jimi and some of every other crazy bastard who ever picked up a guitar. And, of course, there was plenty of Clyde Hominy. Now and then Jimmy had the feeling it was the guitar that was playing him.

But there was much more going on than a mere blending of odds and ends. Out of the wild mixture something else was growing, stretching itself and gradually taking over; call it music or medicine or magic, there was now a new thing that had never been before. . . .

And Brother Seth Abadon, who had been trying to get in with an occasional frustrated lick of his own, suddenly gestured Maranatha to silence, and unslung his own guitar and let it dangle by the neck from his left hand, and stood there listening, unmoving as the audience, while Jimmy finished. Because—Jimmy understood it somehow, looking at him—for all his abilities and powers and attributes,

creation just wasn't a part of what Brother Seth was about.
His talents lay in the other direction.

At the end, when Jimmy had wound up with a fast
fingerpicking run, Brother Seth smiled once again.—*Well.
You seem to have made your point.*

He nodded toward the still-frozen crowd.—*Not, of
course, that it matters. This pathetic handful of aboriginal
relics? Less than a trifle, in the great game.*

The smile widened.—*And I'll get most of them anyway,
in the end.*

"You went to a lot of trouble," Jimmy said, "for a trifle."

Brother Seth shrugged.—*I thought this would be amus-
ing. As it has been, though in unexpected ways, thanks to
you. One does require one's diversions.*

"You got some damn mean ways of getting your
laughs."

—*I?* Brother Seth's eyebrows rose. *What about my
worthy opponent, whom these fools adore? He grows
bored and mountains fall, seas rise, stars explode. Whole
worlds and their inhabitants vanish, usually in painful
ways. And you think me cruel?*

"Wouldn't surprise me that's so," Jimmy said. "But
then I never took much stock in either of you."

—*Interesting.* Brother Seth seemed to use that word a
lot. *You refuse to serve me. Yet neither do you serve my
adversary.*

"Guess I'm just not servant material."

—*Ah, yes.* Brother Seth shook his head. For just a second he looked tired. *I said much the same, a very long
time ago. . . .*

He fell silent, looking off past Jimmy at nothing in
particular. Jimmy realized the sky in the east was getting
light.

—*Still.* Brother Seth waved a hand at the crowd. *I had
a deal.*

"Not with me you didn't. Not with them, either."

—*And yet one hates to leave empty-handed.*

"Take what's yours," Jimmy said. "No problem."

Brother Seth crooked a finger. Down in front of the stage the Sparrowhawk brothers began moving, walking stiffly and clumsily—actually it wasn't all that different from their usual gait—back to the rear of the truck. They climbed the metal ladder and crossed the stage, not looking at anything or anybody. As Jimmy watched, Luther Sparrowhawk stepped into the front of the huge black speaker and was gone. A moment later Bobby Sparrowhawk followed.

—*And so much for that.*

Brother Seth snapped his fingers and Maranatha began packing away their instruments and clearing their equipment off the stage, moving with the same brisk efficiency as before. In hardly any time they had loaded everything back into the white van and were climbing aboard. The white van pulled out of the parking area, making no sound whatever, and disappeared down the road in the direction of Fort Gibson.

At that exact moment the bright disk of the sun cracked the eastern horizon. Immediately the crowd in front of the stage began to move and mill about, heads turning this way and that, arms stretching. There was a low murmuring and a few voices raised in vague surprise, nothing more. A baby started crying.

Jimmy got off the stage before anybody could notice him up there. As he reached the ground Idabel Grasshopper came up and clutched his arm. "Jimmy! Where'd you get to?" She looked up at the empty stage. "What happened to those nice men? I was just enjoying their music so much—"

Suddenly, on the front row, old Nettie Blackfox—nobody knew how old, over ninety for sure and blind as a rock for the last twenty—stood up and began to sing:

> *"Ga-do de-ju-ya-dv-hne-li Ji-sa?*
> *O-ga-je-li ja-gv-wi-yu-hi—"*

Others joined in, rising to their feet if they weren't already standing, raising their voices in the old hymn that had come all the way from the eastern homeland, that the people had sung on the Trail of Tears while a third of the Cherokees in the world died:

> *"O-ga-hli-ga-hli yv-ha-quu-ye-no*
> *Jo-gi-la-wi-sdv-ne-di-yi."*

Jimmy found himself singing too, coming in on bass, while Idabel's voice beside him went for the highs; one thing you had to give Idabel, she could sure as hell sing:

> *O-ga-je-li-ga*. . . . .   *ja-gv-wi-yu-hi*. . . . .
>   *(o-ga-je-li-ga)*   *(ja-gv-wi-yu-hi)*
> *Ja-je-li-ga-no*. . . . .   *ja-gv-wi-yu-hi*. . . . .
>   *(ja-je-li-ga-no)*   *(ja-gv-wi-yu-hi)*

—while the sun continued to climb above the trees and somewhere a redbird began warming up for a song of his own.

After the singing ended Eli Blackbird climbed up onto the truck long enough for a quick closing prayer, saying the words almost mechanically, occasionally pausing and shaking his head. After the amen he climbed slowly back down and made his way through the crowd to the parking lot, where Jimmy Hominy was already standing beside the Mercury, putting the big seven-string guitar back in its case.

"Boy," the preacher said, "I think I must have dozed off there for a while. I didn't even notice when our guests left. Wish I'd thanked them for coming."

He watched as Jimmy snapped the case shut. "I hate to admit it," he added, "but I missed your part, too. Sorry."

He looked Jimmy up and down. "From the look of you, you've been playing to beat the Devil."

Jimmy closed his eyes. "Don't say that, *chooch*," he said softly. "Don't say that. . . ."

BELUTHAHATCHIE

Andy Duncan

"Beluthahatchie" appeared in the March 1997 issue of Asimov's, *with an illustration by Anthony Bari. "Beluthahatchie" was Andy Duncan's first fiction sale, but he quickly made others, to* Starlight, Amazing, Science Fiction Age, Dying for It, *and* Weird Tales, *as well as several more sales to* Asimov's. *In 2000, his acclaimed story "The Executioner's Guild," an* Asimov's *story, was on both the final Nebula ballot and the final ballot for the World Fantasy Award. The first collection of Duncan's work,* Beluthahatchie and Other Stories, *has just appeared. A graduate of the Clarion West writers' workshop in Seattle, he was born in Batesberg, South Carolina, and now lives in Tuscaloosa, Alabama, with his new bride, Sydney.*

In the lyrical, wry, and scary story that follows, he sends us to Hell on a very slow train. Be careful what stop you choose, though!

Everybody else got off the train at Hell, but I figured, it's a free country. So I commenced to make myself a mite more comfortable. I put my feet up and leaned back against the window, laid my guitar across my chest and settled in with my hat tipped down over my eyes, almost. I didn't know what the next stop was but I knew I'd like it better than Hell.

Whoo! I never saw such a mess. All that crowd of people jammed together on the Hell platform so tight you could faint standing up. One old battle-hammed woman hollering for Jesus, most everybody else just mumbling and crying and hugging their bags and leaning into each other and waiting to be told where to go. And hot? Man, I ain't just beating my gums there. Not as hot as the Delta, but hot enough to keep old John on the train. No, sir, I told myself, no room out there for me.

Fat old conductor man pushed on down the aisle kinda slow, waiting on me to move. I decided I'd wait on that, too.

"Hey, nigger boy." He slapped my foot with a rolled-up newspaper. Felt like the Atlanta paper. "This ain't no sleeping car."

"Git up off me, man. I ain't done nothing."

"Listen at you. Who you think you are, boy? Think you run the railroad? You don't look nothing like Mr. George Pullman." The conductor tried to put his foot up on the seat and lean on his knee, but he gave up with a grunt.

I ran one finger along my guitar strings, not hard enough to make a sound but just hard enough to feel them. "I ain't got a ticket, neither," I bit off, "but it was your railroad's pleasure to bring me this far, and it's my pleasure to ride on a little further, and I don't see what cause you got to be so astorperious about it, Mr. Fat Ass."

He started puffing and blowing. "What? What?" He was teakettle hot. You'd think I'd done something. "What did you call me, boy?" He whipped out a strap, and I saw how it was, and I was ready.

"Let him alone."

Another conductor was standing outside the window across the aisle, stooping over to look in. He must have been right tall and right big too, filling up the window like that. Cut off most of the light. I couldn't make out his face, but I got the notion that pieces of it was sliding around, like there wan't quite a face ready to look at yet. "The Boss will pick him up at the next stop. Let him be."

"The Boss?" Fat Ass was getting whiter all the time.

"The Boss said it would please him to greet this nigger personally."

Fat Ass wan't studying about me anymore. He slunk off, looking back big-eyed at the man outside the window. I let go my razor and let my hand creep up out of my sock, slow and easy, making like I was just shifting cause my leg was asleep.

The man outside hollered: "Board! All aboard! Next stop, Beluthahatchie!"

That old mama still a-going. "Jesus! Save us, Jesus!"

"All aboard for Beluthahatchie!"

"Jesus!"

We started rolling out.

"All aboard!"

"*Sweet* Je—" And her voice cut off just like that, like the squawk of a hen Meemaw would snatch for Sunday dinner. Wan't my business. I looked out the window as the scenery picked up speed. Wan't nothing to see, just fields and ditches and swaybacked mules and people stooping and picking, stooping and picking, and by and by a porch with old folks sitting on shuck-bottomed chairs looking out at all the years that ever was, and I thought I'd seen enough of all that to last me a while. Wan't any of my business at all.

When I woke up I was lying on a porch bench at another station, and hanging on one chain was a blown-down sign that said Beluthahatchie. The sign wan't swinging cause there wan't no breath of air. Not a soul else in sight neither. The tracks ran off into the fields on both ends as far as I could see, but they was all weeded up like no train been through since the Surrender. The windows over my head was boarded up like the bank back home. The planks along the porch han't been swept in years by nothing but the wind, and the dust was in whirly patterns all around.

Still lying down, I reached slowly beneath the bench, groping the air, till I heard, more than felt, my fingers pluck a note or two from the strings of my guitar. I grabbed it by the neck and sat up, pulling the guitar into my lap and hugging it, and I felt some better.

Pigeons in the eaves was a-fluttering and a-hooting all mournful-like, but I couldn't see 'em. I reckon they was pigeons. Meemaw used to say that pigeons sometimes was the souls of dead folks let out of Hell. I didn't think those folks back in Hell was flying noplace, but I did feel something was wrong, bad wrong, powerful wrong. I had the same crawly feeling as before I took that fatal swig—when Jar Head Sam, that harp-playing bastard, passed me a poisoned bottle at a Mississippi jook joint and I woke up on that one-way train.

Then a big old hound dog ambled around the corner of the station on my left, and another big old hound dog ambled around the corner of the station on my right. Each one was nearbouts as big as a calf and so fat it could hardly go, swanking along with its belly on the planks and its nose down. When the dogs snuffled up to the bench where I was sitting, their legs give out and they flopped down, yawned, grunted, and went fast to sleep like they'd been poleaxed. I could see the fleas hopping across their big butts. I started laughing.

"Lord, the hellhounds done caught up to me now! I surely must have led them a chase, I surely must. Look how wore out they are!" I hollered and cried, I was laughing so hard. One of them broke wind real long, and that set me off again. "Here come the brimstone! Here come the sulfur! Whoo! Done took my breath. Oh, Lordy." I wiped my eyes.

Then I heard two way-off sounds, one maybe a youngun dragging a stick along a fence, and the other maybe a car motor.

"Well, shit," I said.

Away off down the tracks, I saw a little spot of glare vibrating along in the sun. The flappity racket got louder and louder. Some fool was driving his car along on the tracks, a bumpety-bump, a bumpety-bump. It was a Hudson Terraplane, right sporty, exactly like what Peola June used to percolate around town in, and the chrome on the fender and hood was shining like a conk buster's hair.

The hound dogs was sitting up now, watching the car. They was stiff and still on each side of my bench, like deacons sitting up with the dead.

When the car got nigh the platform it lurched up out of the cut, gravel spitting, gears grinding, and shut off in the yard at the end of the porch where I was sitting. Sheets of dust sailed away. The hot engine ticked. Then the driver's door opened, and out slid the devil. I knew him well. Time I saw him slip down off the seat and hitch up his pants, I knew.

He was a sunburnt, bandy-legged, pussel-gutted li'l peckerwood. He wore braces and khaki pants and a dirty white undershirt and a big derby hat that had white hair flying out all around it like it was attached to the brim, like if he'd tip his hat to the ladies his hair would come off too. He had a bright-red possum face, with beady, dumb black eyes and a long sharp nose, and no chin at all hardly and a big goozlum in his neck that jumped up and down like he couldn't swallow his spit fast enough. He slammed the car door and scratched himself a little, up one arm and then the other, then up one leg till he got to where he liked it. He hunkered down and spit in the dust and looked all unconcerned like maybe he was waiting on a tornado to come along and blow some victuals his way, and he didn't take any more notice of me than the hound dogs had.

I wan't used to being treated such. "You keep driving on the tracks thataway, hoss," I called, "and that Terraplane gone be butt-sprung for sure."

He didn't even look my way. After a long while, he stood up and leaned on a fender and lifted one leg and looked at the bottom of his muddy clod-hopper, then put it down and lifted the other and looked at it too. Then he hitched his pants again and headed across the yard toward me. He favored his right leg a little and hardly picked up

his feet at all when he walked. He left ruts in the yard
like a plow. When he reached the steps, he didn't so much
climb 'em as stand his bantyweight self on each one and
look proud, like each step was all his'n now, and then go
on to claim the next one too. Once on the porch, he sat
down with his shoulders against a post, took off his hat
and fanned himself. His hair had a better hold on his head
than I thought, what there was of it. Then he pulled out
a stick and a pocketknife and commenced to whittle. But
he did all these things so deliberate and thoughtful that it
was almost the same as him talking, so I kept quiet and
waited for the words to catch up.

"It will be a strange and disgraceful day unto this
world," he finally said, "when I ask a gut-bucket nigger
guitar player for advice on auto-MO-bile mechanics, or
for anything else except a tune now and again." He had
eyes like he'd been shot twice in the face. "And furthermore, I am the Lord of Darkness and the Father of Lies,
and if I want to drive my 1936 Hudson Terraplane, with
its six-cylinder seventy-horsepower engine, out into the
middle of some loblolly and shoot out its tires and rip up
its seats and piss down its radiator hole, why, I will do it
and do it again seven more times afore breakfast, and the
voice that will stop me will not be yourn. You hearing
me, John?"

"Ain't my business," I said. Like always, I was waiting
to see how it was.

"That's right, John, it ain't your business," the devil
said. "Nothing I do is any of your business, John, but
everything you do is mine. I was there the night you took
that fatal drink, John. I saw you fold when your gut bent
double on you, and I saw the shine of your blood coming
up. I saw that whore you and Jar Head was squabbling
over doing business at your funeral. It was a sorry-ass
death of a sorry-ass man, John, and I had a big old time
with it."

The hound dogs had laid back down, so I stretched out

and rested my feet on one of them. It rolled its eyes up at me like its feelings was hurt.

"I'd like to see old Jar Head one more time," I said. "If he'll be along directly, I'll wait here and meet his train."

"Jar Head's plumb out of your reach now, John," the devil said, still whittling. "I'd like to show you around your new home this afternoon. Come take a tour with me."

"I had to drive fifteen miles to get to that jook joint in the first place," I said, "and then come I don't know how far on the train to Hell and past it. I've done enough traveling for one day."

"Come with me, John."

"I thank you, but I'll just stay here."

"It would please me no end if you made my rounds with me, John." The stick he was whittling started moving in his hand. He had to grip it a little to hang on, but he just kept smiling. The stick started to bleed along the cuts, welling up black red as the blade skinned it. "I want to show off your new home place. You'd like that, wouldn't you, John?" The blood curled down his arm like a snake.

I stood up and shook my head real slow and disgusted, like I was bored by his conjuring, but I made sure to hold my guitar between us as I walked past him. I walked to the porch steps with my back to the devil, and I was headed down them two at a time when he hollered out behind, "John! Where do you think you're going?"

I said real loud, not looking back: "I done enough nothing for one day. I'm taking me a tour. If your ass has slipped between the planks and got stuck, I'll fetch a couple of mules to pull you free."

I heard him cuss and come scrambling after me with that leg a-dragging, sounding just like a scarecrow out on a stroll. I was holding my guitar closer to me all the time.

I wan't real surprised that he let those two hound dogs ride up on the front seat of the Terraplane like they was

Mrs. Roosevelt, while I had to walk in the road alongside, practically in the ditch. The devil drove real slow, talking to me out the window the whole time.

"Whyn't you make me get off the train at Hell, with the rest of those sorry people?"

"Hell's about full," he said. "When I first opened for business out here, John, Hell wan't no more'n a wide spot in the road. It took a long time to get any size on it. When you stole that dime from your poor old Meemaw to buy a French post card and she caught you and flailed you across the yard, even way back then, Hell wan't no bigger'n Baltimore. But it's about near more'n I can handle now, I tell you. Now I'm filling up towns all over these parts. Ginny Gall. Diddy-Wah-Diddy. West Hell—I'd run out of ideas when I named West Hell, John."

A horsefly had got into my face and just hung there. The sun was fierce, and my clothes was sticking to me. My razor slid hot along my ankle. I kept favoring my guitar, trying to keep it out of the dust as best I could.

"Beluthahatchie, well, I'll be frank with you, John. Beluthahatchie ain't much of a place. I won't say it don't have possibilities, but right now it's mostly just that railroad station, and a crossroads, and fields. One long, hot, dirty field after another." He waved out the window at the scenery and grinned. He had yellow needly teeth. "You know your way around a field, I reckon, don't you, John?"

"I know enough to stay out of 'em."

His laugh was like a man cutting tin. "I swear you are a caution, John. It's a wonder you died so young."

We passed a right lot of folks, all of them working in the sun. Pulling tobacco. Picking cotton. Hoeing beans. Old folks scratching in gardens. Even younguns carrying buckets of water with two hands, slopping nearly all of it on the ground afore they'd gone three steps. All the people looked like they had just enough to eat to fill out the sad expression on their faces, and they all watched the devil as he drove slowly past. All those folks stared at me hard, too, and at the guitar like it was a third arm waving at 'em. I turned once to swat that blessed horsefly and saw a group of field hands standing in a knot, looking my way and pointing.

"Where all the white folks at?" I asked.

"They all up in heaven," the devil said. "You think they let niggers into heaven?" We looked at each other a long time. Then the devil laughed again. "You ain't buying that one for a minute, are you, John?"

I was thinking about Meemaw. I knew she was in heaven, if anyone was. When I was a youngun I figured she musta practically built the place, and had been paying off on it all along. But I didn't say nothing.

"No, John, it ain't that simple," the devil said. "Beluthahatchie's different for everybody, just like Hell. But you'll be seeing plenty of white folks. Overseers. Train conductors. Sheriff's deputies. If you get uppity, why, you'll see whole crowds of white folks. Just like home, John. Everything's the same. Why should it be any different?"

" 'Cause you're the devil," I said. "You could make things a heap worse."

"Now, could I really, John? Could I really?"

In the next field, a big man with hands like gallon jugs and a pink splash across his face was struggling all alone with a spindly mule and a plow made out of slats. "Get on, sir," he was telling the mule. "Get on with you." He didn't even look around when the devil come chugging up alongside.

The devil gummed two fingers and whistled. "Ezekiel. Ezekiel! Come on over here, boy."

Ezekiel let go the plow and stumbled over the furrows, stepping high and clumsy in the thick dusty earth, trying to catch up to the Terraplane and not mess up the rows too bad. The devil han't slowed down any—in fact, I believe he had speeded up some. Left to his own doin's, the mule headed across the rows, the plow jerking along sideways behind him.

"Yessir?" Ezekiel looked at me sorta curious like, and

nodded his head so slight I wondered if he'd done it at
all. "What you need with me, boss?"

"I wanted you to meet your new neighbor. This here's
John, and you ain't gone believe this, but he used to be
a big man in the jook joints in the Delta. Writing songs
and playing that dimestore git fiddle."

Ezekiel looked at me and said, "Yessir, I know John's
songs." And I could tell he meant more than hearing them.

"Yes, John mighta been famous and saved enough
whore money to buy him a decent instrument if he hadn't
up and got hisself killed. Yes, John used to be one high-
rolling nigger, but you ain't so high now, are you John?"

I stared at the li'l peckerwood and spit out: "High
enough to see where I'm going, Ole Massa."

I heard Ezekiel suck in his breath. The devil looked
away from me real casual and back to Ezekiel, like we
was chatting on a veranda someplace.

"Well, Ezekiel, this has been a nice long break for you,
but I reckon you ought to get on back to work now. Looks
like your mule's done got loose." He cackled and speeded
up the car. Ezekiel and I both walked a few more steps
and stopped. We watched the back of the Terraplane getting smaller, and then I turned to watch his face from the
side. I han't seen that look on any of my people since
Mississippi.

I said, "Man, why do you all take this shit?"

He wiped his forehead with his wrist and adjusted his
hat. "Why do you?" he asked. "Why do you, John?" He
was looking at me strange, and when he said my name it
was like a one-word sentence all its own.

I shrugged. "I'm just seeing how things are. It's my
first day."

"Your first day will be the same as all the others, then.
That sure is the story with me. How come you called him
Ole Massa just now?"

"Don't know. Just to get a rise out of him, I reckon."

Away off down the road, the Terraplane had stopped,
engine still running, and the little cracker was yelling.

"John! You best catch up, John. You wouldn't want me to leave you wandering in the dark, now would you?"

I started walking, not in any gracious hurry though, and Ezekiel paced me. "I asked 'cause it put me in mind of the old stories. You remember those stories, don't you? About Ole Massa and his slave by name of John? And how they played tricks on each other all the time?"

"Meemaw used to tell such when I was a youngun. What about it?"

He was trotting to keep up with me now, but I wan't even looking his way. "And there's older stories than that, even. Stories about High John the Conqueror. The one who could—"

"Get on back to your mule," I said. "I think the sun has done touched you."

"—the one who could set his people free," Ezekiel said, grabbing my shoulder and swinging me around. He stared into my face like a man looking for something he's dropped and has got to find.

"John!" the devil cried.

We stood there in the sun, me and Ezekiel, and then something went out of his eyes, and he let go and walked back across the ditch and trudged after the mule without a word.

I caught up to the Terraplane just in time for it to roll off again. I saw how it was, all right.

A ways up the road, a couple of younguns was fishing off the right side of a plank bridge, and the devil announced he would stop to see had they caught anything, and if they had, to take it for his supper. He slid out of the Terraplane, with it still running, and the dogs fell out after him, a-hoping for a snack, I reckon. When the devil got hunkered down good over there with the younguns, facing the swift-running branch, I sidled up the driver's side of the car, eased my guitar into the back seat, eased myself into the front seat, yanked the thing into gear and drove off. As I went past I saw three round O's—a youngun and the devil and a youngun again.

It was a pure pleasure to sit down, and the breeze coming through the windows felt good too. I commenced to get even more of a breeze going, on that long, straight-away road. I just could hear the devil holler back behind:

"John! Get your handkerchief-headed, free-school Negro ass back here with my auto-MO-bile! Johhhhnnn!"

"Here I come, old hoss," I said, and I jerked the wheel and slewed that car around and barreled off back toward the bridge. The younguns and the dogs was ahead of the devil in figuring things out. The younguns scrambled up a tree as quick as squirrels, and the dogs went loping into a ditch, but the devil was all preoccupied, doing a salty jump and cussing me for a dadblasted blagstagging liver-lipped stormbuzzard, jigging around right there in the middle of the bridge, and he was still cussing when I drove full tilt onto that bridge and he did not cuss any less when he jumped clean out from under his hat and he may even have stepped it up some when he went over the side. I heard a ker-plunk like a big rock chunked into a pond just as I swerved to bust the hat with a front tire and then I was off the bridge and racing back the way we'd come, and that hat mashed in the road behind me like a possum.

I knew something simply awful was going to happen, but man! I slapped the dashboard and kissed my hand and slicked it back across my hair and said aloud, "Lightly, slightly, and politely." And I meant that thing. But my next move was to whip that razor out of my sock, flip it open and lay it on the seat beside me, just in case.

I came up the road fast, and from way off I saw Ezekiel and the mule planted in the middle of his field like rocks. As they got bigger I saw both their heads had been turned my way the whole time, like they'd started looking before I even came over the hill. When I got level with them I stopped, engine running, and leaned on the horn until Ezekiel roused himself and walked over. The mule followed behind, like a yard dog, without being cussed or hauled or whipped. I must have been a sight. Ezekiel shook his head the whole way. "Oh, John," he said. "Oh, my goodness. Oh, John."

"Jump in, brother," I said. "Let Ole Massa plow this field his own damn self."

Ezekiel rubbed his hands along the chrome on the side of the car, swiping up and down and up and down. I was scared he'd burn himself. "Oh, John." He kept shaking his head. "John tricks Ole Massa again. High John the Conqueror rides the Terraplane to glory."

"Quit that, now. You worry me."

"John, those songs you wrote been keeping us going down here. Did you know that?"

"I 'preciate it."

"But lemme ask you, John. Lemme ask you something before you ride off. How come you wrote all those songs about hellhounds and the devil and such? How come you was so sure you'd be coming down here when you died?"

I fidgeted and looked in the mirror at the road behind. "Man, I don't know. Couldn't imagine nothing else. Not for me, anyway."

Ezekiel laughed once, loud, boom, like a shotgun going off.

"Don't be doing that, man. I about jumped out of my britches. Come on and let's go."

He shook his head again. "Maybe you knew you was needed down here, John. Maybe you knew we was singing, and telling stories, and waiting." He stepped back into the dirt. "This is your ride, John. But I'll make sure everybody knows what you done. I'll tell 'em that things has changed in Beluthahatchie." He looked off down the road. "You'd best get on. Shoot—maybe you can find some jook joint and have some fun afore he catches up to you."

"Maybe so, brother, maybe so."

I han't gone two miles afore I got that bad old crawly feeling. I looked over to the passengers' side of the car and saw it was all spattered with blood, the leather and the carpet and the chrome on the door, and both those

mangy hound dogs was sprawled across the front seat
wallowing in it, both licking my razor like it was something good, and that's where the blood was coming from,
welling up from the blade with each pass of their tongues.
Time I caught sight of the dogs, they both lifted their
heads and went to howling. It wan't no howl like any dog
should howl. It was more like a couple of panthers in the
night.

"Hush up, you dogs!" I yelled. "Hush up, I say!"

One of the dogs kept on howling, but the other looked
me in the eyes and gulped air, his jowls flapping, like he
was fixing to bark, but instead of barking said:

"Hush yourself, nigger."

When I looked back at the road, there wan't no road,
just a big thicket of bushes and trees a-coming at me.
Then came a whole lot of screeching and scraping and
banging, with me holding onto the wheel just to keep from
flying out of the seat, and then the car went sideways and
I heard an awful bang and a crack and then I didn't know
anything else. I just opened my eyes later, I don't know
how much later, and found me and my guitar lying on the
shore of the Lake of the Dead.

I had heard tell of that dreadful place, but I never had
expected to see it for myself. Preacher Dodds whispered
to us younguns once or twice about it, and said you have
to work awful hard and be awful mean to get there, and
once you get there, there ain't no coming back. "Don't
seek it, my children, don't seek it," he'd say.

As far as I could see, all along the edges of the water,
was bones and carcasses and lumps that used to be animals—mules and horses and cows and coons and even
little dried-up birds scattered like hickory chips, and some
things lying away off that might have been animals and
might not have been, oh Lord, I didn't go to look. A
couple of buzzards was strolling the edge of the water,
not acting hungry nor vicious but just on a tour, I reckon.
The sun was setting, but the water didn't cast no shine at
all. It had a dim and scummy look, so flat and still that

you'd be tempted to try to walk across it, if any human could bear seeing what lay on the other side. "Don't seek it, my children, don't seek it." I han't sought it, but now the devil had sent me there, and all I knew to do was hold my guitar close to me and watch those buzzards a-picking and a-pecking and wait for it to get dark. And Lord, what would this place be like in the dark?

But the guitar did feel good up against me thataway, like it had stored up all the songs I ever wrote or sung to comfort me in a hard time. I thought about those field hands a-pointing my way, and about Ezekiel sweating along behind his mule, and the way he grabbed aholt of my shoulder and swung me around. And I remembered the new song I had been fooling with all day in my head while I was following that li'l peckerwood in the Terraplane.

"Well, boys," I told the buzzards, "if the devil's got some powers I reckon I got some, too. I didn't expect to be playing no blues after I was dead. But I guess that's all there is to play now. 'Sides, I've played worse places."

I started humming and strumming, and then just to warm up I played "Rambling on My Mind" cause it was, and "Sweet Home Chicago" cause I figured I wouldn't see that town no more, and "Terraplane Blues" on account of that damn car. Then I sang the song I had just made up that day.

> I'm down in Beluthahatchie, baby,
> Way out where the trains don't run
> Yes, I'm down in Beluthahatchie, baby,
> Way out where the trains don't run
> Who's gonna take you strolling now
> Since your man he is dead and gone
>
> My body's all laid out mama
> But my soul can't get no rest
> My body's all laid out mama
> But my soul can't get no rest

Cause you'll be sportin with another man
Lookin for some old Mr. Second Best

Plain folks got to walk the line
But the Devil he can up and ride
Folks like us we walk the line
But the Devil he can up and ride
And I won't never have blues enough
Ooh, to keep that Devil satisfied.

When I was done it was black dark and the crickets was zinging and everything was changed.

"You can sure get around this country," I said, "just a-sitting on your ass."

I was in a cane-back chair on the porch of a little wooden house, with bugs smacking into an oil lamp over my head. Just an old cropper place, sitting in the middle of a cotton field, but it had been spruced up some. Somebody had swept the yard clean, from what I could see of it, and on a post above the dipper was a couple of yellow flowers in a nailed-up Chase & Sanborn can.

When I looked back down at the yard, though, it wan't clean anymore. There was words written in the dirt, big and scrawly like from someone dragging his foot.

DON'T GET A BIG HEAD JOHN

I'LL BE BACK

Sitting on my name was those two fat old hound dogs. "Get on with your damn stinking talking selves," I yelled, and I shied a rock at them. It didn't go near as far as I expected, just sorta plopped down into the dirt, but the hounds yawned and got up, snuffling each other, and waddled off into the dark.

I stood up and stretched and mumbled. But something was still shifting in the yard, just past where the light was. Didn't sound like no dogs, though.

"Who that? Who that who got business with a wore out dead man?"

Then they come up toward the porch a little closer

where I could see. It was a whole mess of colored folks, men in overalls and women in aprons, granny women in bonnets pecking the ground with walking sticks, younguns with their bellies pookin out and no pants on, an old man with Coke-bottle glasses and his eyes swimming in your face nearly, and every last one of them grinning like they was touched. Why, Preacher Dodds woulda passed the plate and called it a revival. They massed up against the edge of the porch, crowding closer in and bumping up against each other, and reaching their arms out and taking hold of me, my lapels, my shoulders, my hands, my guitar, my face, the little ones aholt of my pants legs—not hauling on me or messing with me, just touching me feather light here and there like Meemaw used to touch her favorite quilt after she'd already folded it to put away. They was talking, too, mumbling and whispering and saying, "Here he is. We heard he was coming and here he is. God bless you friend, God bless you brother, God bless you son." Some of the womenfolks was crying, and there was Ezekiel, blowing his nose on a rag.

"Y'all got the wrong man," I said, directly, but they was already heading back across the yard, which was all churned up now, no words to read and no pattern neither. They was looking back at me and smiling and touching, holding hands and leaning into each other, till they was all gone and it was just me and the crickets and the cotton.

Wan't nowhere else to go, so I opened the screen door and went on in the house. There was a bed all turned down with a feather pillow, and in the middle of the checkered oilcloth on the table was a crock of molasses, a jar of buttermilk, and a plate covered with a rag. The buttermilk was cool like it had been chilling in the well, with water beaded up on the sides of the jar. Under the rag was three hoecakes and a slab of bacon.

When I was done with my supper, I latched the front door, lay down on the bed and was just about dead to the world when I heard something else out in the yard— swish, swish, swish. Out the window I saw, in the edge of the porch light, one old granny woman with a shuck broom, smoothing out the yard where the folks had been. She was sweeping it as clean as for company on a Sunday. She looked up from under her bonnet and showed me what teeth she had and waved from the wrist like a youngun, and then she backed on out of the light, swish swish swish, rubbing out her tracks as she went.

RENAISSANCE

Nancy Kress

*"Renaissance" appeared in the mid-December 1989
issue of* Asimov's, *with an illustration by Hank Jan-
kus. It was one of a long sequence of elegant and
incisive stories by Kress that have appeared in Asimov's under four different editors over the last
twenty-one years, since her first* Asimov's *sale to
George Scithers in 1979—stories that have made her
one of the most popular of all the magazine's writers.
In the chilling little story that follows, she shows us
how something very Ancient indeed is introduced
anew into the world . . .*

Nancy Kress's books include the novels The Prince
of Morning Bells, The Golden Grove, The White
Pipes, An Alien Light, Brain Rose, Oaths & Mira-
cles, Maximum Light, Beggars in Spain *(a novel version of her Hugo and Nebula–winning novella, an*
Asimov's *story), and a sequel,* Beggars and Choos-
ers. *Her short work has been collected in* Trinity and
Other Stories *and* The Aliens of Earth. *Her most recent books are a new collection,* Beaker's Dozen, *and
a new SF novel,* Probability Moon. *She has also won
Nebula Awards for her stories "Out Of All Them
Bright Stars" and "The Flowers of Aulit Prison,"
another* Asimov's *story. Born in Buffalo, New York,
Nancy Kress now lives in Silver Spring, Maryland,
with her husband, SF writer Charles Sheffield.*

Her ladyship was late to breakfast again, and when she
did appear it was in a cobwebby lace robe stained with
Bloody Marys, blonde mane hanging in artful mats, eyes
big and shadowed with Gray-Violet No. 6. So we were
doing Camille this morning. Brad, already through his
melon and severe in pinstripes, glanced up and frowned.
The tiniest possible frown, almost imperceptible: you
don't upset a wife eight months pregnant with God-
knows-what, *no matter what*. But the frown said he was
not prepared to play Armand. Not dressed for the part,
my dear. Did her ladyship care? She did not.

"Mother Celia, such a dream I had!" she breathed. I
detest being called "Mother Celia." Cherlyn knows this.

"What did you dream, darling?" Brad asked fondly. His
tie was wrong for his suit: too flashy, too slick. Unlike
his father, Brad had no style. Was there a gene for tack-
iness? And if so, had they edited it out of the monstrous
bulge under Cherlyn's Bloody Marys?

Cherlyn breathed, "I was walking up these stone steps,
right? White marble steps, like at a state capitol or something? Only it was in a foreign country, like in a Club
Med ad, and I'm the only one there. The sun is beating
down. It's very hot and the sky is very blue and the steps
are very white and the place is very quiet and I'm very
all by myself."

Not a dialogue writer, our Cherlyn. In the old days,
Waldman would have had her off the set for that sing-
song voice and sticky-cheery expression, as if just below
the smooth flawless skin lay smooth flawless marzipan.
But Brad only leaned forward, elbows on the table and
face wrinkled in concern—my son does this very well—
to prompt, "Were you afraid, darling?"

"Not yet. That's the weird thing. On either side of the
steps were these two humongous stone things, really
strange, and even when the first one spoke to me I wasn't
scared. They were half lion and half some kind of bird."

"Griffins," I said, despite myself. "Fierce predators who
guard treasure and eat humans." Both looked at me

blankly. I added—also despite myself—"Paramount once did the movie. You must have seen it, Cherlyn, you pride yourself on your knowledge of your profession's history. B-movie. Nineteen, uh, thirty-seven. *The Griffin That Ate Atlanta*."

"Oh, yes," Cherlyn said vaguely. "Wasn't that Selznick?"

"Waldman," I said. Brad shot me a warning look.

"I remember now," Cherlyn said. "I remember thinking there was a part in there I would have been *great* for."

"I'm sure," I said. In her present condition, she could play Atlanta.

"Anyways," Cherlyn said, "in my dream this griffim spoke to me. Actually, they both did. The one on the left—no, wait, it was the one on the right—the one on the right said, 'Soon.' Right out loud, real as life. Then the one on the left said, 'We shall return.' "

"Old griffins don't die, they just fade away," I said.

"Huh?"

Brad frowned at me. I said, "Nothing."

"Well, *anyways*, that did sort of give me the spooks, right? This weird stone griffim looks me right in the eye and says, 'We shall return.' No, wait—it was 'We can return.' No, no, wait—it was '*Now* we can return.' That was it."

In the midst of the dialogue editing, the phone rang. The quality of mercy, and it wasn't even raining. I reached backwards from my chair to answer it, but Brad leapt up, knocked over his coffee, and made an end run around the table to get there first. Excilda appeared with a sponge, clucking. Brad listened and handed the receiver to me without meeting my eyes.

"Expecting a call, are we?" I said. Excilda disappeared, still clucking. Brad's eyes met Cherlyn's, then slid sideways to the table in nonchalance as phony as his tie. I felt a brief cold prickling at the back of my neck.

"Celia?" the phone said. "You there, darling?"

It was Geraldine Michaelson, nee Gerald Michaelson,

my lawyer and oldest friend. She had on her attorney voice, which was preferable to his all-us-girls-together voice, and I prepared to listen to whatever she had to say. But she was merely confirming our monthly lunch date.

"There's one or two things we might discuss, Celia."

"All right," I said, watching Brad. His blue eyes did not meet mine. Handsome, handsome man—his father had been gorgeous, the dear dead bastard.

"Some . . . irregularities," Gerry said.

"All right," I said. There are always irregularities. The biggest irregularity in the world kicked under my daughter-in-law's negligee.

"Fine," Gerry said. "See you then."

I passed the phone to Cherlyn, who instead of hanging it up as anyone else would, sat holding it like a party drink. "And *then* in my dream, the stone griffim sort of shook itself on the steps—"

"You told someone," I said to Brad. He turned on his dazzling grin. I was not dazzled; I knew him when. "Cut the bullshit. You broke your word and leaked it. And that phone call was supposed to be the story breaking. Who did you give it to?"

"—even though it was *stone*," Cherlyn said loudly. "And then—"

"Who, Brad?"

"Really, Mother, you worry too much. You always have." More grin: his repertoire is limited. If he were an actor instead of a broker, he'd be as execrable as Cherlyn. He took the phone from her limp hands and hung it up. "You shouldn't have to worry now, at your time of life. You raised your family and now you should just relax and enjoy life and let us worry about this baby."

"*Who*, Brad?"

"—the griffim stood right up—are you listening, Mother Celia?—stood *right up*—"

"You could have waited. You promised the doctors and researchers. You signed a contract. There would have been plenty of money later, without selling a tawdry scoop."

"Now just wait a minute—"

"—on the stone steps big as life and said again 'Soon,' and I liked to died because—"

"You never did have any style. Never."

"Don't you—"

Cherlyn half-rose in her chair and shouted, "—like to died because those stone lion-things just shook out this huge set of stone-cold wings!"

We turned our heads slowly to look at her. Cherlyn's pretty vapid eyes opened wide enough to float L.A.

The phone rang.

Reporters. TV cameras. Cherlyn in a blue maternity smock, blue bows in her hair, no more Camille. Auditioning for the Madonna. Brad in his flashy tie, good suit, coffee-stained cuff, reveling with a sober face. Sleaze and charm. My son.

Miss Lincoln's pregnancy has been completely normal. No, we are not apprehensive about the baby's health. All fetal monitoring shows normal development.

Got two dice?

My wife and I regard it as a singular honor to be chosen to bear the first child with this particular genetic adaptation, the first in a breathtaking breakthrough that will let mankind finally realize all its century-long aspirations.

Got two hundred dice?

Ten years ago, it was barely possible to genetically select for hair color. Ten years from now, the human race will be poised at the start of a renaissance that will dwarf anything which has gone before. And our little Angela Dawn will be among the first.

I had not heard the name before. From the window, I could imagine Brad and Cherlyn scanning the crowd of reporters before them on the lawn, looking beyond for the next wave: agents, book publishers, studio people. How much did a story like this go for these days? Yahweh and Technicolor Mary.

My wife and I talked this over at great length, and agreed it was momentous enough to interrupt her film career for a brief time in order to participate in this, uh, momentous research. We both felt it's what my father, the late Dr. Richard Felder, would have wanted.

He wasn't missing a trick. But Richard, whatever else he was, was not stupid. Physicists seldom are. Richard would not have stood there in the wrong tie speaking over-confident platitudes. Richard could have told Brad something about the unseen risks, the unseen connections, in universes more complex than Universal Pictures.

This opportunity represents the greatest treasure any parents could give their child. But Miss Lincoln and I do regret that the story has broken prematurely. I have asked Dr. Murray at the Institute to investigate how this could have happened. However, since it has happened, it seems better to answer your questions honestly than to permit possibly irresponsible speculation.

I didn't stay to hear any more. While the reporters were still enthralled, I ducked out the back door, struggled over the orchard wall, and called a cab from the Andersons' housekeeper's room. Juana eyed my torn skirt with bemusement, shrugged, and went back to polishing silver. She once, in a burst of confidence after seeing Cherlyn's sole film, told Bruce Anderson that Cherlyn looked like "Alicia in Wonderland, only Alicia, in that book, she keep on her clothes," a remark which endeared Juana to me for life. The Mad Tea Party. The Queen of Hearts. Off with her head. In Cherlyn's case, redundancy.

I suddenly remembered that it was a griffin who conducted Alice to the trial of the Jack of Hearts.

It must have been that thought which gave me Cherlyn's dream. Eyes closed in the cab on the way to Gerry's office, I walked up the shallow marble steps to the temple. The griffins, *en regardant*, watched me from wild carved eyes, but did not speak. I crept towards the one on the left. The great predatory stone head swung toward me, so that I was forced to step back to avoid the hooked beak. Manes of spiral curls, writhing as if alive, stretched towards me. The lion's tail swished from side to side. Stone talons gripped tighter on unhewn rock. But the beast remained silent.

I said, "Are you returning?" Dreams permit one inanity.

The griffin remained silent. But then the eyes suddenly changed. They turned black, a black deeper than any night, more ancient than the marble underneath my feet. The griffin rose and shook its wings: pointed, deeply veined, stone flesh over muscled bone.

But to me it said nothing.

"Celia!" Gerry cried, coming toward me with both hands extended and both eyes averted. That was bad; Gerry considered eye contact very important. In the days when he was an agent and I was Waldman's chief scripter, he would make eye contact on the L.A. Freeway at seventy.

"What is it," I said.

"You're looking wonderful."

"What is it?"

Gerry rubbed her jaw. Under the make-up, she needed a shave. "Your portfolio."

I found that somewhere inside, I'd known. "How bad?"

"Pretty bad. Come inside."

She closed the office door. I sat by the window. Brad had had my portfolio for a little over a year. *To get the business started, Mother.* Desperate dignity in his unemployed voice. A gesture of maternal faith.

"He's been stock churning," Gerry said. "Turned over the entire damn portfolio twenty times in the last ten months. And chose badly. There's almost nothing left."

"How do you know? I gave him complete power of attorney. He wouldn't tell you."

"No."

"How do you *know?*"

"Don't ask. I know."

"You never trusted him." She didn't answer me. I said, "The real estate?"

"I don't know yet. Being looked into now. I only found out about the other this morning."

"When will you know?"

"Possibly tonight. I'll call you if . . . the portfolio was a *lot* of money, Celia. What'd he need it for?"

"Had your TV on this morning?"

She hadn't. We both stared out the window. Black dots whirled in the blue distance. They might have been sea gulls. Finally Gerry said, "This much churning is actionable."

"He's my son."

She didn't look at me. I remember Gerry when he was married to Elizabeth. After Geraldine's operation, Elizabeth took the boys back to Denmark and changed all their names. I was the one who scraped Gerry up off the bathroom floor, called the ambulance, stuck my fingers down his throat to make her vomit however many pills were still in her stomach.

We sat watching the flying black dots, which at this distance might have been anything at all.

I took a cab to the Conquistador, stopping on the way at the Book Nook on Sunset. The cabbie was delighted to go all the way up the coast to the Conquistador. He had even heard of it. "You know, industry people used to stay there. Sam Waldman and his people, they used to go there all the time. Take over the whole place for planning a movie or editing or maybe just partying. Place was a lot grander then. You know that?"

I told him I did.

Nobody recognized me. Nobody commented that my only luggage was three hundred dollars worth of oversized books. Nobody appeared to carry the books to my room, which had one cracked window pane and a bedspread with cigarette burns. My books were the newest thing in the room, and the *Historia Monstrorum* was a 1948 reprint.

I learned that the griffin was the most mysterious of tomb symbols. That it dated back to the second millennium. That the Minoan griffin was the one with the mane of black spiral curls. That the griffin was the most predatory of all mythical monsters, guarding treasures and feeding on live human hearts. That Milton had mentioned a "hippogriff," presumably a hybrid of a hybrid. The Sumerians, Assyrians, Babylonians, Chaldeans, Egyptians, Myceneans, Indo-Iranians, Syrians, Scythians, and Greeks all had griffins. And so did Greater Los Angeles.

I sat by the window past midnight, smoking and watching the sky, waiting for Gerry to call. Clouds scudded over the moon: fantastic shapes, writhing and soaring. Smoke rose from the end of my cigarette in spiral curls. Somewhere, beyond the window in the unseen darkness, something snapped.

Once, when Brad had been very small, I had fallen sick with something-or-other; who can remember? But there had been fever, chills, nausea. The housekeeper had run off with the gardener and sixteen steaks. My soon-to-be-ex had been off doing what already-ex's do; Richard always did like a jump on deadlines. The phone line had gone down in a windstorm. For forty-eight hours, it had been me, Brad, and several million germs. And at one point I had lost it, wailing louder than both wind and baby, lead performer in the Greek chorus.

Brad had stopped dead and crept close to my bed. He peered at me, screwing up his small face. Then he had called jubilantly, "Towl! Towl!" and run to fetch a grimy dish rag with which to smear Liquid Gold across my face. This had become one of my most precious memories. *What will I be when I grow up, Mommy?*

There was wind tonight, blowing from the sea. I could smell it. Sometime past midnight, the phone rang.

"Celia? Gerry. Listen, love—I'm coming up there."

"That bad? Come on, Gerry, tell me. We're both too old for drama."

I could hear her thinking. As an agent, he used to conduct deals while pulling leaves off the *ficus benjamina* by his office phone. In a good year, his exfoliation topped United Logging's.

"He sold the waterfront properties, Celia. Both of them. Not a bad price, but invested wildly. And he's too far extended. You can recover some if you clip his wings right now, today, but the whole house of cards will still be shaky. You'll come out with less than a fourth of what you had, with the stock churning counted in. You're not a bag lady on Sunset yet, but it's not good. And it's actionable."

"I hear something else you're not telling me."

"The media is going wild. Cherlyn's in labor."

"Now?"

"Now."

"It's only eight months!"

"Yeah, but with this . . . baby, they're saying the womb just couldn't hold on any longer. That's what they're saying—what the hell do I know? I'm leaving now to get you."

"I'll take a cab."

"You can't afford it," Gerry said brutally, and hung up. I understood. She would do whatever she could to persuade me to sue Brad. Maybe I would let her. I packed up my books and called a cab. Then I left the books on the ratty unused bed. The Conquistador seemed a good place for them.

The cab could only get a block away from the hospital. I pushed my way on foot through the crowds, argued my way through the police cordon, slunk my way past the TV cameras, blustered my way through the lobby. "I'm Miss Lincoln's mother-in-law." "I'm Miss Lincoln's mother." "Miss Lincoln . . . the baby . . . the grandmother . . ."

More TV, more reporters. Shouts, chaos, trampled styrofoam cups. A huge nurse in a blinding pink uniform grabbed my arm and hauled me into an elevator, closing the doors so fast I lost my purse.

"Pretty fierce, huh?" she said, and laughed. Jowls of fat danced on her shoulders. She winked at me. I wished Brad had married *her*.

He was in the recovery room with Cherlyn, but the main show was already over and a helpful intern hauled him out and then tactfully disappeared. I wished Brad had married *him*. Half-lit, the corridor had the hushed creepiness of all hospitals late at night.

"Mother! You're a grandma!"

He wore a surgical gown and mask, looking like a natural. I opened my mouth to say—what? I still don't know—but he rushed on. "She's perfect! Wait till you see her! Little Angela Dawn. Perfect. And Cherlyn's fine, she's resting up for the press conference. Of course, we want you there, too! This is a great day!"

"Brad—"

"*Perfect*. You never saw such a baby," which had of course to be true enough. "We're going to bring her out wrapped up at first, let them see her face and hair—she's got all this hair, dark like yours, Mother—and just gradually be persuaded to unwrap her. Maybe not even today. Maybe not even tomorrow. We've forbidden cameras in the hospital, of course."

"I—"

"Wait till you see her!" And then he stopped.

And I knew. Knew before he turned to me in the middle of the hall, before he took my arm, before he smiled at me with that blinding sincerity that could sell vacuum tubes to Sony. I knew what he was going to say, and what I was going to say, although up till that moment it had been as much in doubt as Cherlyn's cerebrum.

He laid his hand on my shoulder. "You'll want to set up a trust fund for your first grandchild."

"I'm suing you for mismanagement of funds."

We stared at each other. I felt suddenly exhausted, and sickened, and old. *Towl, towl.*

"Wait!" a voice croaked. "Wait, wait, don't start the press without me, you bastard!"

Cherlyn wheeled herself around the corner in a pink motorized wheelchair, followed by a shocked and gibbering nurse. Cherlyn wore a pink gown with bunnies on it, but her hair still lay against her head in damp coils and sweat glistened on her forehead. One of the nurses grabbed at her hand to snatch it away from the "Forward" button; Cherlyn half-turned in her chair, clawed with three-inch nails at the nurse, and gasped with pain herself. I winced. An hour ago she had been in labor.

"You were going without me! You were going *without* me!"

I saw Brad's state-of-the-art calculation. "Of course we weren't, darling! Cherlyn, honey, you shouldn't be up!"

"You wanted to start without *me*, you bastard!"

The nurse gasped, pressing a tissue to the wicked scratches on her arm. Brad knelt tenderly beside the wheelchair, murmuring endearments. Cherlyn gave him the look of Gorgon for Perseus. She tried to slap him, but winced again when she raised her hand.

Brad shuffled backward to avoid the slap and backed into the knees of a scandalized nurse carrying the baby. "Miss Lincoln! Miss Lincoln! You shouldn't be up!"

"Well, that's what *I* told her," said the first nurse, still holding her arm and glaring at Cherlyn.

The baby nurse tried to squeeze past. Brad reached out and tried to take the baby, a pink-wrapped bundle, from her arms.

"Mr. Felder! You don't have on your surgical mask! This baby is going straight to the high-security nursery!"

"Nuts," Brad said. "This little darling has a press conference to go to."

He reached for the baby with both hands. The nurse held it tighter. Cherlyn reached up from the wheelchair, grimacing with pain and fury. "Give me that baby! I *had* that baby!"

I leaped forward to—what? Add two more hands to the

ones pulling the baby? Brad, being the strongest, won. He wrenched the blanketed bundle from the nurse and pushed her hard enough so she staggered back against the corridor wall. Somewhere in the distance I heard a low rumble, like an advancing horde of barbarians.

"Brad!" Cherlyn shrieked. "Give me that baby!" She began to pound at his knees.

Brad hesitated. One nurse huddled, wild-eyed, against the wall. The other, made of sterner stuff, suddenly sprinted down the corridor in the unblocked direction, probably going for help. That seemed to decide him. He turned on his blinding grin and lowered the baby—tenderly, tenderly—into its mother's arms.

"There, Cherlyn, darling—don't fret, you've been through hell, poor darling. Here she is. You have her now, everything's all right, here she is."

Cherlyn clutched the baby, shooting him a look of pure hatred. "You were *going without me!*"

"No, no, never, darling, you misunderstood. God, look at you, look at both of you!" Overcome by the sight of so much maternity, Brad passed his hand in front of his eyes.

Cherlyn glared at him. "That nurse will have doctors here to take her to the nursery in a minute. If we're going to hit the press, let's go!"

"In one second. Just after *Mother* sees the baby. Your first grandchild, Mother—God, I remember how important Grammy was to me growing up! I would have known a real and profound loss if that special grandparent-grandchild bond had ever been interfered with!"

There were tears in his eyes. Until he was six, Grammy had thought his name was Rod.

Brad took my arm and led me over to the wheelchair. At the other end of the corridor, doors were flung open. I saw a long look pass between Cherlyn and Brad, and then I forgot them both because Cherlyn was peeling the pink blanket back from the quiet bundle.

The baby opened her eyes.

I looked at little Angela Dawn and stepped back. The room faded, righted itself. There were people in it: doctors ordering, Cherlyn shouting, Brad. Brad, my son. He was looking at me levelly, for the moment giving me his whole attention, that treasure all children are supposed to want from their parents. Backward, backward. It's always been clear who holds the treasure, who is the thief that risks being torn apart to approach it. Who is the predator that feeds on whose human hearts.

Brad said softly, "Isn't she beautiful?"

"Yes," I said. She was.

He went on, "You wouldn't wreck her future, would you, Mother? You wouldn't let her little life start with her grandmother suing her father?"

I said nothing, but he knew. With a satisfied smile he kissed me and went back to fighting off the doctors who would interfere with his press conference for such a trivial purpose as the baby's health. I slipped away in the other direction, past the elevators, down corridors till I found an empty waiting room and sat down.

He didn't know. Being Brad, he might not know for a long time. Being Brad, he might never know. But *I* knew. The second I saw the baby, I *knew*.

The unseen risks, the unseen connections. I started to laugh. Poor Brad—and he might never even really know. And neither would anyone else unless Cherlyn related her dream, which I doubted she could even remember. Probably not even Angela Dawn, beautiful little Angela Dawn, would ever know. Only I. Unless one day, in a fit of grandmotherly affection, I held her firmly from rising up off my lap and told her. I would tell her about the moment I first knew: the moment she opened her beautiful eyes.

They were black, not the blue of most newborns but black: night-black, ancient-black. Silky black curls spiraled over her soft head. Babies are not supposed to see well, but it seemed to me that she saw me, saw us all with those dark fierce predator's eyes fixed on her parents' faces.

Someone rushed into the little room, jabbered at me, and turned on the TV. I didn't stay. I didn't need to see the press conference for this little genetically engineered living marvel. I had seen Angela Dawn's eyes.

I didn't need to see the wings.

DIKDUK

Eliot Fintushel

*"Dikduk" appeared in the October 1995 issue of As-
imov's with an illustration by John McGee. New
writer Eliot Fintushel made his first sale in 1993, to
Tomorrow magazine, followed shortly thereafter by
his first sale to Asimov's. Since then, he has become
a regular here, with a large number of stories in the
magazine throughout the last part of the nineties; he
has also appeared in Amazing, Crank!, and other
markets, and is beginning to attract attention from
the cognoscenti as one of the most original and in-
ventive writers to enter the genre in many years, worthy to be ranked among other practitioners of the
fast-paced Wild and Crazy gonzo modern tall-tale
such as R. A. Lafferty, Howard Waldrop, and Neal
Barrett, Jr. Fintushel, a baker's son from Rochester,
New York, who is a performer and teacher of mask
theater and mime, has won the National Endowment
for the Arts' Solo Performer Award twice, and now
lives in Santa Rosa, California.*

*Here he gives us a, yes, Wild and Crazy expla-
nation of just what "Dikduk" means. In case you
were wondering.*

In the unspoken competition among the children at Temple *B'nai Israel* as to who was the most *frum*—ceremo-
nially observant—Ishky Menken won hands down. His

ancient father, Shmuel, was not only the synagogue's sexton, but a cabalist to boot.

It was Shmuel who led the old men in their mystical studies down in the temple's musty basement, with its moldering books and mildew, covered over by the smell of Lysol. It was Shmuel who blew the *shofar*—the ram's horn—on the Day of Atonement, to seal the Book of Life. It was Shmuel who mended the Rabbi's *tzitzit* and the coverlet for the Holy of Holies, the sacred scrolls in the Ark of the Covenant. And Zelafet Safim, the Chachem of Istanbul, was Shmuel Menken's house guest.

In all this, Ishky helped.

Who could match such piety? Certainly not me! What was *my* example? My father, Harry Suss, was a short-order cook at Mendel's Kosher Deli. Actually, he made book. Half the men who came to Mendel's for breakfast were attracted more by the trifecta than by the salami and eggs.

You think that was all? I wish! In fact, my father was one of the men who conducted "auction" on the High Holy Days. "Auction" was our orthodox Jewish equivalent of passing the plate. Since it was ritually forbidden to touch money or to write on the Holy Days, my father and his cronies took pledges from the faithful, and, selecting one of the prepared cards with a number corresponding to each member's pledge amount, attached it with a rubber band to the member's name card, and put them together in a little box, for future redemption.

In practice, however, depending on the schedule at the race tracks and how it happened to synchronize with our Jewish, lunar year, there were often two *extra* cards. These were prepared in a sort of pidgin Aramaic code which meant, on one card, "WIN," "PLACE," or "SHOW," and, on the other, the name of a horse.

The avowed purpose of "auction" (which, up until the time I was twelve, I believed was strictly a Yiddish word, and doesn't it sound like it?) was the awarding of ceremonial honors—such as opening the Ark, reading the holy

text, or closing the Ark—to members who showed gen-
erosity in supporting our synagogue. When my mother
found out about Papa's scheme and reproached him for
it, he showed her in his books how half of his take from
the operation went back into the synagogue as a contri-
bution—and he never even got to hold the Torah! What
a *mensch!* All this I heard through the furnace grate from
my room, where I was supposed to be asleep, but what I
had really been doing was studying the *Sixth and Seventh
Books of Moses* with a flashlight under my blanket. Papa
and Mama's fights were just a sideshow.

But I was telling you about Ishky, the champion *tsaddik*, the righteous one, about how head-and-shoulders
above us all he was when it came to heavenly matters. I
played at his family's apartment sometimes, so I know.
In those crowded four rooms, teeming with *chotchkes*,
with *shmattes*, with *zachen*, with *stuff*, where his father,
Shmuel the Cabalist, squinted and labored over the sewing
machine—and this was America in the 1950s, not Czarist
Russia—his father in the black yarmulke, with the fringes
of his *tzitzit* peeking out over his belt, where nobody answered the phone on Saturday or touched a light switch,
lifted a pencil, cut paper, or cooked, and where everything
stopped three times a day for the recitation of the *Amidah*,
Ishky and his baby sister played with me.

I liked the smell of that place: bubbling soup with
chicken bones. Later, I learned, it's the fenugreek. I liked
his mother's legs, thick as Samson's pillars, with frilly
skirts that always showed when she brought us in something to eat—a cracker with chopped liver, a cookie, or
sometimes even bone marrow, a delicacy we called
markh.

Also, usually, though not lately, the Menkens' home
was a haven of orderliness and calm. Lately, it was nearly
as messy as *my* house. "Papa lost something," Ishky told
me, and his mother added, "He won't say *what*." So
Shmuel was constantly excavating for the lost article.

"Maybe it's under the planter," I'd say, or ". . . the red

chair? . . . the umbrella stand? . . . What about the roll-top desk?" But as likely as not, the named object would *itself* be gone. The Menkens were spring cleaning, it seemed; Shmuel Menken was selling off superfluous items of furniture. And still the lost treasure, whatever it was, did not appear.

Shmuel's work table was still there, piled high with swatches and spindles and bobbins and shears, and other notions of the trade. One afternoon, Ishky and I were pitching baseball cards under it—our favorite stadium when Shmuel was at *shul* for his cabala group. "Sigalofski really *klopped* you one, didn't he, Michael?" Ishky asked me. He was getting back at me for winning his New York Yankees Team card.

"It wasn't so bad," I said. Actually, it was. Sigalofski, our Hebrew School teacher, a frustrated Yiddish author (and what Yiddish author isn't?) had the nasty habit of throwing books at children like me, who didn't pay attention. I had to go to Hebrew School because Sigalofski owed my father a hundred dollars, and this was the only way it could be paid off, quid pro quo. Things had gotten so bad for me there that I had developed this unconscious tick: I rocked back and forth at my desk as if I were praying at *shul*, a defensive maneuver against incoming biblioprojectiles. Sigalofsky eyed me warily for it, but didn't object—the semblance of piety silenced him.

"Don't give me that!" Ishky said. "I heard you grunt. So, what was inside your lesson book—a dirty picture?"

I was taking Ishky to the cleaners. I had his Roger Maris. I had his Yogi Berra. I had his New York Yankees Team card. There was this special way I had of snapping my middle finger against my thumb and *spinning* the cards toward the wall; even a *tsaddik* couldn't beat me. Exactly when Ishky was about to release his coveted Mickey Mantle rookie card, I said, "If you promise not to tell anybody, I'll show you what I was looking at," and his card landed a foot away from the wall. "But it's not a picture, Ishky."

Ishky didn't really care about the cards anyway. He
nodded. I made sure to throw my pot-sweeping Red Sox
Team card—it ended up leaning against the mopboard—
and then to gather my winnings into my book bag and
throw it over my shoulder. Then we ran outside—"Nowhere, Mama! We'll be right back! Michael wants to
show me something!"—and Ishky followed me two
blocks to the alley behind the RKO Palace Theatre, a de-
funct vaudeville venue that was now a movie house. I
showed him how to climb up the fire escape and scramble
across the gravel-covered roof to the top of the elevator
shaft, where I kept my secret throne: a ragged lawn chair
folded just out of sight in a narrow recess.

"Watch your step," I warned him. "The wood's no good
over there." The boards covering the shaft were split and
rotting. Most of the nails had popped out; some littered
the tar paper underneath.

I pulled out my lawn chair and a cigar box that was
hidden under it. Then I sat Ishky down in the lawn chair.
"You're the first person I ever let sit there," I told him.
"This is the throne that I rule the sun and the stars from,
Ishky."

"Michael, you're *meshugge!*" he said. "When are you
going to show me the picture?"

"It's not a picture," I said. "It's a *book.*" I zipped open
the book bag and, pushing aside my gum card boodle,
pulled out the thin, green volume, handsomely grooved
along the binding, that had been sharing my bed for several weeks, flashlit, and creeping into my notebooks at
school. This, however, was my favored place to study and
to experiment with the beloved book—the rooftop of the
RKO, above the city and its houses, alone with my God.

"There are only *five*, you *shlemiel!*" Ishky laughed.
"Pentacle, pentagram, Pentateuch! There aren't any sixth
and seventh books of Moses! Where did you get that *far-
kakte* thing?"

"Don't laugh, Ishky," I said. "I found it in a used book
store. I was looking for *Supermans* and stuff when I saw

it in a cardboard box with a bunch of other books and some *Looks* and *Lifes*. It just came in, see? They didn't even price it yet! I got a deal. They don't know *what* a deal I got, Ishky! And I got the *Supermans*, too!"

"What a deal!" He couldn't stop laughing. "You got more deals in the cigar box, Mickey?"

So I showed him the virgin parchment I'd bought, ten square inches for a dollar fifty, mail order. Actually, it was a vegetable parchment imitation of the virgin parchment called for in the incantations and spells described in the *Sixth and Seventh Books of Moses*. I figured that would be good enough, if the other stuff was fairly authentic. I also showed him my peewee jackknife—it came from a plastic egg inside a bubble-gum machine—and the empty Heinz mustard jar I kept inside the cigar box along with the parchment, the knife, and some stale bread.

"The bread is for bait," I explained.

"Bait for what?" he asked me. Interested by my neat little knife, Ishky had stopped laughing for a moment.

"For doves," I said. "They come to get the bread crumbs, see? Then I sack them with my book bag."

"It'll make your bag stink," Ishky put in.

"No, it won't," I said. "You don't know anything about it. Then I'll cut their throats and bleed them into the mustard jar. Then I'm *ready*, boy."

"Ready for what?"

"Aciel, Mephistopheles, you *name* it! You make a circle of blood, you write some stuff on the paper, and you shout some stuff in Hebrew with all your heart and all your mind, and that's all there is *to* it, Ishky. The sky opens up and everything!"

Ishky said, "You haven't got a pen. You need a dip pen, and you haven't got one."

"I'm going to use my finger," I told him.

"You'll get a disease," Ishky said. "My father has an old dip pen somewhere. I'll get it for you, Mickey."

Everything was going along perfectly. I needed Ishky the Tsaddik to make everything work. I didn't know my

Hebrew well enough, and *my* heart and mind weren't pure enough to raise even spirits of ammonia. "You can stand in the magic circle *with* me when I do it," I said. "It's all in here, Ishky." I tapped the book. I opened it to the diagram of the circle to draw for summoning Spirits of the Air. "You have to stand inside the circle or the spirits get you. As long as you stay inside and keep your mind pure, you're okay."

Ishky looked at the curious diagram with its mishmash of alchemical symbols, astrological signs, and Hebrew lettering in an archaic script. "This isn't the real thing," he announced.

"It is *too*," I said. "They didn't know what they were selling me!"

"I'll do it with you, though," Ishky said, "because if I don't, you'll get in some awful trouble for sure. You're a *shlimazl*, Mickey."

I'm *not* a *shlimazl*. I had most of Ishky's baseball cards in my book bag. I still had the New York Yankees Team picture, which a lot of people today would kill for. I had *The Sixth and Seventh Books of Moses*, and a throne from which I ruled the sun and the stars without adult intervention, including biblioprojectiles from Sigalofski. In addition, after Ishky, the genuine *shlimazl*, went home to supper, I stayed there on the roof of the RKO, and, that very evening, an autumn twilight so magically crimson that I felt as if I were being inhaled by God, along with the whole warm world, right up there into the Holy Presence, not ten yards from my lawn chair I found a pigeon that had brained itself against the skylight and was lying dead in a little pool of blood.

Between a pigeon and a dove, as far as I could see, nobody but a Talmudic scholar could quibble a difference, especially as concerns the blood, which, once out of the body, makes the same ink, I bet. This particular spill was viscous and red-brown. I scooped it into my Heinz jar and shook it up with some water standing in the gutter, lest it turn to pudding or powder before I could draw my circle.

Then I tucked everything away and hightailed it home, where my mother was waiting for me, fuming.

"Where have you been?"

"On top of the RKO Palace, Mom, getting ready to invoke Mephistopheles."—No! I didn't say that! I said, of course, "Out," and I wolfed down my cold lamb chop and mashed potato while Papa handicapped his horses.

"Guess what? Menken placed a bet," he said. "Can you believe it?"

"Impossible!" my mother said. "The man's a *tsaddik*."

"The *tsaddik* blew two hundred and forty dollars," Papa told her. "He hung around Mendel's all afternoon, noshing, kibitzing, getting up the courage to place his bet—a very stupid one, if you want to know. Him and his new cabalist sidekick, the Turk with sidecurls, the one who snores on his sofa, Zelafet Safim."

I swallowed my last mouthful of cold potatoes and said, "He wasn't at Mendel's. He was at *shul*. Mrs. Menken said so." All of a sudden, it was bedtime.

But under the covers: Mephistopheles!

What a dope I am! Did I tell you about *dikduk* yet? Of course not! It's half-way through already, and the Spirits of the Earth and Air are clamoring between the floorboards, itching to explode into view, and you don't yet understand the main thing of all—*dikduk!*

Dikduk was Shmuel Menken's specialty. Old-timers used to come from all over and sleep on a pallet next to Ishky and his sister just so they could visit and confer with Shmuel on some deep question of *dikduk*. I would see them walk round and round the block in their ratty immigrant coats, waving their arms and talking an impenetrable mixture of Yiddish, Ladino, Russian, or German, and Hebrew, unraveling the secrets of the universe. Tears would flow, like drunken poets', or like lovers'. And Ishky and I would have to pitch cards at *my* house.

There are secret *meanings* to things. These meanings are hidden in the seams of things, like money sewn into

a miser's jacket. God put them there for the *tsaddikim*,
the saintly ones, and the *chachamim*, the wise ones, to
figure out—guys like Shmuel Menken, for example. Take
the first few words of the Bible: "In the beginning God
created . . ." In the Hebrew, it's just three words. You take
the last letter of each of these words and arrange them a
certain way, and guess what? It spells the word for truth,
emes, which means that everything in the Bible is true.
That's *dikduk*.

Or take the last three letters of the best cards I won
from Ishky that day—Roger Maris, Yogi Berra, and New
York Yankees Team. The last letters spell out "Sam,"
which is what "Shmuel" is in English. There are three
capital Y's, meaning how wise Shmuel was, and the M
and R in Roger Maris, for "Mr.," because he was my
friend Ishky's father. Like that. The one capital letter I
left out, which I should have paid attention to if I'd had
any *chachem* in me, which I didn't, and it would have
avoided a bloody catastrophe for the entire congregation
of B'nai Israel, not to mention the RKO Palace Theatre,
and my eyesight—which I don't regret—was the capital
letter N in the "New" of "New York." Meaning "NOT."

"Don't do it," the baseball cards were telling me, but I
just couldn't hear them.

Red-eyed, with drooping lids and a hangdog look, Ishky
collared me on the way to school. "Did you get the dove's
blood?" he asked me.

"Of course," I said. "Everything on my end is ready.
So, have you got the dip pen?"

"Yeah," he said, "but Mickey, you don't know what it
cost me." And he started to cry.

That's when I taught Ishky the Tsaddik to play hooky.
"C'mere," I said, and I grabbed his elbow. I turned him
right around and took him back to my throne room, to the
rooftop of the RKO, where we could have a moment of
peace and sanity away from the world of grown-ups. I sat
him down in my lawn chair, I fed him the Baby Ruth I

was saving for lunch, and I showed him my new *Supermans*, including my favorite, where he tricks MXYZPTLK back into the fifth dimension by getting him to say his name backward.

"Hey!" says Ishky. "I know this one. I know *all* these! These are mine, that my Papa sold to the Used man."

"That's luck for you, Ishky," I said. "Now they're mine. I bought them. And you can read them again." After a few comics, I got this little story out of him at last:

"Papa's not so good, Mickey. He's all the time worrying. Late at night, if I get up to pee, he's awake. He keeps tearing the house apart looking for something he says he lost, and then he gets all quiet and sad to put it back together again. And you know what Mr. Safim does? He laughs at Papa!

PICKMAN'S MODEM

Lawrence Watt-Evans

"Pickman's Modem" appeared in the February 1992 issue of Asimov's. *Although Watt-Evans was already a well-known novelist, and had sold some short fiction to gaming magazines, he made his first short fiction sale to a mainline science fiction magazine in 1988, with his widely popular* Asimov's *story "Why I Left Harry's All-Night Hamburgers," a story that won our annual Readers' Award, and later went on to win a Hugo Award as well. Watt-Evans has won the* Asimov's *Reader's Award on two other occasions as well, including a win for the year's Best Poem. He has also published widely in markets such as* Amazing, Pulphouse, Aboriginal SF, *and* The Magazine of Fantasy and Science Fiction, *and to many anthologies. His many books include the novels* The Wizard and the War Machine, Denner's Wreck, The Cyborg and the Sorcerers, With a Single Spell, Shining Steel, *and* Nightside City, *as well as the anthology* Newer York, *and a collection of his short fiction,* Crosstime Traffic. *He lives in the Maryland suburbs of Washington, D.C., with his wife and two children.*

In the wry but Eldritch story that follows, he warns us of an Indescribable Horror that could even now be traveling over your *telephone line . . .*

I hadn't seen Pickman on-line for some time; I thought he'd given up on the computer nets. You can waste hours every day reading and posting messages, if you aren't careful, and the damn things are addictive; they can take up your entire life if you aren't careful. The nets will eat you alive if you let them.

Some people just go cold turkey when they realize what's happening, and I thought that was what had happened to Henry Pickman, so I was pleased and surprised when I saw the heading scroll across my monitor screen, stating that the next post had originated from his machine. Henry Pickman was no Einstein or Shakespeare, but his comments were usually entertaining, in an oafish sort of way. I had rather missed them during his absence.

"From the depths I return and greet you all," I read. "My sincerest apologies for any inconvenience that my withdrawal might have occasioned."

That didn't sound at *all* like the Henry Pickman I knew; surprised, I read on, through three screens describing, with flawless spelling and mordant wit, the trials and tribulations of the breakdown of his old modem, and the acquisition of a new one. Lack of funds had driven him to desperate measures, but at last, by judicious haggling and trading, he had made himself the proud owner of a rather battered, but functional, second-hand 2400-baud external modem.

I posted a brief congratulatory reply, and read on.

When I browsed the message base the next day I found three messages from Pickman, each a small gem of sardonic commentary. I marveled at the improvement in Pickman's writing—in fact, I wondered whether it was really Henry Pickman at all, and not someone else using his account.

It was the day after that, the third day, that the flamewar began.

For those unfamiliar with computer networks, let me explain that in on-line conversation, the normal social restraints on conversation don't always work; as a result, minor disagreements can flare up into towering great arguments, with thousands of words of invective hurled back and forth along the phone lines. Emotions can run very high indeed. The delay in the system means that often, a retraction or an apology arrives too late to stop the war of words from raging out of control.

These little debates are known as "flamewars."

And Pickman's introductory message had triggered one. Some reader in Kansas City had taken offense at a supposed slur on the Midwest, and launched a flaming missive in Pickman's direction.

By the time I logged on and saw it, Pickman had already replied, some fifty messages or so down the bitstream, and had replied with blistering sarcasm and a vituperative tone quite unlike the rather laid-back Pickman I remembered. His English had improved, but his temper clearly had not.

I decided to stay out of this particular feud. I merely watched as, day after day, the messages flew back and forth, growing ever more bitter and vile. Pickman's entries, in particular, were remarkable in their viciousness, and in the incredible imagination displayed in his descriptions of his opponents. I wondered, more than ever, how this person could be little Henry Pickman, he of the sloppy grin and sloppier typing.

Within four or five days, both sides were accusing the other of deliberate misquotation, and I began to wonder if perhaps something even stranger than a borrowed account might not be happening.

I decided that drastic action was called for; I would drop in on Henry Pickman in person, uninvited, and talk matters over with him—*talk*, with our mouths, rather than type. Not at a net party, or a convention, but simply at his home. Accordingly, that Saturday afternoon found me on his doorstep, my finger on the bell.

"Yeah?" he said, opening the door. "Who is it?" He blinked up at me through thick glasses.

"Hi, Henry," I said, "it's me, George Polushkin—we met at the net party at Schoonercon."

"Oh, yeah!" he said, enlightenment dawning visibly on his face.

"May I come in?" I asked.

Fifteen minutes later, after a few uncomfortable silences and various mumbled pleasantries, we were both sitting in his living room, open cans of beer at hand, and he asked, "So, why'd you come, George? I mean, I wasn't, y'know, *expecting* you."

"Well," I said, "it was good to see you back on the net, Henry . . ." I hesitated, unsure how to continue.

"You're pissed about the flamewar, huh?" He grinned apologetically.

"Well, yes," I admitted.

"Me, too," he said, to my surprise. "I don't understand what those guys are doing. I mean, they're *lying* about me, George, saying I said stuff that I didn't."

"You said that on-line," I said. "But I hadn't noticed any misquotations."

His mouth fell open and he stared at me, goggle-eyed. "But, George," he said, "*look* at it!"

"I *have* looked, Henry," I said. "I didn't see any. They were using quoting software; they'd have to retype it to change what you wrote. Why would anyone bother to do that? Why should they change what you said?"

"I *don't know*, George, but they *did!*" He read the disbelief in my face, and said, "Come on, I'll show you! I logged everything!"

I followed him to his computer room—a spare bedroom upstairs held a battered IBM PC/AT and an assortment of other equipment, occupying a second-hand desk and several shelves. Print-outs and software manuals were stacked knee-deep on all sides. A black box, red lights glowering ominously from its front panel, was perched atop his monitor screen.

I stood nearby, peering over his shoulder, as he booted

up his computer and loaded a log file into his text editor. Familiar messages appeared on the screen.

"Look at this," Henry said, "I got this one yesterday."

I had read this note previously; it consisted of a long quoted passage that suggested, in elaborate and revolting detail, unnatural acts that the recipient should perform, with explanations of why, given the recipient's ancestry and demonstrated proclivities, each was appropriate. The anatomical descriptions were thoroughly stomach-turning, but probably, so far as I could tell, accurate—no obvious impossibilities were involved.

The amount of fluid seemed a bit excessive, perhaps.

To this quoted passage, the sender had appended only the comment, "I can't believe you said that, Pickman."

"So?" I said.

"So, I *didn't* say that," Pickman said. "Of course I didn't!"

"But I read it . . ." I began.

"Not from *me*, you didn't!"

I frowned, and pointed out, "That quote has a date on it—I mean, when you supposedly sent it. And it was addressed to Pete Gifford. You didn't send him that message?"

"I posted a message to him that day, yeah, but it wasn't anything like *that!*"

"Do you have it logged?"

"Sure."

He called up a window showing another file, scrolled through it, and showed me.

"PETE," the message read, "WHY DO'NT YUO GO F*CK YUORSELF THREE WAYS ANYWAY."

I read that, then looked at the other message, still on the main screen.

Three ways. One, two, three. In graphic detail.

I pointed this out.

"Yeah," Pickman said, "I guess that's where they got the idea, but I think it's pretty disgusting, writing something that gross and then blaming me for it."

"You really didn't write it?" I stared at the screen.

The message in the window was much more the old Henry Pickman style, but the other, longer one was what I remembered reading on my own machine.

"Let's look at some others," I suggested.

So we looked.

We found that very first message, which I had read as beginning, "From the depths I return and greet you all. My sincerest apologies for any inconvenience that my withdrawal might have occasioned."

Pickman's log, showed that he had posted, "BAck from the pits—hi, Guys! Sorry I wuz gone, didja miss Me?"

"Someone," I said, "has been rewriting every word you've sent out since you got your new modem."

"That's silly," he said. I nodded.

"Silly," I said, "but true."

"How *could* anyone do that?" he asked, baffled.

I shrugged. "Someone is."

"Or something." He eyed the black box atop the monitor speculatively. "Maybe it's the modem," he said. "Maybe it's doing something weird."

I looked at the device; it was an oblong of black plastic, featureless save for the two red lights that shone balefully from the front and the small metal plate bolted to one side where incised letters spelled out, "Miskatonic Data Systems, Arkham MA, Serial #R1LYEH."

"I never heard of Miskatonic Data Systems," I said. "Is there a customer support number?"

He shrugged. "I got it second-hand," he said. "No documentation."

I considered the modem for several seconds, and had the uneasy feeling it was staring back at me. It was those two red lights, I suppose. There was something seriously strange about that gadget, certainly. It buzzed; modems aren't supposed to buzz. Theories about miniature AIs rambled through the back corridors of my brain; lower down were other theories I tried to ignore, theories about forces far more sinister. The brand name nagged at something, deep in my memory.

"It probably is the modem that's causing the trouble," I said. "Maybe you should get rid of it."

"But I can't *afford* another one!" he wailed.

I looked at him, then at the screen, where the two messages still glowed side by side in orange phosphor. I shrugged. "Well, it's up to you," I said.

"It isn't really *dangerous*, anyway," he said, trying to convince himself. "It just rewrites my stuff, makes it better. More powerful, y'know."

"I suppose," I said dubiously.

"I just need to be more careful about what I say," he said, wheedling.

"You don't need to convince *me*," I said. "It's your decision."

We were both staring thoughtfully at the screen now.

"I've always wanted to write like that," he said. "But I just couldn't, you know, get the *hang* of it. All those rules and stuff, the spelling, and getting the words to sound good."

I nodded.

"You know," he said slowly, "I've heard that some magazines and stuff will take submissions by e-mail now."

"I've heard that," I agreed.

"You ready for another beer?"

And with that, the subject was closed; when I refused the offer of more beer, the visit, too, was at an end.

I never saw Pickman in the flesh again, but his messages were all over the nets in the subsequent weeks—messages that grew steadily stranger and more lurid. He spoke of submitting articles and stories, at first to the major markets, and then to others, ever more esoteric and bizarre. He posted long diatribes of stupendous fury and venom whenever a piece was rejected—the usual reason given was apparently that his new style was too florid and archaic.

Sometimes I worried about what he might be letting out into the net, but it wasn't really any of my business.

And then, after the last of April, though old messages continued to circulate for weeks, new ones no longer appeared. Henry Pickman was never heard from on the nets again, except once.

That once was netmail, a private message to me, sent at midnight on April 30.

"Goerge," it began—Henry never could spell—"I boroed another modem to log on, I couldn't trust it anymore, but I think its angry with me now. Its watching me, I sware it is. I unplugged it, but its watching me anyway. And I think its calling someone, I can hear it dialing.#$"

And then a burst of line noise; the rest of the message was garbage.

Line noise? Oh, that's when there's interference on the phone line, and the modem tries to interpret it as if it were a real signal. Except instead of words, you get nonsense. The rest of Henry's message was all stuff like "Iä! FThAGN!Iä!CTHulHu!"

I didn't hear anything from Henry after that. I didn't try to call him or anything; I figured it might all be a gag, and if it wasn't—well, if it wasn't, I didn't want to get involved.

So when I went past his place a couple of weeks later, I was just in the neighborhood by coincidence, you understand, I wasn't checking up on him. Anyway, his house was all boarded up, and it looked like there'd been a bad fire there.

I figured maybe the wiring in that cheap modem had been bad. I hoped no one had been hurt.

Yeah—bad wiring. That was probably it. Very bad.

After that, I sort of tapered off. Telecommunicating made me a bit uneasy; sometimes I almost thought my modem was watching me. So I don't use the nets any more. Ever.

After all, as I've always said, the nets will eat you alive if you let them.

THORRI THE POET'S SAGA

S. N. Dyer and Lucy Kemnitzer

*"Thorri the Poet's Saga" appeared in the June 1995
issue of Asimov's, with an illustration by Steve Cavallo.*

*S. N. Dyer is the pseudonym of an author who
made her first sale in 1978, and subsequently made
eighteen sales to Asimov's—as well as sales to
Omni, Amazing, and other markets—before decid-
ing, for personal reasons, not to write under her real
name anymore. Thus was S. N. Dyer born and made
"her" first sale to Asimov's in 1991; by now, with
a slew of other sales under "Dyer's" belt, both here
and elsewhere, she's creeping up on her old record,
and her stories have proved equally popular with the
readership no matter what name they're published
under.*

*This was new writer Lucy Kemnitzer's first and so
far only sale to Asimov's, although we're keeping an
eye out for her stuff, and hope to see more from her
in the magazine one of these days. Kemnitzer writes
a "left-wing mother's column" for a community
woman's newspaper, has two children, enjoys listening to Indonesian jazz and Finnish folk-rock revival
music, and can read Old Norse.*

Here, they join forces to take us to Ancient Iceland

*for a most unusual detective story . . . one featuring
some extremely unusual "criminals."*

I

Njal Thorgeirsson was one of the three greatest lawyers
in Iceland, and knew something of the future.

"You see that man?" Njal pointed to a short man walking along the booths of Thingvellir, speaking anxiously to
those seated outside. "He is looking for me."

Gunnar of Hildarend shook his head. "You will need
more than this to impress me with your prescience, my
friend. I can see Hilda Hot-head pointing out your booth
to him."

"Then I will tell you that his visit will cause great sorrow
for some, and small joy for others; but I think no great harm
will come to us from it. I ask that you remember my words,
and judge them next summer at the Althing."

They waited, speaking in low voices, until the stranger
approached. His clothes were of well-made homespun, and
his striped cloak was bordered with Irish embroidery; the
brooch was foreign. The short man walked with an air of
confidence not expected in so unprepossessing a figure.

"You have been a Viking," said Njal in greeting.

"In my youth, yes," said the stranger, taken aback by
this.

"Anyone can see this," said Gunnar. "Again, I am un-
impressed."

The stranger said, "I am Ari Tryggvasson. Can you tell
me if Njal of Bergthorsknoll has arrived at the Althing?"

"It is said that the men of the Land-Isles have tented
their booths. I would presume that you have legal problems."

Gunnar snorted.

Ari replied, "My neighbors in Thorthesdal have chosen
me to seek Njal's advice in a matter that involves us all."

"The men of Thorthesdal have a reputation," Njal said, not specifying what it might be. "Will you know Njal Thorgeirsson when you see him?"

"I have heard that he is a handsome well-formed man, though unable to grow a beard, and that he is always accompanied by his sworn friend Gunnar Hamundarsson, who killed many pirates for Jarl Haakon and is said to be tall and strong . . ." Ari paused, and turned red as molten brass.

Njal laughed and clapped him upon the shoulder. "Tell me the problems of the men of Thorthesdal." They went into the booth and spoke by the hearthfire. Skarp-Hedin Njalsson had been out purchasing buttermilk. He passed it round, then sat to hear Ari's tale.

"This midwintersday I held a feast to celebrate the first tooth of my son Glum. All the neighbors came, excepting only Haakon Snakevision, who is our chieftain and thinks himself very grand. All was well until a strange man in a blue cloak entered the hall. He stood away from the fire, in shadow, refused the ale-horn, and would speak with no one. I thought he must be an outlaw or a dead man.

"The children were playing with cooled ashes, arranging them like our beach, with a bit of wood for the cliffs. Grim Arasson was being very loud. The stranger called him over. We all stopped talking, and I sent my wife for my sword. But the stranger only handed my son a ring and said,

> 'The king's body burns.   Brave man's reward;
> Sand has swallowed   the ill-fated singer.'

or something like that. It was not a very good poem, but at least it did not have double kennings or court meter."

"I too prefer the poetry of our fathers," said Gunnar, but Njal held up a hand. Ari continued.

"After the couplet he walked out into the night. I ran out and saw him standing in the home meadow in strong moonlight; then he disappeared. We'd never had a fetch in Thorthesdal before, and were concerned. A week later my bondsmen and I were collecting driftwood and we found a corpse, uncovered by the sea.

Njal leaned forward. "He was buried on the beach? That is very improper."

"The man must have been tall and thin. His hair was yellow as yours, Gunnar, and we found bits of a yellow silk jacket and green-striped trousers and a cloak of blue homespun. I notified Haakon Snakevision, and summoned a jury to witness the wounds. The skull had been flattened in back, and we think the neck had been broken also, but it was hard to tell, the body was not at all fresh. There were no other wounds we could find. He seemed to have a crooked left forefinger, and most of his teeth. No one remembered a man of this description."

"What did your chieftain suggest?"

"Haakon said 'The man is dead, bury him.' And this is the only sound advice he has ever given."

"That is a strong comment. Women have been widowed for less," said Skarp-Hedin with a grin. He was a capable well-built man with pale skin and chestnut hair, but his teeth were prominent.

"I would hear more of your tale," said Njal.

Ari continued. "The fetch has returned several times, always at celebrations. He is quiet and well-mannered but recites some poem which is quite gloomy. My sister took up her wedding ale and the ghost said,

'Happy is the husband   Who falls to wolves and ravens.' "

Skarp-Hedin began to laugh, and his father asked him to be quiet.

"You may imagine that this did my sister's temper no good," said Ari.

"Has the ghost never said anything which might be helpful?"

"One time he watched my wife at her loom. This annoyed her. She said, 'The trolls take you, why do you bother us?' He replied,

'*The wolf's hawk-ground of the ice of the wolf-field
Has stolen the breath of the speaker of Odin's theft.*' "

Gunnar groaned. "I never could tolerate these kennings
within kennings."

"This is a simple riddle," said Skarp-Hedin. "Wolf-field
is a battle; the ice of battle is the sword; the hawkground
is the arm holding the sword. All this signifies a warrior.
Odin's theft is poetry. . . ."

Njal sighed, and stroked his chin. "And so this long
and complex puzzle only tells us that a warrior has killed
a poet, which we had rather suspected. . . . Ari Tryggvasson of Thorthesdal, you fear that this unnamed ghost may
grow bored with visiting your hall peacefully. Next he
may upset boats, or ride the cows, or wrestle with the
shepherds. Did you search the body?"

The short man nodded eagerly. "Haakon would have
kept the effects, but I refused to surrender them." He unwrapped a package of rough wool cloth. Gunnar reached
over and lifted the objects one by one, to examine them
in the firelight.

"A brass cloak pin, very ordinary. An iron crucifix—
he was a Christ's man. An armring. An inlaid silver
horsehead brooch. One and a quarter marks of unrefined
silver. A sword—Norwegian, recent design but unorna-
mented." He stood and hefted it. "It must have been a fine
weapon before this rust. You have been treated disrespect-
fully, my friend." He set the sword down. "A brass box
with silver latticework and runes. What is this?"

"A sample of embroidery from his jacket."

"You have been very thorough," said Njal. "If all the
men of Thorthesdal are so, it must be a fine district. We
will try to put a name to your ghost. I ask that you speak
to me here next year. If you have any news, send to me
at Bergthorsknoll.

"Well, Gunnar," he said when Ari had left. "What do
you make of it?"

"He must have been a foreigner, one of those nosey

Eastern Christ's men who speak only of their god. I would say he must have insulted Thor or Frey, and fought a duel."

Njal shook his head. "I think that someday we shall all give up our gods, and accept the one from Norway. But see the cross—Thor is on the reverse, so he had not sworn loyalty to a single god. And these are not battle wounds. I think he must have fallen from the cliff—or was pushed, then was buried in haste at sea's edge."

"Secret murder? That is a grave offense," said Gunnar. "We must seek to find the criminal who would not admit his killing, and has thus caused such inconvenience to Ari and his family."

2

The next day Njal went to the Court of Legislature on the assembly plain, and after that to the Law Rock to hear the announcements. There was a freedman named Otkel who lived near Thingvellir, and kept his milch ewes nearby so that he might sell curds and fresh butter at the Althing. His products were overpriced and not good, but he sold them to many important men. He had brought a lawsuit, and that evening Njal told Gunnar about it.

"Otkel's shieling is nearby, and some men came there yesterday night and lay with his dairymaid and killed his shepherd, who is also his kinsman. These men were Hoskuld, the illegitimate son of Haakon Snakevision of Thorthesdal, and the Easterners Bjorn and Bjorn Bjarnarsson, who are called the Bjornings and are bear-shirt men. They are the cousins of Haakon. I have never seen such ill-visaged, haughty men, and their chieftain seemed the worse of them."

"This is odd, for I have not heard of them before, and you would think news of such men would travel."

"It is not a prosperous district and few ships go there," said Njal. "Otkel stated his suit very poorly. He had not named the correct number of jurymen, and those he named were from the wrong jurisdictions, and one was a hired man and another a slave. Otkel must have thought that those chieftains who bought from him were his friends and would support his suit.

"Haakon brought a countersuit for wrongful proceedings, and demanded that Otkel be outlawed. The Bjornings promised to sharpen their swords and visit him soon. But the Law Speaker said that this was foolish behavior, and chieftains ought not to abuse their power. He recommended the case to arbitration, and it was decided that Haakon's kinsmen should have all Otkel's sheep, and leave the man alone. Haakon has invited all the important men to a feast, for they do not wish to drive the ewes home with them. I believe that I might have saved Otkel's case, if only he had spoken with me first."

"It is an ill time when men commit manslaughter without paying legal compensation," answered Gunnar. "I think we should investigate this ghost as swiftly as possible, and have done with the contentious men of Thorthesdal."

3

Skarp-Hedin Njalsson and his brothers attended Haakon Snakevision's feast, and had many scandalous tales to tell. "The Bjornings are cruel berserks; even King Harold of Denmark would not allow them to fight for him."

"You ordinarily admire bold men, kinsman," Njal said. "I find it significant that you speak ill of these warriors."

Gunnar went later that day to the booth of Ulm the Mender. He found him at his forge, staring moodily at a German blade broken at the hasp.

The smith rose to meet him. "What brings you here, Gunnar Hamundarsson? Have you damaged your famous halberd?"

"I do not require a wounded weapon to visit you," said

Gunnar. "I recalled that you favor puffin eggs, and my brother Hjort has found some."

"You might have sent a boy with these eggs," said Ulm. "I think you have something else on your mind."

"As to that, I have a question, nothing important. Someone found this arm ring, and it looks unusual. Can you tell me anything of it?"

Ulm turned the ring over in his hands. It was made of two intertwined bands of silver. "Eastern work," he said finally, "and not very fine. Perhaps if an Icelander had gone to the Norwegian court and not offended anybody, and not pleased anyone either, an earl might give him such a thing when he left. Of course, a person who did not know much of his business might trade for it there; I think it comes from Stavanger."

"Smith's eyes are sharp," laughed Gunnar. "I would never see so much story in a circle of metal. Here is another riddle—the same person found this brooch. What can you tell me of it, you with Hugin's own eyes?"

Ulm folded back the cloth around the brooch. "For that, you must ask Arnolf No-nose, the thrall of your old shipmate Sigurd the Unruly. For he has made the thing."

4

Weapontake arrived, and men armed and rode home from the Althing. After haymaking, Njal came to Hildarend to visit Gunnar. Gunnar was grooming his stallion Hrafnfaxi, who had been brought in from the summer pastures. Hrafnfaxi was a dun with a black mane and a stripe down his back; he had fathered many foals and won many fights, and would allow only Gunnar to ride him.

"This has been a good year for milk and cheese," said Njal, "but the corn crop is small. I think not all your men will be needed to harvest it."

"You are about to ask me to do something," said Gunnar. "You see, I can read the future as well."

"I would like you to visit Sigurd the Unruly and speak with his slave regarding the brooch."

"This has been on my mind," said Gunnar, "and I was wondering when you would ask me to make the journey."

Gunnar left his mother and brothers in charge of the farm, and was gone three weeks. He returned near the end of summer, and sent his men into the pastures to gather the cattle and sheep and slaughter those who could not be overwintered.

Gunnar killed the fine ram he had been fattening in the home meadow, and carried the head to Bergthorsknoll and gave it to Njal's wife Bergthora. That evening they feasted. Njal and Gunnar sat in the center of the room, facing Skarp-Hedin and Kolskegg Hamundarsson across the fire. Bergthora and Gunnar's mother Rannveig Sigfusdottir sat upon the dais.

Gunnar told of his visit with Sigurd the Unruly, who was a quiet man and very generous. He had been much taken with Hrafnfaxi, and gave Gunnar a mare, also a dun, who was consecrated to Frey. "I think there will be many back-striped foals," said Gunnar, "and I would like you, Njal, to have the second one. The first, I think, should go to Sigurd."

"Did you learn anything of interest from the thrall?"

"The silversmith Arnolf No-nose has bought his freedom, and Sigurd had settled him on a small farm nearby. They are on close terms."

"I am tired of stories about old jewelry," said Skarp-Hedin. "Tell me of Sigurd's bold-speaking wife."

"This is why I did not ask you to make the trip, kinsman," his father said. "Did Arnolf recognize the brooch?"

"Yes, and that is why it seemed Irish, for Arnolf was an important man in Ireland before his capture.

"There was a man named Thord Thortharsson, who ran into trouble in Norway due to some killings. He settled Thorthesdal and became chief there. His wife was the granddaughter of Asborn the Noisy, who they say was an illegitimate son of King Ragnar Hairy-Breeks."

"That is said of many men," said Skarp-Hedin. "I think he was a busy king."

The other Njalssons and Gunnar's brother laughed with him.

"Thord had two sons, Thorolf Openhand, who inherited the chieftainship, and Thorkel Squint, a man of good nature but little account. One summer a ship from the East arrived bearing timber; it was manned by men from the Hebrides. Thorolf invited them to stay with him. The captain was named Haakon Snakevision and he had stolen a wife in Norway. She was called Jorunn the Unfortunate. Thorolf Openhand decided to wed her sister Unn Olafsdottir."

"This is a mystery—how did Haakon acquire Thorolf's chieftainship?" mused Njal.

"And when will the brooch finally enter the story, I wonder," asked Skarp-Hedin.

Gunnar continued the story. "There was much unrest in the household—Haakon and his cousins the Bjornings were very quarrelsome, and Thorolf had to pay compensation for some killings. The district now seemed unpleasant to Thorolf. He heard of the new fertile farmlands in Greenland, and thought this might be a pleasant place to live.

"Thorolf refitted Haakon's ship and asked him to move his goods and his family there. They left Thorkel Squint and Haakon's wife Jorunn in charge of the land. Nothing was heard for some time, and then Haakon came back and said that Thorolf and his wife and son were dead and that Jorunn had inherited the property. Thorkel was a timid man, but he decided to take the matter to the local Assembly, and acted as his own lawyer."

"Too many men think they understand the law," said Njal sadly.

"Haakon Snakevision had bought the friendship of the other local chieftains, who came with armed men. So Thorkel moved away to the Westfjords. He was not well off there.

"Thorkel had three sons. The youngest was Thorri the Poet, who had seemed a promising child. When he was grown his father told him to find work. Thorri put off looking for work until all the good jobs were taken, but Sigurd the Unruly hired him as summer shepherd. Thorri would sit writing poetry while the cattle strayed off, and then many men would have to search for them. Next Sigurd put him to work making charcoal, but one day while he was daydreaming the fire got away from him and some woods burned down. So they set him in charge of drying the fish, but he forgot to turn them.

"Sigurd had promised to watch over the boy; he was an old friend of Thorolf Openhand. Then Thorri made a praise-poem about their chieftain, Gizur the Learned. Gizur exiled him for it, but he and Sigurd bought him passage to Norway. Sigurd gave him the brooch then, and that is the last that anyone saw of Thorri the Poet."

Njal looked into the fire, as if he were seeing a vision. Finally he spoke. "It may be that we will need to converse with Ari Tryggvasson sooner than I had expected."

5

Gunnar worked at home quietly until early winter. Then one night he awoke with a cry. His mother and brothers beat on the outside of his bedcloset until he emerged. He rode immediately to Bergthorsknoll and woke Njal to tell him the dream.

"The cattle were grazing in the cornfields after harvest, but it seemed I had forgotten to mend the walls, so they got loose. I followed them across the fells and found many milchcows dead, torn apart as if by wolves. There was a polar bear there, dead as well, and he had runes inscribed in bright blood on his white fur, but I could not read them. A bull came upon the scene and called for the barren cattle to help him, and they mourned the cows and raised a tomb over them."

"This is an odd dream indeed," said Njal. "The bull must be your fetch. I will ask you to promise me this—When you go upon your trip, you must treat everyone, man and beast, with equal courtesy and respect."

"This seems an unusual request, but I will honor it," said Gunnar. The next week he set out to Thorthesdal. He rode Hrafnfaxi. Skarp-Hedin rode a red mare, and both led pack-horses.

They came at length to Thorthesdal, and were directed to the farm of Ari Tryggvasson. The grazing land was poor there, but Ari had driftage rights, a boatshed, and several huts for drying and storing fish, and seemed to be industrious.

The farmhouse had thick turf walls, and the green of their grass made the house invisible from a distance. At first they thought it was a hillock on which some sheep were grazing, but as they drew closer they realized that milch ewes were loose upon the roof. Ari was attempting to get them down. The boy helping him seemed to have been responsible for the prank.

Ari greeted his visitors, and called for a kinsman to tend their horses. Skarp-Hedin said, "You have a problem here, it is clear, and I am the man to help you, for I have the widest experience in such matters." And he showed Ari and his son the best way to bring the animals down.

Then they went inside. The slaughter that year had not been large, but Ari offered them porridge and dried fish with butter. Some of his men had gone up the coast to see to a beached whale, in which he owned partial rights, and when they returned there would be fresh meat.

"Tell me of your chieftain," said Gunnar.

"Haakon Snakevision is not well-liked," said Ari, "but he is a powerful man and most people here are bound to him by loans and duty. He never gives advice or promises support in lawsuits except for money, and he has let the temple fall to ruins and never sacrifices. His cousins the Bjornings run rampant—they are bear-shirt men, and it would not surprise me if they were also werewolves. They have committed many killings, though none yet on my land, and never pay compensation."

Skarp-Hedin fingered his axe. "These sound like men to meet."

Ari looked about, then spoke brave words. "It would do us more good if we had no chieftain. Things were better when Thorolf Openhand lived at Thorhof."

"Thorolf had a brother Thorkel Squint. How is it that the wife's brother-in-law inherited, and not he?" asked Gunnar.

"This is the story that Haakon and his cousins swore to in court. They said that their ship foundered off Greenland, and all were tossed into the sea. Thorolf Openhand died immediately as the ship capsized. This meant that the property passed to his only surviving child, Thord Thorolfsson. The boy lived a while, hanging onto some lumber, but then he drowned as well. Thus his mother Unn Olafsdottir inherited from him; she was clinging to a barrel and making loud lamentations. Soon she became silent, which made her sister Jorunn, Haakon's wife, heir to everything. Haakon Snakevision and the Bjornings were rescued, and came back to claim the land."

Skarp-Hedin laughed, and said,

> *"The wolf-like waves fed well*
> *Off the children of the water-steed."*

"That's a kenning, I know what it means," Grim Arasson said proudly. It was clear he admired the Njalsson.

"Thorkel Squint owned the chattels, and he stayed on a while, but Haakon quarreled with him. I think he wanted to provoke him to violence, but Thorkel and his household left hastily one night when Haakon was out collecting loans. Jorunn had known about it, and Haakon was so furious he slapped her. Many men observed this."

"Why did she not divorce him straightaway?"

"That is easy to say," replied Ari's wife, a refined and skillful woman named Gudrun Grimsdottir. She had been pouring the ale herself for the visitors, but now had stopped to nurse young Glum. "She has tried many times, poor woman, but everyone so fears her husband they will not bear to witness."

"Are there no children?"

"She has none," said Gudrun, "but Haakon takes dairymaids into the woods. Now many slave's babies and poor men's grandchildren bear his evil features. Also he has an illegitimate son he brought with him from home and has set over all the others."

Ari sighed. "It is a shame the woman has no kinsmen, and a hard thing, to live with such neighbors. Sometimes I think I should sell out and move, but I like the land." He took his infant son's fingers in his, as if comparing the child's hand to his own, and it was clear that he feared he might be forced into some action which would make his sons orphans.

"I am not surprised the Bjornings have left you alone, Ari Tryggvasson. You do not seem to be a man who would ignore a wrong done you," said Gunnar.

"They have called upon me only once, and I think they were trying to provoke me."

"Tell us about it," grinned Skarp-Hedin. "I am interested in everything about these bear-shirt men."

"It was last spring. The Bjornings rode up to my house, fully armed but clad only in skins. I sent Grim to fetch the men sowing, and I carried my sword and shield. 'What can I do for you, neighbors?' I asked.

"Bjorn Bjarnarsson spoke nonsense. 'It will be said of us that we did a great wrong to kinsmen.'

"Then the older Bjorn Bjarnarsson said 'The Bjornings will be seen to be the cause of worse events. Many a life is lost in trying to make a point.' I am a peaceful man, but I told them they were drunk. They rode away." He shuddered at the memory, and his wife hid her face. It seemed that she was crying.

"This is significant," said Gunnar. "I do not need Njal's counsel to understand these events. The Bjornings had just killed someone, and they were telling you of it in such a way that they did not reveal things, but might later absolve themselves of a charge of secret murder."

"The ghost? The dead man on the beach?"

"Indeed," said Gunnar. "I would like to continue to enjoy our rest today, but tomorrow I think we must visit Thorhof."

6

That night a storm came up, and they spent the next several days inside, venturing out only to feed the stock. Gudrun had a fine game board that had belonged to her father, with pieces made of glass and amber. Gunnar showed himself adept at playing the surrounding army, but never won as the besieged kingsmen. No one could defeat Skarp-Hedin except for Grim, who cheated and threw some warriors into the hearth.

The fourth morning the weather cleared, and the sea was calm and peaceful, the color of the sky.

"What did the ocean say?" asked Gunnar. " *'Many men have died in my bed yesterday. Come, I invite you to join me.'* "

"Those foreign poems are odd and do not translate well," said Ari. "But many are appropriate." He sent most of his men to repair storm damage to roof and fence, and he went to his beach to hunt for driftwood. His guests offered to accompany him, but he urged them to follow their earlier plans.

Gunnar and Skarp-Hedin rode to Thorhof. This had been a prosperous property, but seemed in ill repair. Wet sheep looked unhappy as they gleaned in the corn pastures, and while there were stables and byres enough, even the cows looked as if they had not been sheltered. Shepherds and housecarls were at work on the field walls, piling turf upon stone. Much of this stone seemed to have been taken from the temple, of which little remained.

Gunnar and Skarp-Hedin halted before the farmhouse. A huge man with uncombed hair and beard came forth. He wore a blue cape and scarlet shirt, and carried an axe.

"I am Gunnar Hamundarsson of Hildarend, and this is Skarp-Hedin Njalsson of Bergthorsknoll. We have been visiting our friend Ari Tryggvasson at Arasted, and thought to pay our respects to his chieftain."

"Ari Tryggvasson? It is said that he fattened a pig on the home meadow, and his butcher mistook him for the dinner and was not stopped until he had removed something of importance. Gunnar, is it? I have heard of you, pretty-man. You won the favor of Jarl Haakon of Norway, and spent many a winter in style at court."

Gunnar stared at the man, but did not answer.

"I am surprised you ride a stallion. I have heard you rode a mare, and the Jarl would let his horse mount you both."

"You speak harsh words to innocent travelers," replied Gunnar. "Is your axe so thirsty that you offer it the hospitality you deny us?" He looked sternly at Skarp-Hedin, warning him to ignore any insults.

The berserker now turned his attention to the youth. "And look, this child is growing a beard. I hear his father has none—perhaps he had to farm his wife out to a more manly fellow."

Skarp-Hedin turned pale, with a spot of red upon his cheeks, but he grinned. "It is well I met you, rude fellow, before my beard is full. I now know the importance of grooming."

Before any more might be said a seemly woman appeared at the doorway. She was dressed in coarse striped homespun, and had no ornament save an old brooch from which hung the housekeys and her comb—poor garb for the mistress of so large a property.

"Bjorn Bjarnarsson!" she cried. "I have heard your evil words and deplore them. I am still the owner here, and will not have it said that we refused hospitality to honest guests."

Bjorn scowled, drawing down thick eyebrows to hide his eyes, so that his entire face seemed covered by fur save his nose. "I will go tell my cousin Haakon that his wife is making sheepeyes at womanish strangers."

He stalked away, brandishing his axe, and the woman called for a boy to tend the horses. "I am Jorunn the Unfortunate," she said, "and I bid you welcome. Please come warm yourselves by the fire until my husband returns."

She led them into the house, and it was much finer on the inside. The walls were covered with rich hangings with figures woven upon them, though many seemed to have been slashed by knives and then repaired. Jorunn put the men upon the high seat, and brought them ale in a transparent horn. Then she sat at her loom. The high seat pillars seemed to have once been ornately decorated, but now obscene pictures were carved upon them.

"If you have questions needing honest reply, then you must ask swiftly," said the housewife.

"You are a respectable and refined woman. Why do you stay with these unpleasant Hebrideans?"

"I have no choice," she answered. "A hundred times I have walked around the bed reciting 'Haakon I divorce thee.' I have worn trousers in public. I have knitted my husband a shirt that showed his nipples and tricked him into wearing it, I have performed every honorable divorcible act known to the law—but no men will witness my actions."

"I will be straightforward with you," said Gunnar, "for I can tell that you can hold a confidence, and if you help us things may work out to your benefit. A secret murder has been committed, and we intend to prosecute it to the fullest. Do you know of Thorri the Poet?"

"That would be Thorri Thorkelsson, the son of the brother of my sister's husband. My poor kinsman, even as a child he was thin and ineffectual. He came to me one night early in Cuckoo Month, when winter had barely turned to summer. I recognized him immediately. The men were out sowing corn. Thorri told me he had returned from the East, where he had been a Queen's man, and had wintered nearby. Then my husband came home, and struck the alehorn from my nephew's hand. He sent me into the dairy, but I could hear loud voices arguing.

"My husband then called me back. Thorri was gone. Haakon gave me some papers with writing, and bade me burn them. I heard him tell the Bjornings the boy was dangerous. They took up their axes and left."

"They threw Thorri over a cliff, then buried him on the beach," said Gunnar. "He is the fetch who has been haunting Ari Tryggvasson."

A man entered, with sharp and devious features. "I am the chieftain Haakon Haakonarsson. I welcome you, travelers. I see my wife has brought you ale, but surely I can offer more to such notable men."

He ordered a table to be set up, and told his wife to bring curds, salt mutton, and bread of imported flour. He himself drank from an expensive mug made of glass. Haakon spoke very pleasantly, telling them of foreign events and local lawsuits, and asked for news of their own quarter. Nothing untoward occurred, and no criticism might be given of the afternoon, except perhaps the way that both Bjorns sat at the end of the fire and sharpened their swords. The brothers were equally large and ill-favored, and could be told apart only by their hair. One had dark curls. The other had gone gray.

Gunnar and Skarp-Hedin rose the next morning and thanked their host. Jorunn ran to intercept them as they left. She bore a large cheese wrapped in cloth.

"It said that the people of the north coast are no good at the dairy-arts. I would like your judgment. Give this cheese to your father, Skarp-Hedin Njalsson, for I have heard he appreciates such things."

They thanked her and rode away. The horses pranced upon the rocky path.

"Hrafnfaxi is pleased to leave. Even Haakon's stable must harbor villains," remarked Skarp-Hedin.

They rode along some meadows, between outcroppings

of lava, then came to a small birch wood. The horses snorted and shied away from the trees. Gunnar's halberd rang loudly, as it always did when about to taste blood.

"Someone who means us ill is in there," said Gunnar. As they emerged from the trees, he dismounted and stood ready with his halberd in one hand and his sword in another. Skarp-Hedin tethered his mare, then joined Gunnar.

A pair of wolves came out of the woods and began to circle. Each wolf was large as a man. The horses screamed.

Skarp-Hedin fingered his axe. "They feed the dogs well around here," he remarked.

The black wolf came at him, and he drove it back with a wound on its hip.

The gray wolf lunged at Gunnar, and he struck it with his sword. The weapon shattered.

Then Hrafnfaxi rushed forward, reared up and brought his hooves down upon the wolf's back.

"Thank you for your help," said Gunnar. The wolf turned upon the stallion, rending his belly so the entrails spilled onto the ground.

"My sword has failed me, but my halberd will not." Gunnar threw it so that it passed entirely through the gray wolf, anchoring it to the turf. Skarp-Hedin struck off its head with a single blow. The other wolf had fled.

Hrafnfaxi neighed piteously, unable to rise.

"You have done me great service today, fosterling," Gunnar told the horse. "See now how poorly I repay you," and he thrust his halberd into the stallion's heart.

"Few have been of such service as he," said Skarp-Hedin. "I would be well served if more of my friends were horses."

Remembering Njal's admonition to treat man and beast with equal courtesy, Gunnar told Skarp-Hedin they would raise a tomb there about Hrafnfaxi. They built it of stone and turf, and the place ever since has been known as Horse Hollow. They put Gunnar's saddle upon the mare and led her away. Gunnar stopped some herdsmen.

"We have killed a wolf by the birchwood," he announced. "I thrust my halberd through it, and Skarp-Hedin struck off its head. Another wolf was cut about the leg. I ask that you go there and witness the wounds." They returned to Arasted, and told of what had happened.

"This is most unusual," said Ari. "I have never heard of wolves in Iceland. Perhaps they were Irish dogs; King Myrkjartan is said to have one as tall as a horse."

"I have never seen wolves before, but they seemed to match the description," replied Gunnar. "Let us go examine the body."

Ari's shepherd came in, with the tale that Haakon's herdsmen had been unable to find the wolf. They had seen the blood, though, and tracks, and thought its comrade must have dragged it off.

Ari gave Gunnar a grey stallion, young and unproven in fights but full of promise, and he and his men rode with them until they were out of the district. Then his men loaded their packhorses with a good stock of flour and dried fish, to supplement their winter fare.

"I worry that this gift may be misinterpreted," Ari said, concerned. "Spiteful men may say that I bought your favor with cod."

"A lord buys friendship with golden armrings, a chieftain with silver marks," said Gunnar. "A brave man offers his right arm."

They parted in friendship.

7

They returned to Bergthorsknoll. Gunnar sat beside Njal, Skarp-Hedin across the hearth-fire, and they told their tale.

"I am pleased you followed my advice and announced the wolf's slaying," said Njal. "This will avoid future trouble. It has been said that the Bjornings are the sons of a werewolf, and it would seem that the leaves fell close to the tree. Now, I would see this gift to me from Jorunn the Unfortunate."

Gunnar fetched the cheese from his pack. Njal unwrapped the cloth.

"We live in amazing times," said Skarp-Hedin. "First ill-mannered men become well-mannered wolves, and now ewes produce books."

"I thought as much," said Njal. "Remember the inlaid box which Thorri the Poet carried? It was a saga case, and here is the saga which it held. The brave woman must have burned some other papers."

He called Bergthora, and asked his wife to put the book in the chest in their bedcloset. Then Gunnar returned to his farm, which his brothers and mother had kept in good repair, and spent the rest of the winter quietly. The snow stayed late that year, and Gunnar had cause to thank Ari for his gift of flour and fish.

On the equinox Gunnar was sowing corn, his halberd beside him. Njal came to him in the field.

"Ogur Freyspriest is sacrificing today, and Gizur the Learned has come to share the horsemeat."

Gunnar went home and dressed in crimson, with the gold armring from Jarl Haakon, and tied his hair with the gold embroidered band that King Harold Gormsson of Denmark had given him for slaying the viking sons of Snae-Ulf. No one looked so fine as Gunnar. They rode in great company to the feast.

Skarp-Hedin galloped before them and arrived first in the homemeadow. Ogur Freyspriest and his household came outside, well-armed.

"Where is Gizur the Learned?" cried Skarp-Hedin.

A bald man with a braided beard stepped forward. "My father's son bears that name."

"Good news, old man. We have heard that you collect poets. We have a sheep which speaks court meter."

Njal rode up beside him and dismounted. "Kinsman, your tongue will someday be the death of you, and of your mother and father and brothers," he said sadly. But

Ogur and his guests were laughing at the jest, and invited them inside.

"I am investigating the secret murder of Thorri the Poet," Njal announced.

"I put the lad on lesser outlawry for a praisepoem," said Gizur. "I do not see the future so well as you, Njal, but I warned him that he should stay in Norway if he would live to be prosperous. The worst of our poets, you know, is better than the best the old country breeds. Secret murder is an awful crime; I would like to help you find those who mock the law."

Njal showed the book to Gizur. He carried it to the edge of the fire.

"It was written by monks in Vikingsholm, luckily in the vernacular. *There was a man named Ketil Cat.* They have put that into Latin and call him 'Ketullus Feles.' Monks have absolutely no feel for language. They are inaccurate copyists also, and always add bits praising their White Christ."

"Ketil Cat. I have heard of him," said Gunnar. "He attributed his riches to a red English cat he brought aboard to keep down the mice. He named the creature his sworn brother, and when Jarl Sigurd's sister's son killed it he refused compensation."

"Do not ruin the story," said Skarp-Hedin, and the others agreed. Gizur began to read. He continued for several hours. Finally Njal stopped him.

"Please repeat that chapter."

On the return voyage to Greenland the cat climbed the masthead and began to yowl. Then they saw a wrecked ship. Four men clung to lumber. The captain had been an Icelander. He caught fever and lived not long. There were three Hebrides men who lived all that winter at Ketil's expense. They were quarrelsome and not well-liked, but Ketil protected them.

When summer came Ketil asked Haakon Haakonarsson what he wished to do.

"I must return to Iceland and tell my wife of her kin's deaths."

"I think your wife would have preferred that you had met the fate of the others," answered Ketil. But he purchased the three men passage and gave them fine gifts. Ketil was a generous man. The shipwrecked men are now out of the saga.

Gizur turned a page. "Now we go on to another fight with the Skraelings in Markland."

"We have learned what we need to know," said Gunnar.

Njal nodded. "We know now why the Bjornings had to kill Thorri Thorkelsson. He had heard this saga, and learned that the survivors had lied about the outcome of the shipwreck. They had claimed that Thorolf's wife Unn Olafsdottir died last, making her sister Jorunn heir to Thorhof. Instead, Thorolf Openhand survived the rest of his family, so that Thorri's father Thorkel Squint was rightful owner of the land."

"It is a sad time when the law is flouted," said Gizur. "Haakon Snakevision is a powerful man and the Bjornings are greatly feared. You will not find many willing to challenge them."

"I will not ask you to risk yourselves directly, as this is none of your concern," said Njal. "But I will ask you to stand ready to assist me at the Althing. It does not take prescience to know there will be trouble."

"In that event, I will also make sure I bring enough silver to pay compensation for any killings I may find necessary," said Gizur. "Is there anything else you require?"

"I would like you to continue reading," answered Skarp-Hedin. "I am anxious to hear of Ketil's vengeance for his sworn-brother."

8

In Lamb's Fold Month Njal sent for Gunnar. "It is time for me to ride to Thorthesdal and serve Haakon Snake-vision his summons, and gather a jury."

"I will get my horse," replied Gunnar.

"I would prefer that you not accompany me; I will take my nephew Thorgeir, who is a promising young man."

"I do not trust those Thorhof people to behave properly," protested Gunnar. "At least allow me to ask my uncles Thrain Sigfusson and Ketil of Mork to accompany you."

Njal agreed, and added that he hoped all the Sigfussons would come to the Althing that year with their followers, for he required support.

"I have made a grave mistake, my friend," said Njal. "We have proceeded in this investigation without considering that we lack a proper plaintiff. This is a serious legal error."

"Ari Tryggvasson required our help."

"The ghost troubles him, it is true, and it is unlikely we could get the ghost to court, or hold him accountable. But the actual murder is a matter for kin to prosecute, and I was not hired by Thorri the Poet's blood. That is what you must do, Gunnar—find some relative of the dead man and get him to ask my help. Otherwise I face outlawry and confiscation for illegal suit."

"I will go alone this time," said Gunnar. "Skarp-Hedin's wit will not convince anyone to aid us."

9

Njal, his nephew and the Sigfussons stayed with Ari Tryggvasson. Ari called for the eight nearest householders. Njal took each man aside and questioned him carefully, as it would break his case if any juror could be disallowed. Indeed, one man did not live as close as necessary and another owned insufficient property, and a third was an outlaw, but new jurors were swiftly found. All promised to attend the Althing.

The company rode to Thorhof, passing along the way the tomb of Hrafnfaxi. Njal paused, and looked away.

"There will be many more barrows, with dead men sitting upright holding broken axes, before this matter is concluded."

"I do not envy you the sight of the future," said Ari.

Haakon Snakevision stood before his home with his son Hoskuld and with the black-haired Bjorn Bjarnarsson, who walked now with a limp. All three had swords in one hand and spears in the other, and there were many householders with axes.

Njal recited the summons, that Haakon and Bjorn were to come to the Althing to answer charges of secret murder.

Haakon laughed. "Go away, Beardless. When we have done with your case, you will need to dress as a woman to sneak away from Thingvellir." All his household laughed loudly.

Njal's brother's son Thorgeir spurred his horse forward, but Njal blocked him. He also held up a hand to stop Gunnar's uncles.

"We shall address these insults before the Law Rock."

Then the jury dispersed, and Njal and his companions returned to their homes.

10

Gunnar went to visit his friend Sigurd the Unruly, and told him his problems. Sigurd recommended that he speak with the silversmith Arnolf No-nose, whose niece had worked for Thorkel Squint.

Arnolf made him welcome and sat him before the fire. His small daughter came and sat upon Gunnar's lap and braided his beard. Thorkatla was a pretty child, with flaxen hair to her waist, and was also good-tempered and accomplished.

"I will not congratulate you for having a beautiful daughter, as this is not a matter over which you have control," Gunnar said. "But you govern her temperament and education, and this you have done admirably." Gunnar gave Thorkatla his red headband, which she could use as a belt.

Arnolf led Gunnar into the mountains, through inhospitable peat bogs and along lava beds. Only one familiar with the land could find his way through the mires. "This is not good land," said Gunnar. Barely enough lyme-grass was found to feed their horses.

They came upon Thorkel's home in ruins. An aged bondsman lived there, and told them the property belonged to creditors now. Thorkel had not raised enough corn and hay to last the winter, and had been forced to slaughter or sell all the stock. Then Thorkel traded a cow for a very poor boat, and thought to go fishing.

"Every man thinks himself a sailor," said Arnolf scornfully.

The housecarls had had sense enough not to go in that vessel, but Thorkel's pride or foolishness forced him to go anyway. His sons went with him. All had perished when the boat foundered. The bondservants took anything left of value and went their own way, except this one slave who thought himself too old to travel.

"Is there no kin left?" asked Gunnar.

"Thorkel's father came from Norway."

Arnolf invited the old man to stay with him, and promised to send someone to fetch him and his goods.

Gunnar did not speak much during the trip back.

"You seem gloomy," Arnolf said. "One would think you Thorkel's next of kin, as only you seem to mourn him."

"I have no choice. Njal is summoning Haakon Snakevision for the secret murder of Thorri the Poet, and we can do this only for a relative. If I do not find a proper plaintiff, Njal will be outlawed, and I will not allow him to suffer this alone."

"Thorri cannot be worth two hundred ounces of silver. I would not think the renowned Njal Thorgeirsson so greedy that he would risk his life for the lawyer's half of the settlement."

"There is more than a man's compensation at stake here. Haakon has stolen much property and a chieftainship."

"I can see risking outlawry for those."

Gunnar reined in his horse, much angered. "You are wrong if you think we do this for gain. An honorable man named Ari Tryggvasson is being haunted by the fetch of Thorri the Poet; we sought only to help Ari, and this is where the path has led."

Arnolf said that he had mistaken Gunnar's intentions. "You have shown yourself a true hero, and I will now help you," said the silversmith.

Arnolf then told this tale. His sister's daughter had been in the service of Thorkel Squint, and slept with him in his bedcloset. Thorkel gave her the keys and referred to her as his goodwife. She died giving birth to a girl. Thorkel declared there were mouths enough to feed, nor could he afford to hire a wet nurse, and ordered a thrall to expose the child at the crossroads. The thrall secretly carried the baby to Arnolf.

Arnolf told everyone that his wife had borne the girl. Indeed, when they put the infant to Hallgerd's breasts she began to give milk, which seemed a sign that it was meant to be.

"So Thorkatla is the daughter of Thorkel?" Gunnar smiled, greatly relieved. Then his face changed, as if the sun had been covered with clouds. "But he did not sprinkle her with water or name her; she is not legally his heir."

Arnolf told him to be cheerful, and continued. The next summer he had contracted to mend Thorkel's housegoods and weapons, and brought his wife and daughter with him. One day he came to Thorkel Squint.

"You are a wise man," Arnolf told him. "My wife and I cannot agree on something. We would like you to settle the argument."

"I will help if I might," answered Thorkel, much flattered.

Arnolf put the baby upon Thorkel's knee. "I want you to look closely at her, and decide which of us she most resembles. If it is me, then I will name her Gudrun after my mother. But if you think she looks more like Hallgerd, then we will call her Thorkatla, for her grandmother."

"My mother was also named Thorkatla," said Thorkel. The baby had some ashes upon her cheek. At that moment a bondswoman came by with the water for washing; Thorkel took some and dropped it on the child's cheek, then wiped it with his sleeve. He looked carefully at the baby. "She shall be named Thorkatla."

Hearing of this subterfuge, Gunnar laughed long and hard. "You are wasted as a smith, my friend. Your cleverness belongs to a lawyer."

He rode back to Hildarend with an improved spirit.

11

In midsummer Njal and Gunnar rode to the Althing and tented their booths. Njal went to visit chieftains and other powerful men to ask their support in his suits, for there were several minor matters of property he was also involved with. Those men who were bound to him by kinship or friendship or gratitude for past assistance agreed to help. But some refused to become involved; their names are lost but they were important men and were later shamed by their inaction.

The Njal went to hear the Law Speaker recite the laws.

Gunnar rode to the shieling of Otkel the dairyman. The man was honored by the visit, and offered him fresh whey to drink. "Your manslaughter case against Hoskuld Haakonarsson was never finished," said Gunnar. "I would like you to assign me the rights to the case."

Otkel readily agreed.

Then Gunnar went to Ari Tryggvasson and gave him a message from Njal, who requested that he agree to foster a little girl. Ari said that his family had too many boys as it was, and his wife would not be unappreciative of the company.

Next Gunnar found Gizur the Learned and Ogur Freys-priest, and asked them to walk with him. They went up Almanna Gorge, and climbed the cliffs. There they had a good view of Thingvellir. They looked down upon brightly dressed men standing about the Law Rock, and the booths and grazing grounds.

"Do you see the Stronghold Booth?" asked Gunnar.

"There seems to be a giant outside it," replied Ogur.

"It seems to me that I am seeing a wolf," said Gizur, who had a touch of the second sight.

"That is Bjorn Bjarnarsson, a villain and a berserk. His chieftain has bought the friendship of many well-armed men of little account. I think that they plan to shed blood at the Courts, and then retreat to this booth."

"Armed men could hold up there a long time, until their besiegers wearied and went home to harvest," Ogur said.

"They could be burned out," said Gizur.

"That is too cowardly a crime to contemplate," said Gunnar. "I would ask you this—when Njal goes to present his suit, arm your men. I will not ask you to fight with us, but I would like you to bar the way to this booth, if it is within your power."

"That seems a reasonable request," the chieftains replied.

12

That night Skarp-Hedin woke his father. "Let me tell you my dream, kinsman. I thought I would swim in the Oxar

River, but when I came to the standing stones there were many men lying deep in the water, dead upon the bridge. The river was red as blood, but I was able to cross by walking upon the bodies."

"This is no false dream," said Njal. "There will be a great battle tomorrow, and many will fall. This is deplorable. There should not be bloodshed at the Althing."

"You become an old man before your time," replied Skarp-Hedin. "This is an opportunity to advance ourselves."

But Njal was unquiet and did not sleep the rest of the night.

The next day Njal went to the Law Rock. He went unarmed, but his sons wore helmets and carried weapons and shields. There they met Gunnar with his brothers and the Sigfussons, his mother's brothers; they were all well-armed. Others had come to support them. It was said that so many well-built and brave men had seldom been gathered together. There were also many armed men with Haakon Snakevision. They wore cloaks of raven blue. Haakon and his son had gilded helmets, bright coats of chainmail, and painted shields. Bjorn Bjarnarsson wore a bearskin, and stood chewing upon his shield; men avoided him.

Njal stood up on the Law Rock and announced his case. He had a good voice, and it was well heard echoing against the cliff behind him.

"I summon Haakon Snakevision of Thorhof for the secret murder of Thorri the Poet." He listed the wounds on Thorri, and summoned Haakon for inflicting those as well, and called upon his nine jurors to testify that he had made the summons properly. Then he repeated the summons for Bjorn Bjarnarsson. Everyone agreed that he had spoken very well.

Hjalti Prow then stood; he was the son of Einar Thumb and Thorunn Horsehead, and was accounted the best lawyer in the Westfjords. He was a vain man, though his nose

was thought too large. He wore a large new armring of
gold.

"Not many men wear thirty-two cows upon their arm,"
said Skarp-Hedin. "His advice comes dear."

"I invalidate Njal's case against Haakon Snakevision
and Bjorn Bjarnarsson," said Hjalti Prow. "It was improperly done. There is no proper plaintiff. All of Thorri
the Poet's relatives are dead."

Men were surprised to hear that Njal had made such a
basic error.

Hjalti further demanded that Njal be served with outlawry and confiscation for having brought the case improperly. He was eloquent, and convinced many listeners.

Njal spoke again. "I have no rich armrings from my
client, it is true. I have brought the case in behalf of the
dead man's sister Thorkatla Thorkelsdottir."

This news shocked Hjalti, and he went aside to confer
with Haakon.

"We have no knowledge of this relative," he said finally.

Sigurd the Unruly came forward; he was an even-
tempered man and well respected. He testified that Thorkatla was his neighbor, and the daughter of Thorkel
Squint.

Hjalti smiled. He had a sly face. "Then I accuse Njal
of the crime of bringing his case before the wrong quarter
court."

Njal now smiled. "I call upon Ari Tryggvasson of Arasted to testify that he is the foster-father of Thorkatla, so
that she resides in the same quarter as Haakon. The case
has been appropriately managed."

Hjalti then said, "I bring suit against Gunnar Hamundarsson for the secret murder of Bjorn Bjarnarsson."

Everyone looked in surprise at Gunnar, who was the
last man any would expect to kill surreptitiously.

Hjalti went on to call his own jury, who had witnessed
the wounds of the dead man and heard Haakon's summons.

"This is a very serious charge," said Njal. "I will counter with these points. First, Bjorn Bjarnarsson provoked this killing by making vile comments, then by coming upon Gunnar in the guise of a wolf with intent to cause him grievous harm. By all these actions—the insults, the attack, and the shape-changing—he made himself an outlaw so that the killing was legal. Next, it must be said that Gunnar handled the manslaughter legally, by announcing it to some shepherds."

"He did not cover my brother's body," shouted Bjorn Bjarnarsson.

"That was not necessary, as the body was already covered with a wolf skin," Njal replied. "Finally, this suit against Gunnar was announced also at the wrong quarter court. I expect Hjalti to take full responsibility for this infraction.

"Furthermore," continued Njal, "in behalf of Thorkatla Thorkelsdottir I bring suit against Haakon Snakevision for robbery and perjury." He told of the evidence that Haakon had lied in order to obtain his property and chieftainship, and held up the saga which Jorunn had given Gunnar.

Hjalti was conferring in low tones with his client. Haakon pushed him away. "Gunnar Hamundarsson and Skarp-Hedin Njalsson obtained this evidence improperly, by seduction of my wife. My cousin and housecarls will testify that these men spent much time alone with her."

This was a grave charge. Before Njal might answer it, Skarp-Hedin spoke up. "I have been told that The High One recommends one avoid beer and other men's wives. But when a man cannot plow his own field, is he not often jealous of those who seem capable of a man's work?"

At that Hoskuld Haakonarsson screamed out in rage, and threw a barbed spear at Skarp-Hedin. He ducked and it passed over his head. Gunnar then caught the spear in his left hand and threw it back. It passed through Hoskuld's thigh.

He looked down at his leg, which was turning red. "Gunnar has returned my gift," he said, and fell dead.

There was a sudden stillness and in the quiet, Gunnar's halberd was heard to ring loudly.

Then Bjorn Bjarnarsson attacked, leading Haakon's followers after him. The berserker cut down several men. He was very fearsome, with his bloodied axe and the shield with its toothmarks. Njal's supporters fled before him until Ari turned, waiting.

"A small man may fell a tree," he said, and chopped off Bjorn's foot. Then Gunnar ran up. He thrust his halberd through the berserk's shield and into his heart.

13

Gunnar and the others advanced, driving Haakon's men off the Law Rock and among the booths. Women and other non-combatants were cooking and mending weapons or taking the sun; they went to their doorways and watched the battle pass.

Hjalti Prow came up against Arnolf No-nose, and aimed a blow at him with a richly inlaid sword. Arnolf blocked him with his own weapon. Hjalti's sword bent, and he paused to straighten it with his foot.

"A sword should be as good as its ornaments," said the smith. Arnolf then swung his axe and sliced off Hjalti's arm, the one with the gold ring. The limb lay upon the ground. "That is no way to treat good jewelry."

Haakon Snakevision saw his wife's cousin Helgi Starkadsson relaxing beside a booth. Helgi was a Dane, captain of a trading ship. "Will you stand by and watch your kinsman die?" asked Haakon.

"It would seem to be what you deserve," replied Helgi. "But men will not think me worth much if I do not help you." He called to his shipmates and they joined the fight. This evened the odds, and made Njal's faction draw back warily. Helgi himself fought as well as two men, wounding a handful of opponents.

Skarp-Hedin found one of Ari's neighbors, who was

limping away leaning upon a spear. "I have need of your crutch," he said. He ran forward. The spear broke against Helgi's shield, but Skarp-Hedin pushed him back until he fell into a large kettle in which a woman had been making soup. Helgi cried out from the boiling water, and then the Njalsson struck off his head with his axe.

The woman berated him loudly.

"It is true I have ruined your family's nightmeal," said Skarp-Hedin, his cheeks flushing, but he held his temper. He directed the woman to go to his booth and ask Bergthora for better provisions than had been lost.

Haakon's men retreated now toward the Stronghold booth, but found their way barred by Gizur the Learned and Ogur Freyspriest. Haakon's men set down their weapons.

"You are all cowards," cried Haakon Snakevision. Seeking to shame them, he ran at Gunnar, swinging his sword. Gunnar thrust his halberd through shield and mail and deep into Haakon's belly. The chieftain fell to the ground, and was taken inside a booth to die. Then the fight ended, and men bore away the wounded and buried the dead.

14

The next day all gathered again at the Law Rock. Jorunn the Unfortunate sent word that she would accept arbitration, and a dozen chieftains were chosen to consider the case. The wounds and deaths of Njal's followers were set against those of Haakon's, and there was little else to consider, for the fight had been close.

The death of Hoskuld Haakonarsson was set against the case of Otkel's shepherd, and the two canceled each other. The death of both Bjornings were set against the death of Thorri the Poet, the attack on Gunnar and Skarp-Hedin, and their insults. Haakon's demise was considered justified because his crimes had made him an outlaw; many felt that Gunnar had done Haakon's wife a favor.

Hjalti Prow demanded full compensation for his wound. Njal, Gunnar, and Sigurd paid in Arnolf's behalf. Then Hjalti was sentenced to three years outlawry, but it was recommended that he leave the country and not return until all involved parties were dead, in order to keep the peace.

This left only the killing of Helgi Starkadsson to be settled. Jorunn had asked four hundred ounces of silver, double the usual compensation. The judges themselves offered to pay half, and other important men at the Althing reached into their purses so that the full amount was paid immediately. Sigurd the Unruly added a silk cloak with gold embroidery atop the pile of riches, for he had now seen Jorunn and thought her pleasant. He and his own wife had recently divorced due to mutual incompatibility.

It was decided that Thorhof and all of Haakon's property which had been derived from Thorolf should go to Thorkatla; the rest rightfully belonged to Jorunn. Arnolf told her that she might stay at Thorhof in charge of the household so long as she pleased.

Haakon's chieftainship needed to be awarded. Njal said that he would propose they award it to a man who lived in the district, who was skillful, brave, wise, and of good birth.

Gizur the Learned spoke in behalf of the other judges. "We will accept your suggestion in this matter."

"I recommended Ari Tryggvasson," said Njal.

Ari was declared the new priest-chieftain. His neighbors swore allegiance to him immediately, and thought their lot greatly improved.

The rest of the Althing passed peacefully. The men of Thorthesdal rode home together, as did Njal and Gunnar with their followers, and no one was attacked.

15

The next summer Gunnar attended the wedding feast of Jorunn and Sigurd. He learned then that the ghost of Thorri still haunted Thorthesdal. After the harvest he and Njal rode to Arasted.

"I foresee conflict," said Njal.

"This knowledge of the future seems clear even to those of us without prescience," said Gunnar.

They were warmly welcomed, and Ari took them into the firehall and sat them on the high seat, sitting himself on the lower bench. He had not let being chieftain go to his head.

Arnolf No-nose joined them; he and his family lived at Thorhof where they had built a large smithy and planned to raise a new temple, but they spent most of their time at Arasted. Thorkatla and Grim Arasson were very taken with each other, and it was planned that they should wed, if they were still of such a mind when grown.

Ari's wife herself brought the washing water, and then beer. They conversed pleasantly, until Ari said "Here he is."

A silent cloaked man had entered the room and stood at the foot of the hearth. Despite the blazing peat fire, the room suddenly seemed very cold.

Little Thorkatla began to cry. Her brother frightened her.

Grim stood up. He had a sword which Arnolf had made him, wood painted to look like a richly inlaid weapon. "Do not bother us!" said the child, and swung his toy at the ghost's leg.

"Surely I can match this boy's bravery," said Gunnar. He rose, took up his sword, ran to the ghost and struck off the head.

The ghost picked up his head, replacing it upon his neck, then sat down beside the children.

Gunnar reached over and pushed the ghost into the hearth. He did not burn, but spoke.

"Hearty is the homefire   Welcoming warriors."

"You are not welcome. Return to your grave," said Gunnar.

Several of Ari's men stepped forward, emboldened by Gunnar's harsh use of the ghost. They each took one of Thorri's arms and began to pull him toward the door.

Thorri grabbed one servant and threw him into the fire; the other he threw upward so that he was smashed against the rafters. Both were seriously injured.

Gunnar then approached waving his sword again. Thorri retreated before him and at the doorway sank into the ground. But Gunnar would not let him escape. He caught him by his hair and pulled him back out of the ground.

Then he wrestled with the ghost until he got him in an armlock, and forced him to walk before him. All the household followed, until they came to the mound where they had buried Thorri. Ari directed that the mound be opened, and Gunnar shoved the ghost inside.

Njal addressed the ghost. "Thorri Thorkelsson, your presence here is unlawful. You must remain in your home, and no longer bother anyone with unwanted visits or poems."

They placed all of Thorri's effects with him, including his brooch and the saga, and then closed up the mound. Thorri the Poet never left it again, and here the saga of the ghost of Arasted ends.

HE-WE-AWAIT

Howard Waldrop

*"He-We-Await" appeared in the mid-December 1987
issue of Asimov's, with a cover illustration by Dennis
Potokar and an interior illustration by Terry Lee.
Waldrop has only published a few stories in the mag-
azine, far fewer than we'd like, but they have all been
worth waiting for. He is widely considered to be one
of the best short-story writers in the business, and his
famous story "The Ugly Chickens" won both the
Nebula and the World Fantasy Awards in 1981. His
work has been gathered in four collections:* Howard
Who?, All About Strange Monsters of the Recent
Past: Neat Stories by Howard Waldrop, Night of the
Cooters: More Neat Stories by Howard Waldrop, *and*
Going Home Again. *Waldrop is also the author of
the novel* The Texas-Israeli War: 1999, *in collaboration with Jake Saunders, and of two solo novels,*
Them Bones *and* A Dozen Tough Jobs. *He is at work
on a new novel, tentatively entitled* The Moon World.
*A longtime Texan, Waldrop now lives in the tiny town
of Arlington, Washington, outside Seattle, as close to
a trout stream as he can possibly get without actually
living in it.*

*Here he takes us from the Valley of the Kings in
ancient Egypt to the concrete canyons of modern-day
Manhattan, in pursuit of a mystery over five thousand*

years old, a dark and deadly mystery that may de-
termine the fate of humanity . . .

"In the king-list of Manetho, an Egyptian priest who
wrote in Greek in the Third Century B.C., two names
are missing.

They were Pharaohs, father and son. The father,
Sekhemet, by legend reined one hour less than 100
years. Sekhemetmui, his son, a sickly child born to him
in the ninety-first year of his rule, lived less than a
year after his father's kingship ended.

I did not say "after his father died". No one knows
what happened to Sekhemet. Herodotus, who was in-
itiated by the priests into the Mysteries of Osiris, does
not mention either father or son in his list, giving cre-
dence to some kind of sacerdotal conspiracy.

A stele, found in an old temple of Sekhmet, had the
name of Sekhemet defaced in one of the periods of
revision by later kings. The broken and incomplete
stele tells of a great project undertaken in his 99th
regnal year: 10,000 men set out upriver in 600 boats
built for the expedition. Then history is quiet.

That a century of human life in this time-and-death
haunted land are represented only by carvings on a
broken rock is a reminder of all that has been lost to
us for want of a teller."

—Sir Joris Ivane
From the Raj to the Pyramids
Chatto and Pickering, 1888

Always, always were the voices and the cool valley wind.

Ninety-seven times he had made the journey down the
River to pray to Hapi, his brother-god, for a good flood.
Hapi had been kind eighty-six times and had not denied
his prayers for the last nine years in a row, since the birth
of his last, his crippled son.

Sekhemet, Beloved of Sekhmet, Mighty-Like-The-Sun

and Smiter of the Vile and Wretched Foreigner, stood with his retinue on the broad road before his great white house.

Around him was the city he had caused to be built fifty years before, white and yellow in the morning sun. The shadows of the buildings stretched toward the River. Down at the wharf the royal barque was being outfitted for its trip southward up the waters.

Across the Nile were the mastabas of his fathers, and of those before them, cold and grey lumps in the Land of the Dead on the western bank. Here his ancestors slept, their *kas* prayed for, sacrifices offered them, as just in their sleeps as in their lives.

Sekhemet looked back to the balcony of the great house, where his lastborn Sekhemetmui stood watching him. A strange boy, born so twisted and so late, sired in his hundredth year of life, his ninety-first of kingship. Sekhemet did not understand him or his ways.

"The work on the barque awaits your inspection," whispered his chief scribe to him.

Always, always were the voices, more and more voices the older he became, quieter but more insistent.

His ancestors, who had fought up and down the length of the River, had had an easier time of it: uniting the Bee Kingdom and the Reed Kingdom, bringing the Hawk Kingdom under their sway. They had been men and women of action—war pressed on every side, treachery behind every doorway, quick thinking was needed.

Sekhemet had reigned ninety-seven years. All his wars were won while he was still young. Anyone who could offer him treason had long ago been scattered on the desert winds.

The retinue—Sekhemet, his scribes, guards, bearers, and slaves—began its walk in the city he had built across from the tombs of his fathers. His own mastaba was being constructed in the shadow of his father's. The workmen ferried across the River each morning well after sunup and returned long before dark. No one wanted to be caught on the west bank after nightfall.

So it was that they walked in orderly progress, all eyes of persons they met downcast at sight of them, until they happened by the temple of the protecting god of the city, Sekhmet—she with the hippopotamus-head.

There was a commotion at the temple door—it flew open and the doorkeepers fell back. For, coming out of the courtyard, his garments torn, was the high priest, eyes wild and searching.

He shambled toward them.

"Oh Great House!" he yelled. The guards turned toward him, spears at ready. The priest flung himself to the ground, tasting the dirt, his shaven head smeared with ash from the temple fire. "It is revealed to us—wonderful to relate!—a great thing. A few moments ago, a novice, an unlettered boy from the Tenth Nome—but, it is too marvelous!" The priest looked around him, blinking, seeming to regain his composure. He bowed down.

"Oh Great House! Oh Mighty-Like-The-Sun, forgive me! Sekhmet has given a revelation. We come to you this evening in full pomp. Forgive me!" He backed on his knees to the doorway of the temple, bowing and scraping.

Shaken, his heart pounding like the feet of an army at full run, Sekhemet, Smiter of the Vile and Wretched Foreigner, continued on his way to the royal docks.

After the revelation given by the priests a great flotilla was built. Hundreds of ships were loaded with clothing and tools; provisions of garlic, bread, onions and radishes were laid in, jugs of lily-beer trundled aboard. Work on the mastaba across the water stopped.

The armada was filled with slaves and workmen, artisans, scribes, bureaucrats, and soldiers. The ships set out one gold morning following the royal barge up the River.

Somewhere on the long journey south the flotilla put in, for the royal barque carrying Sekhemet and his son Sekhemetmui came alone to Elephant Island where the

Pharaoh made his prayers to Hapi and then returned north-ward.

Nothing was heard of the expedition for a year. The government was run by dispatches sent from somewhere southward of the city on the River.

At the end of the year the royal barge appeared once more at Elephant Island; again Sekhemet and his son sup-plicated to Hapi for a good flood with its life-giving *kemi*. Those of the island's temple who viewed Sekhemet said he looked younger and more fit than in years, transfigured, glowing with some secret knowledge.

Then the barque returned northward down the River. It was the last time the old Pharaoh was seen.

Nine months later a small raft came to the dock of the increasingly-troubled royal city. Foreigners impinged on the frontiers, there was rebellion in the Thirteenth Nome, the flood had not been as great as in earlier years and famine threatened the Canopic delta.

On the raft were one priest and the son of the old Phar-aoh, Sekhemetmui. He was eleven years old and bore on his stunted breast the tablet of succession.

In a few days he was accoutered with the Double Crown of Red Egypt and White Egypt and became Sek-hemetmui "The Glory of Sekhmet is Revealed" and Mighty-Like-The-Sun.

He had been a sickly child. Troubles came in waves, inside his body and out. There was fighting in the streets of the capital. He reigned for less than six months, dying one night of terrible sweats while a great battle raged to the east.

He was put into the hastily-finished mastaba across the River which had been started for his father.

Four hundred years after his death his city was a for-gotten ruin and many miles down the River the first of the great pyramids rose up into the blue desert sky.

In the empty temple of Sekhmet there was a stele devoted to the old Pharaoh. On it were carved the signs: "I, Sekhemet, shall live to see the sun rise 5000 years from now; my line shall reign unto the last day of mankind."

How it was usually done:

The body of a dead person would be taken to the embalmer-priests by the grieving family, their heads plastered with mud, their bodies covered with dust.

The priest would demonstrate to them, using a small wooden doll, the three methods of embalming from the cheapest to the most expensive. In the case of a Pharaoh it would always be the latter.

Then the family would leave and go into seventy days of mourning.

One of the embalmer-priests would be chosen by lot. He would take a knife of Ethiopian flint and with it cut into the left side of the body just below the ribs. The other priests would scream and wail; the chosen priest would drop the knife and run for his life. The others pursued, throwing stones in an effort to kill him, such was their belief about the desecration of a body, and ran him from The House of Death.

Then they would return and dig the brains out of the corpse through the nose with a curved iron hook, procuring most of it in this manner. Then they would pump in a solution of strong cedar oil into the brain cavity and plug the nose and throat.

Other priests reached in through the knife-wound and took out the internal organs, placing them in jars with distinctive tops. In the man-headed jar went the stomach and large intestines. Into the dog-headed they put the small intestines; the jackal-headed vessel got the lungs and heart, and into the hawk-headed went the liver and gall bladder. The jars were sealed with bitumen and capped with plaster.

Into the body cavity they stuffed aromatic spices, gums, oils, resins, and flowers, then they sewed the wound closed. They placed the body in a trough of natrum for sixty-nine days, taking it out only to unplug the nose and

allow the rest of the brains to run out. They spent the
night wrapping the body in linen strips soaked in gum,
and placing it in its wooden coffin, which always had eyes
painted on it so the soul, or *ka*, of the dead could see.

On the morning of the seventieth day the mummy and
jars of organs were given back to the family for burial.
For Pharaohs this usually meant a resting place in some
tomb or mastaba on the Libyan bank of the Nile, the land
of the setting sun and of the dead.

None of this happened to Sekhemet.

When a ruler of Egypt wanted sherbet with his meal next
day, word went out to the royal works.

An hour before dawn next morning, several hundred
slaves would enter a building divided into hundreds of
high-walled roofless cubicles open to the desert air.

The slaves went to the center of the cubicles, from the
floor of which rose a pillar six feet tall and a few inches
in diameter. At its top was a shallow depression, the rim
only a fraction of an inch above the bottom of the con-
cavity. Into this tiny bowl the slave sprinkled a drop of
water and smoothed it into a film.

Each slave did this in several rooms, and there were
hundreds of them.

The temperature of the desert floor never dropped below 34°F. But a few feet off the ground the air, shielded
from any wind by the high thick walls, was colder.

Royal attendants, with a thin spoon made of reed and
bearing triple-walled bowls, waited outside the rooms a
few moments. Entering them and working quickly, turning their heads to avoid breathing in the pillar's direction,
they scraped a fingernail of frost from each pillar-top into
the bowls.

Going from room to room, each gathered the ice. The
many tiny scrapings were placed in one bowl, covered
over, closed and packed in datewood sawdust and carried
to Pharaoh's house.

A few moments before it was to be served it was flavored, one or two small portions to the ruler, his wife, his eldest child and one or two highly-favored guests.

These iceworks, three or four acres in extent, were usually found near the palaces.

Early in the twentieth century A.D., an iceworks was discovered far to the south, where no large cities had ever stood. It covered seventy-two acres and contained eleven thousand cubicles, each with the wonder-working silent pillars.

THE HOUSE OF THE *KA*: I

. . . further into the valley. Perhaps my house will not prove to be safe, will be found out, my resting place defiled, my temple defaced. Surely, though, the priests will not let this happen.

Their hands on me like so many clubs. No pain, just sensation, pressure, as if it were happening to someone else. Things I cannot see.

What if the priests are wrong? Is it possible they tell me these things to put me out of the way? They know my son to be weak: if trouble comes he will not be able to hold the Bee Kingdom and the Reed Kingdom together—the nomarchs of the Delta are too shrewd, as they have always been.

What if they have done these things to be rid of my strength? The thought comes to me now—all their talk, the revelation that I go away from the light to wake to a kingdom my line will rule forever . . .

What madness is this I have done? Guards, to me! Let me up, I say! Take your hands from my divinity!

I cannot move. The cold had seeped through me.

What if the priests do not keep their word? I am lost. My *ka* will be dispersed: I am not dead. They have seduced me, deposed me with only words, words of power and glory I could not resist.

Was ever such a fool on the River Nile?

Now there is no more light, no more feeling. All ebbs, all flows away.

Gods. Sekhmet. Protect me. Thoth, find me not wanting on the scales. Let your baboons weigh me true.

The madness of priests . . .

Outside they came and went, some by design, some because they were lost.

At first they spoke the Old Language, or the black tongue of the south, and the barbaric speech from the northeast. Then they used the long foreign sounds unknown in his time, from far across the salt water, Greek, then the rolling Latin.

Then there were desert languages, and those twisted Latin speech patterns of French and Anglo-Norman, the gutturals of German; Italian and Turkish, then French, English, German again, English, all against the old desert speech.

They brought their gods with them in waves; Shango, Baal, Yahweh, Zeus, Jupiter, Allah and Mohammed, Dieu, Gott, God and Jesus, Jesu, Gott again, Allah, Allah, Money.

Twice people tried to get in—once by accident. They were crushed by a four-ton block balanced by pebbles, one of six. The second intrusion was by design, but when they saw the powdered skeletons of the first they turned away, fearing one, two, ten more deadfalls ahead.

Once there was a tremor in the earth and the remaining blocks fell, leaving a clear passage. Once, water fell from a cloud in the sky.

From inside the sounds—voices, earthquakes, rain, deadfall, praises to gods, the sighing of the gentle dusty wind, the slosh and swing of the Nile itself, the groaning of the earth on its axle-tree—were as the long quiet ticks of a slow, sure, well-oiled metronome.

The man ran through the gates of the small town clutching parchment scrolls to him as he stumbled.

Behind him came the drumming of camels' hooves, the

clang of their harness bells. The cries of the desert people leaped up behind him.

The running man was old; his head was shaven and his face hairless. He ran by the broken and tumbled buildings that had once housed the Christian desert fathers, deserted for more than two centuries.

He fell. One of the scrolls broke into powdery slivers under his hand. He cried out and pulled the others to him.

He looked over his shoulder. The camels were closer. Black-garbed riders, swords out, bore down on him. Eyes wild, he ran behind the broken legs of a statue of Dionysus, trying to climb the jumbled stones of a small amphitheater. He saw far out to his left the ribbon of the Nile, beyond the date-palm orchards. He yelled in his anguish.

The riders surrounded him, their camels spitting and stamping. One of them dismounted from his knee-walking animal, swinging up his sword. He held out his hand.

Weeping, the old man turned the scrolls over to him.

He had been at Alexandria when they came out of the Northeast in black flowing waves, putting all who resisted their holy war to sword and fire. He saw them capture the city and tear down the idols. He followed them to the Great Library. He had wept when they began carrying out hundreds and thousands of books and scrolls and took them to burn to heat the public baths—enough parchment and papyrus and leather to keep them steaming for six weeks.

He had come as quickly as he could to this town, the site of the old temple, for these scrolls. He was the only one of the Society of He-We-Await who had made it this far. No one had disturbed their resting place. But he had been seen as he left the ruins and the cry had gone up.

"These scrolls," one of the mounted men leaned forward and spoke in a thick language the old man hardly understood. "If they contradict the *Koran*, they are heathen. If they support it, they are superfluous."

The man on the ground opened one, then another,

looked at them, puzzled. He handed them up to the one who had spoken.

"They are in the old, old writing," he said. "They are infidel." He handed them back to the swordsman on the ground.

With no trace of emotion, and some effort, the man jumped up and down on them, grinding them to fine shards which sifted away on the breeze.

"We have no time to light a fire," said the mounted leader, "but that will do. Your conversion will come later. First, the books, then the hearts of men."

They turned their camels and sped back toward the wattle-walled village.

Crying, the old man sank down in the mingled dust of writings and bricks, wailing, gnashing his teeth, rubbing his bald head with handfuls of sand.

In the late nineteenth century A.D. artifacts of an especially good quality surfaced on the antiquities market.

The Cairo Museum, responsible for all Egyptian archaeological work, investigated.

They found that a graverobbing family from Deir el Bahrani, near the Valley of the Kings, had made a discovery in the cliffs behind Queen Hatsepshut's tomb about a decade before.

The majority of the tombs which had been uncovered in the Valley had proved empty of goods, the coffins missing their contents.

The graverobbers had found, in a shaft dug into the cliff wall above Deir el Bahrani, a forgotten chapter of history.

There was a marker there, hastily carved, a great quantity of goods from many dynasties, and thirty-six mummies.

The marker told the story—in one of the lawless periods before the XXIst Dynasty, the government fell apart, bandits roamed the towns, foreigners attacked from all

sides. The priests could no longer guard the tombs in the
Valley of the Kings.

Secretly they entered the mausoleums, took out the
royal mummies and brought them to the hidden tunnel,
with such of the grave goods as they could carry, and
secreted them away, hoping their bodies, and the *kas* of
the royal lines, would be safe from marauders.

Of the thirty-six mummies, one—Thutmose the IIIrd—
had been broken into three pieces. The others were intact,
including those of Ramses the Great; Ahmose; Queen Ah-
mes, the mother of Hatsepshut; and Thutmose the Ist and
IInd. The rest were eventually identified, except one. That
of a very young boy about twelve years of age, in wrap-
pings of a much earlier period than the others. He was
entered in the catalogue of the Museum, where the mummies were all taken, as "Unknown Boy (I-IIIrd Dynasty?)."

Doctor Tuthmoses looked at the final reports. They were
magnetometer scans of the west bank of the Nile, from
the Delta, past Aswan to the influx of the Atbara River
above the Fifth Cataract, far longer than the extent of the
kingdoms of the early dynasties.

All the known tombs were marked; all the new ones
found had been checked and proved to be those of later
dynasties, of minor officials. The search had gone much
further out of the Valley than any burials ever found. Still
nothing.

He looked around him at the roomful of books. He was
now an old man. There were others devoted to the cause,
younger men, but none like him. They were content to
sift over the old data again and again, the way it had
always been done since the knowledge of the resting place
was lost twelve centuries before.

He had devoted fifty years of his life to the quest,
through wars, panics, social upheaval, and unrest. He had
seen his mentor, Professor Ramra, grown old and weak,
and embittered, die, with nothing to show for *his* sixty

years of diligent search but more paper, more books, more clutter.

Tuthmoses rang the bell for his secretary, young Mr. Faidul. He came in, thin and dapper in a three-piece suit.

"Faidul," he said. "The time has come to change our methods. Take this down as a record for the Society.

"One: Obtain the best gene splicer possible for a two-day clandestine assignment to be completed on short notice in the near future.

"Two: Send Raimenu and a workaday specialist to Egypt. I want Raimenu to find a woman who wishes to bear a child for a fee of $100,000. Not just any woman. A woman of a family that still worships The Old Way. The specialist is for a mitochondrial check—make sure she's from an African First Mother.

"Three: The first two conditions being met, arrange for a scientific examination of the Deir el Bahrani remains at the Cairo Museum. During this, one of the party is to obtain genetic material from the remains of the "unknown boy," who we know to be the Son of He-We-Await" (Tuthmoses and Faidul bowed their heads).

"Four: The genetic material from Sekhemetmui is to be implanted by the splicer into the egg of the mitochondrial First Mother.

"Five: The child of this operation is to be handed over to the Society and placed in my care to be raised as I see fit.

"End of note."

"So it is written," said Faidul.

"So it shall be done," said Doctor Tuthmoses.

They called him Bobby. He was raised at first by a succession of nurses in an upstairs room which became his world. He was eventually given everything he wanted—toys, games, insects, fish, mammals.

He had large dark eyes, a small head with a high hairline, a short face, an aquiline nose. One of his arms was bent from birth.

What he read and what he saw were censored by Tuthmoses and his staff—everything was tape-delayed and edited. Other children were brought in for him to play with. He was given tutors and teachers.

He grew up self-centered, untroubled, fairly well-adjusted, with a coolness toward the doctor that seemed to be reciprocated.

They were playing one day; Bobby, the teacher-lady and the kids who were brought in after their school let out.

They had been doing some kind of word games, and Deborah the dark-haired girl got up to get something, then had gone over and started talking to Sally Conroe about something. There had been some quiet talk, and then Deborah did a little dance, humming in a whiny voice:

"Yah-ya-ya-ya-yah yoo yah yoo-yah" and then had sung:

"All the girls in France
Do the hoochie-hoochie dance
And the dance—"

The teacher-lady, at that time a Ms. Allen, stopped her with a sharp command.

Bobby found himself staring at Deborah, whom he did not particularly like.

Then Ms. Allen got them all doing something else, and soon Bobby forgot about it.

Deborah never came back to the after-school group after that day. Bobby didn't particularly care.

One evening he was going through some books—the ones he had with the big black places on some of the pages—and he was looking in the one on music, way over toward the back.

He turned the page. There was a bright gaudy photograph of a music machine.

He read the caption: In the 1940s and 1950s, "jukeboxes" (like the 1953 Wurlitzer 150 pictured here) brought music to the customers of malt shops, cafes and taverns.

The machine had disc recordings inside and a turntable he could see. But it was wide and curved, like a box that ended in a smooth round top. It was bright with neon lights, and the sides had what looked like bubbles of colored water inside.

Bobby stared at the picture and stared at it, as if there were something else there.

He held up his hand slowly toward the photo, moving his fingers closer, staring at the page. His hand curved to grip the picture.

"What do you have there?" asked Dr. Tuthmoses, who had come in to check on him.

"A jukebox," he said, still looking.

Tuthmoses peered over his shoulder a moment.

"Yes. They used to be very popular."

Bobby's hand was still held over the page.

"What's wrong?" asked the doctor.

"It's—like—"

"Well, now everybody has music at home. They don't have to go where jukeboxes used to be. They're anachronisms."

"What are anar-ancho—?"

"Anachronism. Something that doesn't belong to its time. Something that has outlived its usefulness. One or the other."

"Oh," said Bobby. He put down the book.

Sometimes, late at night, Bobby thought of the word "anachronism." It conjured up for him a vision of a bright orange, yellow, and green jukebox.

The doctor came to Bobby's room one day when he was eleven.

"I've got some tapes we should watch together, Bobby," he said. "You've never seen anything like them. They're about a faraway country, one you've never seen or heard of."

"I don't want to watch the tube," said Bobby. "I'm reading a neat book about American Indians."

"That will have to wait. You should see these."

"I don't want to," said Bobby.

"This is one of the few times you're not going to get your way," said the doctor. He was old and growing irritable. "It's time you saw these."

Then he gave Bobby a mug of hot chocolate.

"I don't want this, either."

"Drink it. I've got mine here. Watch." The old man gulped the thick hot liquid, leaving himself a dark brown mustache.

"Oh, all right," said Bobby, and did likewise.

Then they sat down in front of the television and the doctor put the tape on. It started with flute music. Then there was a cartoon, a black and white Walt Disney, with sounds and a spider inside a bunch of pointed buildings with carvings on the walls.

Bobby watched, not understanding. He found himself yawning. The carvings on the walls, angular people, came alive; strange things were happening on the screen.

Strange things happened inside him, too. He felt light-headed, like when he had a fever. His stomach was very numb, like the place had been when Dr. Khaffiri the dentist had fixed his tooth last year. He felt listless, like when he was tired and sleepy, only he wasn't. He was wide awake and thinking about all kinds of things.

The black and white cartoon ended and another started—a Gandy Goose and Sourpuss one. They were in army uniforms, in the same place with the skinny curved trees and the pointed big buildings, and Gandy went to sleep and was inside one of them, and stranger things began to happen than even in the first cartoon. Walls moved, boxes opened and things came out, all wrapped—

Things *came out all wrapped.*

There had been a movie after the cartoon and it was ending.

Things came out all wrapped.

It had been about the same things, he thought, but it had been like in a dream, like Gandy had, because Bobby wasn't paying attention—he was watching another movie on his half-closed eyelids.

It was like at the hospital only—

Things came out all wrapped.

Only—

Bobby turned toward the doctor who sat very still, watching him, waiting for something.

Bobby's head was tired but he could not stop, not now.

"I . . . I . . ."

"Yes?"

"I want to go there."

"I know. We're ready to leave."

"I really want to go there."

"We'll be on the way before you know it."

"I . . ."

"Rest now. Sleep."

He did. When he woke up he was in an airplane, miles and miles up, and the air above them and the water below was blue and deep as a Vick's Salve jar, or so it seemed, and he went back to sleep, his head resting on Dr. Tuthmoses' shoulder.

The launch made its way down the brown flood of the Nile. The sun was bright but the air was moderate above the river. There was no feeling of wind, only coolness.

Bobby sat in a chair, watching the river, taking no notice of the other boats they passed, the fellucahs they met. His hands fidgeted on the arms of the deck chair. He would turn from time to time to watch Dr. Tuthmoses. The doctor said nothing; he saw that the wild faraway shine was still in the boy's eyes.

Bobby sat forward. Then he stood. Then he slowly sat back down and slumped in the chair. Tuthmoses, who had his hand up, let it fall again. The launch pilot went back to his fixed stare, whistling a tune to himself.

Another half hour passed in the muddy cool silence.
Bobby shot up so fast Tuthmoses was taken aback.

"Here!" Bobby said, "Put in here!"

Tuthmoses held his hand up, pointed. The pilot turned
the wheel and the nose of the craft aimed itself at a large
rock outcropping. The old doctor sighed; he had been on
an expedition thirty years before which covered this very
part of the River and had found nothing. The boat aimed
at the western bank, the land of the setting sun and of the
dead.

"No, no," said Bobby, jumping up and down. "Not that
way. Over there! That way!"

He was pointing toward the eastern bank, the land of
day. And of the living.

THE HOUSE OF THE *KA*: II

The Light! The light! What place is this?

—is this the room where my soul is weighed? Thoth?
My brother-gods?

Heavy. My limbs are heavy. My brain is a lump. Why
cannot I think? My dreams are troubled. They are swirling
colors.

My son. How he hates the traditions. The things that are
done in the name of being god. He shall have to marry
his half-niece, many years older than he. I should have
had a daughter for him to marry, by his mother also. All
his older half-brothers died before him. But his birth killed
her.

It is too late to sire a queen. I am old. He was so twisted
in his limbs. What pain is that in my knee?

I know you trick me! All of you! These are my last
thoughts. You have left me to die; my *ka* to wither away.
How did I listen to priests?

What great plan, Sekhmet? To put an old man out of
the way?

• • •

Where are my eyes? Have they put me in the jars? How do I think? I am going mad mad mad mad mad

My foot itches.

It took two years and the best people and equipment money could buy and a few times they almost weren't enough.

Bobby was still cared for, but left on his own more and more. He found himself sitting for days, wondering what was happening, what had happened, where he had come in, what his purpose was. He knew he was part of some plan, something to do with the trip he barely remembered.

Dark places in the books disappeared, he could have anything he wanted. Books on Egypt were brought to him when he asked. The television now jibed with the *TV Guide*. He watched the news—depressing stuff on wars, plagues, fires, human misery, suffering, death, live and in color.

Sometimes he thought the old way, the days before the trip were better.

Nothing told him *anything* he really wanted to know.

Dr. Tuthmoses, old and subject to palsy, came to him for the first time in months.

"Tomorrow, Bobby," he said. "Tomorrow we will take you up there with us. There will be a ritual. You will need to be there. We will bring you clothes for it. You get to carry things needed in the ceremony. You're an important part of it. I hope you'll like that."

"I'm going to get to see him?"

Tuthmoses' eyes widened.

"Yes."

"Doctor?"

"Yes?"

"That time, before we went on the trip. When you

showed me the cartoons and the movie. You also put something in my chocolate, didn't you?"

"Yes, I did, Bobby. It was to help you remember."

"Would you give it to me again?"

"Why?"

"If I'm going to be part of this, I want it to *mean* something. I want to understand."

"Don't you have everything you want?"

"I don't have a place," said Bobby. "I don't understand any of this. I've read the books. They're just words, words about people a long time ago. They were interesting, but they've been gone a long time. What do they have to do with *me*?"

Tuthmoses studied him for a few seconds. "Perhaps it's for the best." He got up shakily and walked to the bookcase jammed with titles by Wallis Budge, Rawlinson, Atkinson, Carter. He picked one up, turned pages. "I'll have the drink brought to you tonight. After you finish it, read this chapter." He held the book out to Bobby, held open with his long thumb to a chapter on ritual. "Then you'll understand."

"I want to," said Bobby.

Tuthmoses opened the door. He turned back. "In a year or so you might be able to leave here, go anywhere, do anything you wish. By then it won't matter what you know or whom you tell. But until then, you have to stay."

"I guess I don't understand."

Tuthmoses' shoulders dropped. "I wish I had been a better guardian, a father to you," said the doctor. "It was not to be. Perhaps, later on if I live, and events do not deter, He-willing, we can learn to be friends. I would like to try."

Bobby stared at him.

"Well, that's the way I feel," said the doctor. "Rest now. Tomorrow is the greatest day."

"Of *my* life?"

"Of all lives," said Tuthmoses. He left.

* * *

He was brought into the great long room with the large curtain at the end.

Doctor Tuthmoses, Faidul, and the others were dressed in loose grey robes. Their heads and beards were fresh-shaved.

On the walls were murals, hieroglyphs, evocations to the gods. At one end of the room stood the hippo-headed statue of the god Sekhmet, its thick arms raised in bene-diction. In front of it was a throne of ivory, facing the curtain.

The room was brightly lit though it was early in the morning. When the door opened and Bobby was ushered in, his dark eyes were blinking. He was dressed in a short kilt, he had bare arms, chest and legs. A white headdress spilled down onto his shoulders.

In his crossed arms were a hook and a flail.

Tuthmoses had told him what the ceremony was; the book and drink the night before told him what it meant.

In the early days, once a year, the chief priest would chase the Pharaoh with a flail around a courseway. As long as the Pharaoh could run, his youth and vigor were renewed by the ceremony.

In later years when the kingdoms were united this was changed. A young man was chosen to run the course be-fore the priest, and his vigor would transfer by magic to the ruler. This was the ceremony of *heb-sed*.

Bobby was the chosen runner.

The course was outlined by bare-chested men, standing four feet in from the walls of the room, holding in their hands bundles of wheat.

Before the throne on a low table were symbols of life and death—four empty canopic jars, their effigy-tops un-stoppered, an empty set of scales, an obsidian embalmer's knife, the figure of a baboon.

Another door opened and all in the room, except Bobby and the men holding the wheat along the course, dropped to the ground.

There was the sound of small steps, shuffling feet.

Bobby watched the four men bring the shrunken figure in between them.

He was old, old and bent. They had dressed him in another simple kilt. His skin was pitted and wrinkled, stained in patches of light and dark from chemicals.

He doddered forward, eyes looking neither right nor left. His head had been shaven; there were corrugations in his skull like a greenhouse roof. His legs were twisted. One arm was immobile.

They placed him on the throne, then the attendants fell to their faces.

Dr. Tuthmoses stepped forward, bowed.

On the old man's head he placed first the red crown of the Bee Kingdom, then the white crown of the Reed Kingdom. The old man's eyes focused for the first time at the touch of the crown's cloth.

He looked slowly around him.

"Heb-sed?" he croaked.

"Yes, *heb-sed,"* answered Tuthmoses.

The ancient man leaned back in the throne a little; the edge of his mouth fluttered as if he was trying to smile.

Tuthmoses waved—a priest stepped forward, came to Bobby, took the flail from the hand of his bad arm. Music began to play through hidden speakers, music like in the first of Bobby's dreams while watching the cartoons two years before.

Bobby stepped past the men with the wheat and began to run. The priest's naked feet slapped on the Armstrong tile floor behind him, and the first of the knots on the flail hit him, drawing blood from his shoulder.

He jerked. Faster and faster he ran, brushing by the standing men, and at every third step the flail kissed him with its hot tongue and he yelled.

Some of the wheat covered the floor by the second circuit. On the third Bobby saw spots of blood on the tiles ahead.

They passed the starting point—Bobby kept running. The expected stroke did not come. He looked back over his shoulder. The priest had stopped at the marker, arm still raised. He motioned the boy back and handed him the flail.

Bobby's shoulders twitched as the priest guided him next to Tuthmoses. He was sweating and his chest heaved.

Bobby looked at the old man on the throne—was it only the nearness or did he look less ancient, more human? The music rose in volume, drums, flutes, strings. The old man's eyes grew bright.

"Oh Great House!" said Tuthmoses in the Old Language, "we wait to do your bidding. Behold," he said, waving his arm, "the sunrise 5000 years later!"

The room lights went out.

The curtain pulled back. Dawn flooded the room twenty-two stories up over Central Park. Great towers rose up on all sides, their windows filled with lights. The ocean was a flat smoky line beyond, and the slim cuticle of the sun's red edge stood up.

The old man stared in wonder.

"I have lived to see it," he said. Then he looked at Bobby. His lip trembled.

"Boy," he said. "Here," he lifted his twisted blotched arms toward him. "My flail, my scepter."

Tuthmoses motioned him forward, indicating that Bobby hand them over.

Bobby stepped up on the dais, watching the shaking in the old man's hands as they closed on the sacred objects, pulling them to his breast.

Bobby stepped backwards, picked up the obsidian knife from the table and jammed it under the ribs of the old man and twisted it.

He made no sound but slid up and over his own knees and spilled forward off the throne onto the floor, the scepter breaking on the chair's arm.

"You were the worst father anyone *ever* had!" yelled Bobby.

There was a gasp of breath all around the room, then the sound of someone working the slide on an automatic pistol. The doctors made a rush toward the bloody old man.

"Stop!" said Bobby, turning toward them, knife in his hand.

They froze. Faidul was aiming a pistol at Bobby's head. Tuthmoses stared at him, eyes wide, breath coming shallowly.

"He has seen the sun rise 5000 years from his time," said Bobby. He dropped the Ethiopian knife back onto the table, knocking over the baboon figurine. "*Now*, his line is ready to reign until the last day of mankind."

He walked to the throne, the barrel of Faidul's pistol following him.

"Only this time," said Bobby, "I'll do it *right*."

He sat down.

Beginning with Tuthmoses, and one by one, they bowed down before him, prostrating themselves to the floor tiles. Last to go was Faidul, whose hand began to tremble when Bobby gave him a withering stare.

"What is your first wish, Oh Great House?" asked Tuthmoses from the floor.

"See that my late father is given seventy days' mourning, that his tomb is made ready, that his *ka* be provided for through all eternity."

"Yes, He-We-Await," said Tuthmoses, beginning to tear at his robe and gnash his teeth.

Bobby watched the orb of the sun widen and stand up from the horizon, grow brighter, too bright to stare at.

"Get busy!" he said, turning his head away.

So began the last days of mankind.

THE SHUNNED TRAILER

Esther M. Friesner

"The Shunned Trailer" appeared in the February 2000 issue of Asimov's, *with an illustration by Jason Eckhardt. Friesner's first sale was to* Asimov's, *under George Scithers in 1982, and she's made many sales here subsequently under Gardner Dozois. In the years since 1982, she's become one of the most prolific of modern fantasists, with more than twenty novels in print, and has established herself as one of the funniest writers to enter the field in some while. Her many novels include* Mustapha and His Wise Dog, Elf Defense, Druid's Blood, Sphinxes Wild, Here Be Demons, Demon Blues, Hooray for Hellywood, Broadway Banshee, Ragnarok and Roll, Majyk by Accident, Majyk by Hook or Crook, Majyk by Design, Wishing Season, The Water King's Daughter, The Sherwood Game, Child of the Eagle, *and* The Psalms of Herod. *Her* Asimov's *story "Death and the Librarian" won a Nebula Award in 1996, and she won another Nebula Award the following year. She lives with her family in Madison, Connecticut.*

Here she escorts us through the perilous and low-rent fringes of Lovecraft Territory—White Trash

*Gothic Territory, perhaps—for a very funny visit to
a different kind of trailer park . . .*

When springtime lays its impertinent hand upon the stony
bosom of New England, it is deemed no extraordinary
thing for a young man of my years and education to ven-
ture forth in search of certain genial entertainments such
as may only be procured in sunnier climes than the cob-
bled streets of Cambridge. Alluring though the houris of
sweet Radcliffe may be when snow is drifted deep over
Harvard Square, when the Charles River is a ribbon of
gray between icy banks, and when a man is willing to
date a moose if there is an outside chance that he may get
lucky, it is an indisputable law of nature that the local
ladies lose their former powers to charm once the thaw
sets in. Accordingly I had determined to spend my vernal
academic hiatus from the hallowed halls of Harvard in
pursuit of the Three B's, namely Brew, the Left One, and
the Right One.

I set out upon my pilgrimage of grace with some trep-
idation. Alas, my finances were not of the most robust,
which situation precluded my engaging an aeroplane flight
to the enchanted dream-city of unknown Daytona Beach.
Like some latter-day goliard, it was my misguided inten-
tion to make so long a journey by presuming upon the
kindness of strangers and, in an extremity, upon the reli-
ability of shank's mare.

My expedition into alien lands at first seemed blessed
by my guardian gods, for I was able to engage the atten-
tions of a carload of young ladies passing through Cambridge on their way south from the red-litten towers of
Bennington. It was truly unfortunate that our jolly fellow-
ship came to an abrupt and distasteful end when the
maiden who owned our common conveyance discovered
me paying my compliments to one of her comelier companions. Being of an excitable nature, she was unwilling
to overlook our lack of a chaperone, despite the fact that
it is virtually impossible to engage a trustworthy *duenna*

at three in the morning when one is more or less completely naked.

Thus it was that I found myself engaging alternate transportation somewhere south of our nation's capital. My luck seemed to have departed with my first ride, for the second car to offer me a lift was full of Vassar girls.

I came back to my senses on an isolated stretch of dirt road well below the Mason-Dixon Line. Apart from a vague sense of having been thoroughly exploited in any number of ingenious ways, and the presence of a gaudy tattoo on my left shoulder which referred to Steven Hawking as (I blush) the "Mac Daddy," I had no recollection of my ordeal. In and of itself this was a mercy, save only for the fact that I likewise had no notion of where, precisely, I was nor of in which direction I must now set out in order to find my way back to a more traveled road.

As I stood thus lost and bewildered under the moon's indifferent cyclopean eye, the heavens grumbled their displeasure and it began to rain like an upperclassman pissing on a flat rock. Now my need was both clear and immediate: I must find shelter from the storm. As I staggered along the dirt road, which was rapidly becoming a muddy slough beneath my Nikes, I thought I spied a light in the distance. Hastening toward it, I soon became half-blinded by the rain, which had intensified in both rapidity and vigor. Ere long I could see nothing before me but that one encouraging blur of light, and when ultimately I reached the door that it illuminated, I took no notice of my surroundings but only pounded upon the portal with my last strength.

The door swung open under my unrelenting blows and I toppled into what I thought was a safe haven. Ah, how little I knew then the nameless horrors that awaited me! And yet I must in honesty confess that even had some admonishing angel with a fiery sword appeared to forewarn me of how I then stood in peril, body and soul, I was so grateful to have come in out of the rain that in all likelihood I would have replied to that winged messenger, "Bite me."

No sooner was I under shelter (and ere I was able to take in my surroundings) than the full physical impact of my late hardship manifested itself. My limbs were seized with a mighty trembling, my body was racked by chills and fever, and through my delirium I heard myself declaiming a rather saucy sestina about Voltaire and a well-disposed Merino. I had just arrived at the third iteration of *"Vive les moutons et la France!"* when over-taken by benevolent oblivion.

I awoke to the smell of mildew, stale beer, and deep fat frying. My burning eyes opened to behold a dwarfish, gray-skinned creature which hunched over a miniature gas range, its keg-like bulk swathed in a purple flowered housedress. It clutched a plastic spatula in one paw, and with this it traced arcane symbols in an unknown alphabet within the depths of a black cast iron skillet. Somewhere a recording of Jeff Foxworth routines was playing at top volume. So this was Hell.

As I lay there, amid sheets as damp as the hands of drowned men or importunate Vassar girls, furtively observing the creature at the stove, I was ignorant that other eyes were at the same time observing me. I was made aware of this only when a voice behind me unexpectedly exclaimed, "Look there, Ma! He's woke!"

At this, the spatula-wielding thing turned its head slowly toward me. Ah, pitying heavens! What manner of countenance now met my eyes! It was a face that might be termed human only as a courtesy. The skin thereof was, as I have already remarked, of so drab a cast as must be classified as gray. The few tufts of wiry hair atop the broad, flat head were of no perceptible color at all. The bulging eyes and wide, almost lipless mouth, were batrachian features whose like I had never seen outside of my elementary biology dissection lab. Indeed, as the creature approached me, I imagined that it was preceded by the aroma of formaldehyde, although I quickly realized that this was merely the smell of breakfast.

"So he is," the creature said, and when it spoke I presumed from the timbre of its voice that it was a female. She smiled, a grimace that set my stomach to quaking like a blancmange. In fear for my powers of peristalsis, I sought to revive my intestinal fortitude by diverting my eyes from that uncanny visage and fixing them upon some pleasanter sight.

Fat chance. Above my head a low, curved, poorly lit ceiling stretched off into ill-omened shadows, suggesting a dwelling shaped according to no sane architectural principles but rather based on the Hostess Twinkie (™). It was narrow to the point of inducing claustrophobia in snails, yet these tight confines had not deterred its inhabitants from packing every available inch of wall, shelf, and countertop with the wretched idols of Kitsch, demon-god of yard sales. To my left I beheld a calendar illustrated with a photo of a pig wearing lingerie. To my right loomed a row of syrupy-eyed children, pastel-colored figurines adorned with idiot simpers and odious observations like: "A Friend Returns Your Car Keys But Holds Your Heart." Nor might I evade the horror by staring directly overhead, for someone had affixed to the ceiling a Mylar imitation of a mirror framed by the words *If You Ain't Smiling Yet, It's Not My Fault.*

"Dear God!" I exclaimed. "I'm in a trailer!"

"Whoa, can't hide nothin' from you, college boy," Ma said dryly. She brought the sizzling skillet almost under my nose. "Hungry?"

"Ah . . . maybe?" I replied, pulling the sheets up to my chin. I was fully in my senses now, after having had them frightened out of me, and had just become cognizant of the certitude that I had been sleeping *au naturel*. In a moment of painful epiphany, I knew that what I passionately desired more than anything else in this world—even beyond certain private fantasies I had long entertained concerning the Spice Girls and a large tub of chocolate frosting—was to get my pants back on and myself the hell out of there.

My distress must have painted itself plain to see upon my face, for the creature snickered in a dreadfully *knowing* manner, and even went so far as to make a playful feint at the nether hem of my enshrouding bedlinens with her spatula.

" 'Sall right, honeybug, they's just dryin' out some. Yer jeans, that is. Won't know about them sheets until later if you get my drift and I think you do, heh, heh, *chugger-umpf!*"

"Aw, now, *Ma*—!" The same voice which earlier had declared my waking state now sounded again in my ear. The thin mattress beside me sagged as a second being, marginally nearer the human form than Ma, plopped himself down beside me on the bed. "Don't you mind her none. She always gets kinda brassy to guests when it's our turn to host the sabbat prayer meet."

"Sabbath prayer meeting?" I echoed, or thought I did. The minor difference in our exchange eluded me, although later on its dreadful significance did not. Of course by *then* it was too late. It always is.

"*Brassy,* am I?" Ma's tone hit somewhere between a first alto and a blender full of cockatiels. She boxed her offspring's ear smartly and snapped, "That how I learned you manners? You keep a civil tongue in your head, boy, or I swear I'll—!"

"Shoot, Ma, where else *would* I keep it?" he replied, and with that an unimaginable stretch of flabby blue-black flesh shot out of his mouth and flew the length of the trailer, returning with terrible alacrity and a copy of *TV Guide* stuck to the tip. "Thee?" he concluded as he wrestled with the tongue-tying periodical.

The sight of this unmanning spectacle at first stunned me, then caused me to break into a nonstop stream of mindless chatter, alternately thanking mother and son for their philanthropy and begging them to give me back my clothing that I might no more abuse their hospitality. The monstrous pair was visibly baffled.

It finally devolved upon the son to address me, when he could get a word in edgewise. "Friend," he said, "I can tell you're a little put off by what I just done, but I can't help it; it's my nature. Not the sort of thing you're used to, what with your big city ways and your canned eggnog and your edible underwear and all of them other high-tone delights of civilization. Well, Ma and me, we're just simple, Elder Godsfearing country folk. Our ways ain't your ways, but we don't mean you no personal harm. Less you'd happen to be a virgin—?" His voice trailed off on a hopeful note, which it was my duty to squelch at once. He was crestfallen, but continued. "Too bad, too bad. Anyhow, I'm assuming that you're mostly upset by our looks. That right?"

"Well, you *do* look a bit—" I groped for a way to speak accurately without insulting the folk who had literally taken me in out of the rain "—batrachian." It was a good word to use, for the odds were excellent that these people had never heard it and, rather than taking umbrage, would mistake it for a compliment.

To my shock and chagrin, I was half wrong. The son slapped his meaty thigh and looked extraordinary pleased. "That's *it!* That's just *it*, brother! You have gone and hit the nail smack dab on the head. What we are, see, is New Liturgy Batrachians, the only spawn of Great Cthulhu who have preserved His teachings and commands and assorted hideous gibberings in the *truly proper and orthodox* manner."

"Not like them sinners up north in Innsmouth and Arkham," Ma put in scornfully. "Hoity-toity little shitepokes, ever' last one of 'em, think they're so all-fired great 'cause they got them Dagon churches with store-bought roofs on 'em and a coupla stuck-up high priests that snuck their sorry froggy butts through Yale Divinity. Hunh! Why, they're no more fit to greet the rise of sunken R'lyeh from the depths than a pig to sing Kenny G's greatest hits."

With those words, the full horror of my situation struck me: Cthulhu! Innsmouth! Arkham! Sunken R'lyeh! Names, alas, whose sinister meanings were not unknown to me. When I was a boy at home and a day student at St. Dimmesdale's Prep there had been one among my schoolmates whose pale complexion, grim mien, and demon-haunted eyes had provoked my curiosity. His name was Randolph Akeley, a boarding student who seldom spoke of his family, nor of much else save the occasional froward Latin declension. Intrigued by his reclusiveness, I resolved to learn more of him. One day I stole into his room, on the pretext of borrowing a condom, and nosed about. He came in and caught me studying a large, expensively framed photograph of a smiling angler displaying a fish almost as large as he was himself.

"Nice catch," I remarked, trying to put a bold face on things.

"That's what my sister said when she married him," Randolph replied in his flat, affectless voice.

"I meant the fish," I said.

"So did I. Was there anything else you wanted?"

I stammered out my contrived excuse for calling upon him and he detained me only a moment while he located the item I had requested. I was deeply startled to discover that a person of Akeley's unsociable temperament had such a thing to hand, yet there it was. It was of an unfamiliar make with nothing upon the wrapper save the image of a black goat in one of those red-circle-and-sideways-slash symbols. Later on, when again my inquisitive nature got the better of me and I opened it, to my horror I perceived it to be a *condom of alien and unknown geometry!*

That was enough to put paid to any further fascination young Randolph Akeley might have held for me. We never exchanged another civil word, although shortly thereafter I received in the post a crudely printed pamphlet entitled *Cthulhu Awareness for the Non-Inbred Seeker.* In this manner did I learn of the Elder Gods, of Nyarlathotep, of Azathoth, of Yog-Sothoth and Shub-Niggurath and a dozen others whose names alone seemed to be the product of a demented mind with a bad lisp. Within the pages of that hellish tract did I read of how they had been banished for a time from the sight of man, likewise of the arcane and unspeakable worship still done to these deities from beyond the stars, worship by depraved, half-mad cultists whose ultimate goals were to bring about the Elder Gods' return from well-merited exile and to reestablish their vile reign over all the earth!

I returned the pamphlet to Akeley privately, in politic silence, although I did feel constrained to give him a dollar when he thrust his *Save the Shoggoths* collection can under my nose. At the time it seemed a cheap price to pay for my escape.

What price would such flight be now?

My hosts, mother and son, were somewhat troubled by the silence whither my apprehensive recollections had deposited me. Ma shook her head and sadly said, "Y'know, if'n I had a nickel for every time I heard people like you go on all smarmy-like about how looks don't *really* matter and it's what a body's like on the *inside* what counts, I'd be able to buy me a decent Sunday-go-to-orgy dress and then some. But talk's cheap, even for a bigot like you."

"I am *not* a bigot! I'm a Harvard man!"

"*Ha!* If you was any more fulla shit, your eyes'd be brown. You ready to swear you're not carrying 'bout half a hunnerd prejudicial thoughts 'gin Butchie and me just because we happen to look like frogs and worship the Elder Gods and—?"

"Bu—Bu—Butchie?" I repeated idiotically. It did not sound like a name proper to a potential purveyor of human sacrifice.

It was the first time I had ever seen someone with gray skin blush. " 'S not my real name," he said sullenly.

"Which is—?"

Butchie swallowed hard: "Kermit." The corners of his

mouth turned down, which placed them somewhere in the vicinity of his knees.

In the ensuing awkward silence, Ma left the trailer briefly, returning with my clothes. They smelled of sunshine, fresh air, and Tide. (Though, for all I knew, it was a malign and fantastic Tide that once had swirled about the spires of Great Cthulhu's blasphemous abode in sunken R'lyeh and—Oh, the hell with it, it was plain Tide laundry detergent, probably bought on sale at Wal-Mart.)

"They're startin' to arrive," Ma said as she tossed my apparel onto the bed. "Cousin Ephraim's just now pullin' in with that old family rattletrap of his, and the car don't look too good either. Now, city-boy, I don't mind you talkin' down to me under my own roof, but I'm tellin' you right now I won't have you doin' the same to my blood kin, nor my friends and neighbors, so if you can't get down off your high night-gaunt and act mannerly, you can just hit the road right now. Otherwise you're more'n welcome to stay, and maybe we can scare you up a ride to the bus depot after. Like Butchie says, we're hostin' the sabbat here today and I wouldn't mind an extra pair of hands to help me get the food on the table."

"I'd be more than happy to oblige," I said. "It's the least I can do to thank you for taking me in last night." What evil angel possessed me to give such a reply, so glibly? It must have sprung from some lingering ghost of shame for my indefensible bias against Ma and Butchie, a prejudice based solely on their looks, their creed, their economic and social standing, and their abuse of the Budweiser logo as an interior decorating motif. No sooner were the words out of my mouth than I repented them, but there could be no going back. No stronger bond exists upon this earth than the word of a Harvard man, I don't care *what* that self-styled Camilla-Mistress-of-Pain-person over on Brattle Street claims.

Ma was more than pleased. "Well, that's *mighty* pink of you, city-boy, *mighty* pink. Me and Butchie'll give you some privacy so's you can get decent, and then you just come on out and join the fun." With that they left the trailer.

I dressed with alacrity. I was not in any hurry to become a part of the "fun," as Ma termed it, but reasoned that the sooner I discharged my obligations, the sooner I might be on my way with a clear conscience. Fully clothed at last, I flung wide the trailer door and stepped into nightmare.

I also stepped into something else. I regret to say that this accident caused me to curse loudly enough to draw Ma's attention.

"Gods *damn* it, Billy-Joe Tindalos, you pick *up* after them hounds o'yours!" she bellowed, shying an empty bottle at the head of a snot-nosed abomination from beyond the stars or under the porch or somewhere.

As I scraped the muck from my shoes, I looked around. The space before the trailer teemed with all manner of weird beings, some of the same amphibian appearance as Ma and Butchie, others whose hair had a disquieting tendency to hiss, and still others whose skin bore the leprous cast of a fish's belly. To these, one and all, Ma extended the hand of kinship and greeted them with a cheerful, "Iä, Iä, y'all! Grab a cold one and kick back, we'll start the nameless rites and obscene gibberin' soon's the band tunes up some."

Something tapped me moistly on the shoulder. I turned to face a pair of Ma's guests, beings of such abhorrent and alarming appearance as to make even Jerry Springer think twice before booking them. The male was clad in a grease-stained sweatshirt, the sleeves cut off, the front limned with faded runes proclaiming it stolen from the Miskatonic Co-Ed Naked Chug-a-Lug Team. His mate sported a similar garment, its message to the world simply *I'm With Eldritch.*

"Yo, city-boy," the male said, his breath a musky compendium of all things foul and loathsome, with just a hint of Cheez Doodles. "You seen our kid?"

"I'm sorry, I'm a stranger here," I replied. "I wouldn't

know the little fellow if I tripped over him."

The female snickered. "Oh, if you done that you'd *know* him all right! Right before he sucked your brains out through your eye-holes."

"*I heard that,* Selma Jean!" Ma's words boomed out as her formidable presence manifested among us. "What d'you think yer doin', tryin' to run off this nice young man when he's said he'll help me set out the noon meal? Maybe you don't *want* to eat my prize-winning barbecue after sabbat?"

"*Your* barbecue?" The male licked his lips, a gesture that likewise wetted down all of his face and part of his lady's. (Fortunately this was a sight for which Butchie's earlier display of lingual excess had prepared me.) "Man, your barbecue kicks *cloaca*. Let's get this show on the road, 'cause once we hit that last 'Cthulhu f'thagn,' I'm beatin' feet for the table." He grabbed Selma Jean and dragged her away.

"Services be startin' real soon now," Ma informed me. "I got to go, but meanwhile why don't you see to the spread? All the stuff what's s'posed to go out on the tables's in them coolers under the tree."

There was only one tree she could mean, a titanic, gnarled, lichen-shrouded botanical anathema that only a deeply kinky druid could love. The trailer that had been my haven the previous night was—as I now saw—but one of many that nestled, like scabrous mushrooms, among its far-flung roots. In its distant shade reposed a number of picnic tables, a pyramid of beer kegs, and the prophesied coolers.

As I approached the tree it was my misfortunate necessity to pass between several of the other trailers, a gauntlet of visceral terror. Innumerable lawn flamingos, their plastic beaks twisted into leers of unholy malice, followed my progress with glittering, evil eyes. The incessant creak-creak-creak of spinning pinwheel sunflowers thrust their droning paean to iniquity through my throbbing skull. The one ray of hope that fleetingly lightened my way—the sight of a welcomely prosaic statuette of the kind commonly referred to as Our Lady of the Upended Bathtub—was instantly extinguished when I noticed that the supposed Madonna had more tentacles than conventional iconography generally allows.

I was in a cold sweat and breathing heavily by the time I reached the coolers, but I soon stiffened my backbone and set to work. As I relieved the coolers of their contents, I was only half aware of the muted sounds of Ma's kinfolk raising their voices in worship. The glubberings and whinings, the shrieks and ululations, the bad guitar riffs and worse banjo solos, all united in one quasi-musical discord that would probably go platinum in a heartbeat if anyone from ASCAP showed up in these parts with a tape recorder.

"Purty sound, ain't it, city-boy?"

I looked up from my labors and saw yet another of Ma's relations perched atop the table beside me. She was a young female of certain healthy thoracic dimensions that permitted me to overlook the fact that she had a mouth that even Mick Jagger would have to kiss in installments. The thin fabric of her top (one that announced "My Parents Howled on the Frozen Plateau of Leng and All I Got Was This Lousy T-shirt") was stretched to the point where merely watching her breathe was a religious experience.

"H—how do you do?" I rasped.

"Jus' fine, less'n Daddy catches me," she replied with a grin that covered two zip codes. "Name's Beulah May Waite. Uglier'n a shaved dog's ass, ain't it? I like my nickname better."

"Which is—?" I asked, leaving a cooler still half-full of gelatin salads to look after itself.

"Can't Hardly." My comprehension registered as a beautiful scarlet flush, which only encouraged her to straighten her shoulders in a way designed to bring down empires. "Tsk-tsk, city-boy. Maybe you better reel in that tongue o' yours before someone mistakes you for one o' the family and hauls your butt back to services. They's compulsory, y'know."

"In that case, why aren't *you* over there?" I countered, scrambling to recover some minuscule portion of my self-possession.

" 'Cause Daddy thinks I'm doin' homework." She waved a familiar black-and-yellow booklet at me. I never knew that Cliff's Notes published a study guide to *The Necronomicon.* I was about to ask my bosomy batrachian babe where she'd purchased such an item, as a clever prelude to less academic discourse, but it was not to be. My suave moves perished unmade, my cleverly seductive chit-chat never left my lips. A dire air of cryptic menace fell over the trailer park, an atmosphere redolent with such ominous significance that I found myself immobilized like one who has stumbled upon the site of ancient and un-hallowed sacrifice, or has studied for the wrong subject during finals week.

"Yog have mercy!" Beulah May cried, wringing her hands.

"What is it?" I was at her side, ready to defend her fair person against any peril. "What's wrong?"

"There! Look there!" She pointed to the north and moaned with fear.

Well might she moan! For now I too saw, against a morning sky gone suddenly dark, the unmistakable funnel shape of an onrushing twister in search of its natural prey, the trailer park.

The gravity of our situation had a peculiar effect on me. Rather than run away screaming in mindless panic, I felt instead washed by a great calm. Solemnly I said, "Ms. Waite, we must warn the others."

"Oh, it's no good, not a lick of good at all!" she keened, clutching her hair. "They's all deep into the rites by now; they won't quit in mid-*Iä* for no one or nothin'!"

"That remains to be seen," I replied and, taking her firmly by the hand, we sought out the place where Ma and the rest were calling upon the Elder Gods.

They were conducting their services in an open space behind my hosts' trailer. The same innate curiosity that in former days had made me snoop in Randolph Akeley's room now manifested itself as an unhealthy desire to view the infernal shrine to which they paid their cacophonous homage. After all, I reasoned, with the twister fast bearing down upon us, this stygian fane might soon be literally gone with the wind. Fast in the toils of my own over-weening nosiness, I winkled my way into the crush, Beulah May in tow, for a better look.

I winkled my way out again doubletime and stared at my companion. "That's a wading pool in there," I stated.

"Uh-huh," she said.

"Your extended family is standing there, three deep, chanting barbaric hymns to a child's wading pool."

"Sometimes they do an uptempo number, too," she offered.

"They are standing around a child's wading pool—a child's *Power Rangers* wading pool, might I add—with a folding lawn chair set up in the middle of it."

"Well, they can't just plunk the idol of Great Cthulhu straight in the *water*. That wouldn't be respectful. If you already got a shrine and an idol and a *salaried* preacherman like we do, you gotta have an altar, too. *Anyone* knows that." She spoke disdainfully, like every religious Insider who has ever relished telling an Outsider that he is ignorant, ineffectual, and inferior, a smug state of mind that allowed her to forget our imminent danger.

I did not care to be condescended to by the likes of Beulah May Waite. "Your *shrine* is a Power Rangers wading pool, your *altar* is a folding lawn chair, your *idol* is a stack of Mrs. Paul's frozen fish sticks boxes, and your *preacherman*—salaried or not—has just placed a paper party hat on top of the whole soggy mess."

"I should hope so; it's Great Cthulhu's *birthday*. But I guess you didn't know that *either*, huh, city-boy?" Ms. Waite had fallen out of temper with my reportage of the obvious, and apparently impatience brought out a viciously mean streak in the girl for she then sneered: "I guess they just never taught you anything about that up at *Yale.*"

"*Yale?!*"

That did it. That was the straw up with which my proud Harvard-educated camel's back would not put. Her effrontery had no excuse: I was wearing a crimson and white shirt proud with the name of fair Harvard. She could not hope but know; the insult was deliberate, and one that I would not brook even from a woman of twice Ms. Waite's endowments.

Anger kindled in my belly. Deep within my entrails I felt the old powers churn. My eyes burned with the rage of a thousand demons. Minor lightnings crackled from my fingertips and potent words of austere and fearsome condemnation roared from my mouth. The worshippers around the wading pool broke off their mesmeric chant, although the banjo player wouldn't take the hint. I blasted him to strings, splinters, and moist froggy smithereens with a minor side-spell and inwardly thanked God that I had opted to major in something more practical than English.

The amphibian congregation scattered before me in terror, hopping into their waiting vehicles and speeding off at a furious rate. Beulah May vaulted onto the back of a Harley, straddling the bitch seat behind a jacket-wearing member of the Yuggoth's Angels. I laughed triumphantly to watch her flee my just and awesome wrath.

Silly me: I'd forgotten all about the tornado.

It had not forgotten about me, though. I heard its approaching roar and felt the first lashings of its captive winds at my back. I fell to my knees then and there and raised my voice in prayer. "O Lord," I began, my eyes tightly closed against earthly distractions. "Lord, I implore Thee, save me. And if that's not possible, then at least don't let me have to watch a cow go flying past before I die. If I've got to go, let me do it without suffering the indignity of any stupid movie clichés first, please. Amen."

Hey, I liked *that scene with the flying cow!*

My eyes shot open. "Who's there?" I demanded, though I had to shout my challenge down the throat of the screaming wind.

Me, said the wading pool. And with no more prologue than that, the tentacled countenance, leathern wings, and squamous bulk of Great Cthulhu erupted from the waters. He was wearing the paper party hat and looked like a squid on a toot.

Thus is it written in ancient tomes of forbidden lore: *Verily the Elder Gods do not fart around.* (This sounds better in Latin.) With a single stroke of his gargantuan paw, Great Cthulhu swept the tornado from the sky. A grateful hush fell upon the heavens and the earth. I tried to stammer my thanks as well, but the strain of the moment would not let me do other than raise my voice in a reedy rendition of "Happy Birthday to You."

The Elder God stopped me before I got to the end of the "How old are you now?" verse. Perhaps he was sensitive about such matters. *Look, don't mention it, all right?* he said. *I was summoned anyway, I might as well answer a prayer or two as long as I'm in the neighborhood.*

"But I wasn't praying to *you,*" I felt bound to point out.

Hey, Coke or Pepsi, Mickey D's or Burger King, paper or plastic, who gives a shoggoth's ass? His bat-like wings rose and fell in an affable shrug. *Besides, if you weren't praying to me now, you will be some day.*

"I . . . don't really think that I'm going to—"

Sure you will! My demurral did not seem to affect his good humor at all. *Because it's guaranteed; you won't have a choice. Baby, it's comeback time!*

"This comeback, it's not going to be *too* soon, is it?" The thought of my dear Mummy's reaction if I didn't get married in the Episcopal church scared me worse than Great Cthulhu ever could.

Sooner than you think, college boy. I haven't been

*wasting all my time dreaming the aeons away in sunken
R'lyeh. Damn sharks keep swimming up my nose every
few centuries, for one thing. I figure that since I can't get
any decent REM sleep anyhow, I might as well get off my
thumb, bring about the return of the Elder Gods, overrun
the globe, reward our followers, destroy our enemies, and
yada, yada, yada.*

"Is that why they were invoking you here?" I asked,
unable to repress a shiver. "To begin the conquest of
earth?"

The fearsome being gave me a disbelieving look. *On
my* birthday?!

In a more amicable tone he confided, *Listen, college
boy, these are nice folks out here, so nice that I don't
have the heart to tell 'em how all their rites and sabbats
and pep rallies and frozen ichor socials won't do dick to
bring back the good times. Oh, that sort of thing was all
right once, but it'll take more than faith to float sunken
R'lyeh. If you really want to* accomplish *something these
days, you've gotta have the chops, the tech, the brains.
And to get that, it's not what you know, it's who you
know: Network, network, network!* He slapped one paw
into the palm of the other to emphasize his words. *Which
is exactly what I've been doing. No more seeking out the
debauched mongrel races of the world, no more scattering
my spawn like there's no tomorrow, no more breeding
with cannibal South Sea islanders and barbarian savages
in the cold wastes and people from Massachusetts, nuh-
uh. Besides, who knows where they've been? No sir, nowadays I've got some* really *scary guys on my side, and I
didn't even have to say "Of course I'll respect you in the
morning" to get them!*

"Who are they?" I demanded. "What manner of men
would be so degenerate, so corrupt, so possessed of an
unfeeling lust for pure, ultimate, uncontested power and
worldly dominion that they would betray their fellow human beings and serve you?"

The horrendous creature from between the nighted

gulfs of space winked at me and flicked his party hat to a more rakish angle with the tip of one bloodstained claw. *Tell you what, sport, I'm gonna leave you a clue.*

Something dropped from his paw. It splashed into the water at his feet, creating a plume of fetid smoke and a violent burbling on impact. Ere the last seething hiss died away, he was gone.

I stood for a time recovering my composure. Then, with rapidly beating heart I steeled myself to face the smoldering token which the awful Elder God had left in his wake. By inches I sidled closer to the edge of the deceptively peaceful wading pool and with a manful effort gazed down at what reposed beneath the softly lapping waters.

Ah, the accursed thing! Even now, even here, safe once more within fair Harvard's ivy-swathed incubation pouch, the memory thereof fills me with a griping nausea and a terror whose claws are set into the uttermost depths of my soul. That thing, that damned "clue" that the departing Elder God had left me was no ordinary object, but a warning to all mankind, an omen that wordlessly spoke of our predestined doom, a harbinger of the inevitable extinguishment of all things kind and warm and good and human in the earth, in our lives, and in our very hearts. For you see, it was—it was—

It was the class ring of a graduate of M.I.T.!

THE COUNTRY DOCTOR

Steven Utley

"The Country Doctor" appeared in the October 1993 issue of Asimov's, *one of a lengthy string of sales that Steven Utley made here throughout the decade of the nineties. In the story that follows, he offers us an unsettling study of how even that most familiar of territories, home itself, can suddenly be shown to be alien, ominous, and strange . . .*

Steven Utley's fiction has appeared in The Magazine of Fantasy and Science Fiction, Universe, Galaxy, Amazing, Vertex, Stellar, Shayol, *and elsewhere. He was one of the best-known new writers of the seventies, both for his solo work and for some powerful work in collaboration with fellow Texan Howard Waldrop, but fell silent at the end of the decade and wasn't seen in print again for more than ten years. In the last decade he's made a strong comeback, though, becoming a frequent contributor to* Asimov's Science Fiction *magazine, as well as selling again to* The Magazine of Fantasy and Science Fiction *and elsewhere. Utley is the co-editor, with Geo. W. Proctor, of the anthology* Lone Star Universe, *the first—and possibly the only—anthology of SF stories by Texans. His first collection,* Ghost

Seas, *was published in 1997. He now lives in Smyrna, Tennessee.*

Gardner was drowning, and strangers were laying hands on the bones of my forebears. I felt obligated to see that liberties weren't taken with my grandmother, my great-grandmother, and other good, God-fearing ladies, so I put the business on auto pilot and made the drive as if on auto pilot myself.

I viewed the visit as a familial duty, not a sentimental journey. I hadn't been back to Gardner in twenty-five years. I'd always told myself that, with my grandparents dead and their house taken over by obscure cousins-removed, there was nothing to come back for. Soon there would be nothing to come back *to*. The dam was completed, the waters were rising. Gardner was drowning.

Once in the town, however, I couldn't simply drive to the cemetery. It wouldn't have taken two minutes. Wherever you were in a place the size of Gardner, you weren't far from anywhere else, and now, especially, everything was smaller and closer together than it had seemed when I was a kid. But I found that I had to drive down my grandparents' old street, had to stop in front of what had been their house. I sat with the motor running and stared disconsolately. Throughout my childhood, though I moved wherever the military took my father, my grandparents' house, a big warm clapboard pile, had re-mained the center of the world, the universe—*home*. My earliest memories were of being in that house, surrounded by relatives, loved, safe. Now it sat waiting for the water. My grandfather had been a carpenter, among other things; I could see his shed in back. There had been a vegetable patch back there, too. My grandmother had shelled a lot of peas and snapped a lot of beans from it.

The other houses on the block had once been features of a familiar landscape. Now, curtainless windows gave most of them a look of stupid surprise. One was carefully boarded up, as if the owners fully intended to return. The house next to it looked agape and miserable. Paint hung from it in strips. The owners must have stopped bothering with upkeep when they heard about the dam; finally, they'd just walked away. All but one of the lawns on the block were overgrown. A handful of people still remained, the die-hard element, determined to hold out until the water lapped over their doorsteps, and to keep their yards looking nice in the meantime.

It was three blocks to the cemetery, long blocks for someone dragging an orthopedic shoe. Nevertheless, I told myself. Nevertheless. I turned off the motor, got out of the car. The sun was at zenith. There was no wind. A male chorus of cicadae sang of love's delights to prospective mates. The day felt and sounded exactly like all the summer days I'd spent in Gardner in my childhood. I put my hands in my pockets and started walking, slowly, stunned by the force of the memories crowding in on me. I remembered how my grandmother used to sit in a metal porch chair and, as she put it, have herself a little talk with Jesus while she snapped those beans. Sometimes she sang gospel songs. She only ever sang the melodies, but I had been to enough revival meetings to know the words to whatever she sang. Sometimes, hearing her, I'd stop my playing and sing the words while she hummed. . . .

My eyes began to sting. Gardner was drowning.

Around the corner had lived Blanche, who was my grandmother's age and whose relation to me was, then and now, unclear. Someone lived there still—a green station wagon with a dinged-up fender sat in the driveway, and there were curtains in the windows—but Blanche herself was long dead, killed in an automobile accident. I'd like her a lot. One summer, she had given me the empty coffee can in which I buried my grandmother's dead parakeet Petey. I knew exactly where I'd scooped out Petey's grave and wondered what I might find if I were to open it now. Nothing, probably—at most, a few crumbling shards of coffee-can rust. Tiny little bones dissolve in no time. On the next block was the crumbling brick shell of Cobb's Corner Market, where I'd sometimes spent my entire weekly stipend, twenty-five cents, on comic books and a Coke. Dime comic books and nickel soft drinks—it had been that long ago, and it was all about to pass forever from sight and memory.

Drowning, drowning. . . .

More vehicles were parked by the cemetery than there were in the whole town. I saw many opened graves—it could have been the day after Resurrection Day. At least a dozen people wearing old clothes were working among the headstones. I knew in a very broad way what these archeologists were supposed to be doing here, and I did see individuals sifting dirt through screens or duck-walking around exhumed coffins with tape measures in their hands, but what I mostly saw looked like just a lot of hot, dirty shovelwork with nothing scientific about it.

I came upon two youngish men at the end of the first row of graves. On the ground between them was a new coffin. Its lid was open, and I saw that it was empty. One of the men nodded a hello at me.

"How's it going?" I said.

"Well," he said, "it *is* going."

I gestured vaguely around. "These're all my relatives."

They looked at me as if I'd caught them doing something naughty.

"Well," said the one who'd spoken before, "we're taking real good care of everyone, Mister—"

"Riddle."

The second man pointed away and said, "Most of the Riddle family's still located over on that side."

"Yes," I said, "I know." I did know; it was all coming back; I could have found the Riddles blindfolded, and the Riches and the Bassetts, too. I had seen both of my maternal grandfather's parents buried here, then his wife, finally his own self. The first Riches and Bassetts had been laid to rest here in the 1850s; Riddles came along after the war, when a lot of ruined Southerners were moving around and resettling. Relatively speaking, the concentration of Riddles wasn't great—Riddles, it once was explained to me, tended to die young and tended also to have wanderlust. My father had been orphaned when he was barely into his teens, and members of his line had come to rest in odd places throughout the South, the West, and as far away as the Coral Sea. The first graveside service I'd attended in the Gardner cemetery was for a young cousin of mine, Kermit, who one summer day had succumbed to the fascination of a fallen power line. The last one was for my grandfather.

I nodded at the new coffin. "Who's this for?"

"Whoever," one of the men said. "We try to keep everything together, even the box somebody was buried in. Some of these old graves, though, you find a few splinters of wood and some rusty nails, nothing you could still call a coffin."

"Is Doctor Taylor here?"

"He's somewhere around here." He looked about and nodded off toward the south end of the cemetery. "I think he's over that way."

"Thank you." The two men seemed glad to see me walk on.

When I was a child, I'd sometimes been sent to spend the summer with my grandparents. My grandmother and great-grandmother had visited this cemetery often. Between them they must have known seven out of every ten people buried here. They always brought flowers, and usually they brought me. They'd move among the graves, place the flowers, murmur secrets to the dead or prayers to Jesus, murmur genealogy to me, life histories, accounts of untimely, often horrific, deaths—most of their anecdotes were imbued with pain and tragedy. Sometimes I was interested and listened. Sometimes I was bored, drowsy from the heat, and instead listened to the cicadae. The sound of those summers was one long insect song, cicadae and honey-bees by day, crickets and mosquitoes by night, punctuated by gospel-piano chords, hands clap-

ping time, voices singing, *I'm gonna have a little talk with
Jesus, I'm gonna tell Him all about my troubles. . . .*

It kept coming back, coming back.

It came back as I passed Dr. Sweeny's headstone,
which lay in the grass by the edge of the driveway.
Nearby, a man wearing a faded plaid shirt was excavating
the grave with a shovel. As headstones in this cemetery
went, Dr. Sweeny's was pretty fancy, with some decora-
tive cuts and a longer inscription than most.

Dr. Chester Sweeny
d. June 30, 1900
Erected in respectful memory
by those he tended
these 30 years

Dr. Sweeny was the only doctor, the only Sweeny, and
the only non-relative buried in the cemetery. I had been
filled with dismay and disbelief the first time I saw his
name on that stone. Until that moment, I'd thought that
doctors were immune to sickness and exempt from death.
Mammaw, I said to my great-grandmother, whom I'd
been trailing past the rows, what kind of a doctor *dies*,
Mammaw? "Honey," she told me, "doctors die just like
everybody else. Everybody's got to die. That's why the
important thing in life's to be baptized in Jesus' name, so
you'll go to heaven when you die." But why, I demanded,
do people *have* to die? She didn't answer, just looked at
the stone, and after what was probably only seconds but
must have seemed like a whole minute or a full hour to
an impatient child, she said, "Old Doc Sweeny. I went to
this funeral. I was a girl then. I was nearly as young then
as you are now." She was in her sixties when she told me
this; naturally, I couldn't think of her as a girl or imagine
that she had ever been nearly as young as anybody. "I
remember because everybody in the whole valley come
for it, and thet's when I met your Pappaw for the first
time. He didn't want nothing to do with me then, but later,

well, I changed his mind. But that day everybody come
to pay respects to old Doc Sweeny." Was he as old as
you, Mammaw? "Doc Sweeny was as old as Methuselah.
Why, *my* momma, that was your great-great-gran'maw
Vannie Bassett, wasn't even born when he come here. My
own daddy made the box to bury him in and druv it here
in his wagon, and a man over to Dawson give this stone.
Doc Sweeny was just as poor as everybody else and didn't
have no money set aside. Seems like there never was so
good a one as him again. He druv his buggy all over, day
or night, rain or shine. Not like these doctors we got now.
Poor as he was, too, he always had some candy and play-
pretties for us littlens in his pockets. I remember him visiting my momma when she was sick, and when he was
leaving, he give me a piece of peppermint candy and said,
My child, my child. And I was a sassy thing then, just
like you, didn't have no more manners'n a pig. Instead
of thanking him for the candy, I just said, I ain't neither
your child," and she had laughed delightedly at the memory of her own devilishness.

Thereafter, throughout the remaining summers of my
childhood, Dr. Sweeny occupied a place in my mind as
special as the one he occupied in the cemetery. I soon got
over his being a dead doctor, but I remained impressed
by his anomalous presence in what was effectively an out-
sized family plot. It suggested to me that he must have
been, somehow, one of us. Even now, he had power to
fascinate me. Gazing down at his stone, I found myself
wondering exactly what he must have done, besides giving candy and cheap toys to children, to so endear himself.
Mostly just be there, I guessed, when folks needed a sym-
pathetic ear and a few sugar pills. Doctors in Sweeny's
day had done more nursing than actual doctoring. Much
of the nursing was ineffectual, and most of the doctoring
was downright savage. There was no Food and Drug Ad-
ministration to look over a physician's shoulder as he
dosed people with God only knew what. Maybe this particular country doctor had won his neighbors' trust and

respect simply by not killing inordinate numbers of patients.

I tore myself away, moved on, and found Dr. Taylor and a woman squatting in the shade at the end of a row. He was strongly built, balding, with a sunburnt face. She had long, reddish-brown hair tied back in a ponytail and was covered with freckles everywhere that I could see. A map of the graveyard was spread on the ground between them, with numbers and other marks scribbled all over it. None of the graves at this end of the row had been opened yet. I noticed four narrow, squarish stones set into the ground at the feet of two graves identified by a common headstone as those of John Hellman Rich and Julia Anne Rich.

"Doctor Taylor," I said.

Both of them looked up, and I could tell from his expression that he didn't recognize me. We had met only briefly, weeks before.

"Doug Riddle," I said.

"Mister Riddle!" He stood quickly, brushed dirt off his hands, started to offer to shake, pulled back suddenly. "I don't know if you want to shake hands with me. I've been rooting around in graves all day." He seemed genuinely flustered. He turned to the woman, who had risen with him. "Gertie, this is Doug Riddle. My associate, Gertrude Latham."

"I'm very pleased to meet you," she said. She seemed as ill at ease as he. She had a wonderful accent, German come through the heart of the Deep South.

"Finding out what you came to find out?" I said.

Taylor made an attempt at a smile. "In this line of work, you never know what you'll find out."

"Some people," I said, meaning mainly my irrepressible Uncle G. A., "called this place Gardner Gardens."

They looked uncertain, as if unsure they'd heard me right. He ventured to say, "Oh?"

"The planting ground," I said, then shrugged. "Small-town black humor."

"Ah. Yes." Taylor smiled again, more feebly than before, and tried to make up the difference by adding a chuckle, with results that embarrassed everyone. My own smile began to hurt my mouth.

Gertrude Latham went for a save. She nodded toward Julia Anne Rich's grave and said, "That headstone tell us a great deal about this young woman's life. Do you know anything about her?"

I glanced at the dates on the stone. Julia Anne Rich had died, age twenty-two, before the turn of the century, when my great-grandparents were children. "I remember the name," I said, "from when I used to come here as a kid. I thought Julia Anne was a nice name—" I gave Latham an apologetic look "—for a girl's name. But I don't know anything about her in particular."

Latham nodded at the grave again. "Those are her babies there by her feet. Judging from the dates, she lost four of them in a row. The last one may have killed her."

If this was archeology, I wasn't impressed. I felt sure I could have deduced as much from the information on the stones. Childbirth in the nineteenth century was perilous.

I said, "There're more babies and mothers buried here than anything else. Lot of children's graves, too. Children used to die of everything. After World War Two, though, hardly anyone except old people got buried here. All the young people went into the service or moved to Evansville to work in the P-forty-seven factory. And they just never came back."

The two archeologists were staring at me. There was something like admiration in Taylor's expression. I felt a sheepish sort of pleasure and could not help smiling as he asked me, "Are you Gardner's official historian?"

I shook my head. "But there was a time when I must've known the name on every last one of these headstones. I got to be a whiz at subtraction from figuring out by the dates how old people were when they died. And in the forties people did start going away and not coming back.

My father went into the service and stayed in. And somebody in the family did go build P-forty-sevens, too. There were framed prints of the things hanging in a spare bedroom at my grandparents' house for years. Official prints, with the Republic Aircraft logo."

"Mister Riddle," Taylor said, "we could use your knowledge to interpret this site. I'd appreciate it if you'd consider letting us interview you sometime."

"You'd be what's known in anthropology as an informant," said Latham.

Informant didn't have the ring to it that *official historian* did, but I was flattered all the same. There's little to compare with having people hang on everything you say. Anyway, I told myself, maybe Gardner was too small for a full-fledged historian. Nothing had ever happened here—nothing that mattered to anybody besides Riddles, Riches, and Bassetts, harvest time, tent meetings, weddings, funerals, somebody's barn being raised or burning down. No one famous had ever come from Gardner, or to it, for that matter. And it struck me then, with unexpected and shaming clarity, that I'd never made the effort to bring my own children or grandchildren to this place, that I should have been murmuring genealogy and tragic personal histories to them all their young lives, teaching them about family and the continuity of life. I should have been telling them, "Every one of your ancestors lived and suffered and sometimes all but swam up waterfalls like salmon to make sure you'd be here today and the family would continue and the thread be unbroken. They were brave and wonderful people, and if you don't believe it, just look here at your great-aunt, your great-something Julia Anne, who lost four babies one right after another, which isn't even a record, and it must've seemed to her like the worst thing in the world to lose the first one but then she carried three more, suffered crushing loss every time, died a probably painful and possibly protracted death trying to deliver the last one—" And, *"Doug,"* my wife would've said by then, *"Dad,"* my daughter would've said by now, each with that same disapproving furrow between her eyebrows. I do get carried away at times.

I blinked the thoughts away and looked at the two scientists. "So," I said, "what're you finding out?"

Latham said, "We never really know what we've found until we've finished an excavation and, uh, put all the pieces of the puzzle together."

"Is there a puzzle here?"

She essayed a smile. It was the best smile any of us had managed thus far. "There's always a puzzle."

"And you always find a solution?"

Her smile got even better. "This is what you'd call quick and dirty archaeology. We have to excavate by shovel, get as much information out as we can, as fast as we can, and move on. We don't have a lot of time. All we can do is figure out what the person was buried with and measure the bones. And we try to look for evidence of disease that would show up in the skeletal material."

"Is there evidence of a lot of disease?"

Everything suddenly felt awkward again. I could tell by the look she gave Taylor that she regretted her last statement.

I looked over my shoulder and saw Roy Rich's grave right where I'd left it decades before. "Here's a puzzle for you," I said. "What does this stone tell you about Roy Rich's life?"

Latham glanced at it. "He died at age fifteen."

"He was lucky to live that long," I said. "Or maybe not so lucky. I remember Roy. He was deformed. Not 'differently abled,' not even 'physically handicapped.' Deformed. His sister Betty, too." I pointed to Betty's headstone, next to his. "She died at age twelve. Those two had everything in the world wrong with them. I guess you'll see for yourself when you open the coffins."

The two scientist were silent. It was very hot, and sweat gleamed on Taylor's pate and beaded on Latham's forehead and upper lip. I felt slimy inside my clothing. The cicadae would not shut up.

At last, Taylor said, stiffly, "We'll write a report when we finish the excavation. If you like, I'll send you a copy."

"I'm sure it'd be much too technical for me. Tell me something about my ancestors that I can go home and tell my wife."

Taylor looked about as unhappy as any human being I'd seen lately. Latham looked as if she were trying to wish somebody away—me, of course. The more ill at ease they became, the pushier I felt. Maybe it was the gene for devilishness, handed down from Mammaw.

"It doesn't necessarily have to be something *nice,*" I said, "if that's what's holding you back. Nothing you tell me can be any more horrible than some of the things Granny and Mammaw told me." I looked over the rows. A truck pulled away from the gate, bearing some of my dead away to strange soil. "Doctor Taylor, when we met last month, you said this ground's full of history, and this was a one-time-only chance to get at it."

"Yes," he said, slowly—warily, I thought. "Yes, I did say that."

"This is the last time I'll ever see this place. Living or dead, everyone's being scattered. I know it's true I'll be able to visit my relatives' new graves over in Dawson, but they'll be, they'll seem out of place over there. *This* is where my grandparents and great-grandparents were buried. This little spot in the road was their home. It was my home, too, for a while. Next year, it'll all be gone, the whole valley'll be under water. It'll be like Gardner never existed. So please indulge me. I'm not going to gum up the works for you, I really don't want to be in your way or bother you a lot, but I need ... I need to carry away everything from here that I can this time."

"We try," Taylor said, "we try very hard to be careful of the feelings of living relatives of the people we exhume. It's been my experience that relatives shouldn't,

well, watch. And that despite what they say, they don't
really want to know everything."

"Look. There're a few chicken thieves buried here.
There's even supposed to be a horse thief. And one of my
cousins stabbed her husband with a big sharp kitchen
knife when he beat up on the kids. He isn't buried here,
but the point is, I don't have many illusions about my
family. I'll try not to he shocked by anything you tell me."

He manifestly wasn't convinced. "It's not illusions I'm
talking about. I'm talking more along the lines of—" he
couldn't look at me now, so he compelled me not to look
at him by pointing down at his map of the cemetery—
"grislier facts. Most people don't find it pleasant to contemplate, ah, physical abnormality."

Pleasant or no, I almost said, I contemplate it with
every step. I could've gone on, mentioned my children's
and grandchildren's congenital problems, too. I did say,
"I'm not squeamish, either."

He gave me an okay-but-I-warned-you look. "There's
evidence of pretty high incidences of birth defects, of
bone disorders. Many of them are kind of gruesome and
unusual."

If he was expecting me to flinch, he was disappointed.
If I was supposed to react strongly in any way, I failed.
The only reaction I noticed in myself was some kind of
inward shrug, meaning, approximately, Sure, of course,
so what? In a community like Gardner, with no medical
facilities and not even a resident doctor since Dr. Sweeny,
there had been no avoiding the raw proof that flesh is
weak, treacherous stuff. The maimed, the hideously dis-
eased, and the genetic misfires had at all times been at
least semi-present and semi-visible.

I said, "Unusual how?"

He exhaled a soft, exasperated sound and said to Latham, "Gertie, would you please take Mister Riddle over
to where Dan and Greg are working and . . . show him."

She almost managed to conceal her distress at finding

herself appointed tour-guide. Anger flashed in her blue eyes, but she answered, "Sure, Bob."

We walked past the rows. Up ahead, I could see two men kneeling beside an open grave.

"Doctor Taylor," I said, "seems to think I'm made of glass."

"Please try to understand. Working in recent graveyards is about the least pleasant job there is in archeology. It's very sensitive and very stressful, actually."

One of the archeologists kneeling by the grave was writing in a notebook. The other poked at the contents of a coffin, yellow bones, disintegrating remnants of a dress. They smiled when they saw Latham, went blank when they saw me. Introductions were made: the man with the notebook was Greg, the one doing the poking, Dan. They received the news that I was a relative without cheering.

Latham looked down at the bones and said, "Is this one of the—is this one?"

"Yep," said Dan.

"Would you please show Mister Riddle what you've got here?"

Both of the men regarded me doubtfully for a second, and then Dan said, "Okay. Well, sir. Know anything about human anatomy?"

"Not much more than the foot bone's connected to the ankle bone." I hadn't intended to call anyone's attention to my mismatched shoes, but Dan was the least-stiff person I'd met so far. He just nodded and turned to the bones and began speaking very easily. It was refreshing.

"I won't make this technical," he said, "and I'll skip the small stuff. Um, the long bones in your hand, how long'd you say they are?"

I glanced at the back of my hand. "Three, four inches."

"Close enough." He directed my attention to the remains inside the coffin and pointed out an array of bones as long as cigars. "These are the same bones, and there're the fingers. As you can see, it's a pretty extraordinarily oversized hand."

It was almost an understatement. Whoever the dead girl or woman was—I looked for the name, but glare on the stone obscured it—she must have looked as if she had an oar up her sleeve.

"Typically," Dan went on, "congenital problems left the door open for all sorts of other problems. She must've been in pain her whole life. She was about eighteen or twenty when she died. Most of the others've been much younger."

"There're really a lot of skeletons like this one?"

"Yep." He watched me carefully now. "Awful lot of 'em."

"Enough to make you wonder," said the other man, Greg, "if the local drinking water isn't spiked with uranium dust or thalidomide or something."

Latham shot him a thoroughly dismayed look. Greg cleared his throat and examined a page in his notebook very, very carefully.

"Actually," I said, "my family's probably just dangerously inbred."

Latham and the two men seemed not to know how to take that remark. I let them twist in the wind, stared down at the tormented bones, thought, Roy Rich, Betty . . . I had sometimes glimpsed them through the half-open doors of their back bedrooms when my grandmother visited their mother and hauled me along. My cousin Dorsey would nowadays be called "learning-disabled." Aunt Jean was "movement-impaired." Several of her lower vertebrae were fused together; walking, standing, even sitting, all were torture for her. Once, I eavesdropped fascinatedly on a morbid conversation about her back and hip and knee problems and strange calcium spurs the doctor didn't know what to make of. Once, I was appointed to help her down the aisle at a revival meeting, at a pace glacial and excruciating even for me. The valley resounded with preaching on hot summer nights, and every household brought forth its lame, afflicted, dying, and sent them forward to be healed by faith. Summer after summer, I saw the lines of pain deepen around my aunt's mouth. I saw the microcephalic and the acromegalic, saw the man whose body appeared to be collapsing telescope-fashion, the man with the tumor that sat on the side of his neck like a second head, the woman with calves like some pachyderm's, the girl who was one great angry strawberry mark, saw it all and became inured to it. Faith never healed anyone, but no one ever lost faith. DNA had let us down, but Jesus would yet lift us up.

I was jarred out of this reverie as Dr. Taylor strode up in a hurry. He had a frown on his face and appeared not to notice me. "Gertie," he said, "Rita's got something we better take a look at."

He turned without waiting to see if she followed. She hurried after him, and after a moment's hesitation I went lugging after her. Two men and a woman with her nose painted white stood over a warped coffin. One of the men held the lid like a surfboard. We looked down, and La-tham said, "My God," *mah Gott*.

Lying in the coffin was the apparently preserved body of an elderly man in a dirty funeral suit. Lying in the grass by the edge of the driveway was Dr. Chester Sweeny's headstone. I heard a roaring in my head.

The white-nosed woman, Rita, couldn't contain herself. She said, "It's *not* a cadaver!"

Latham asked, "What do you mean?"

"I'm *saying* this isn't a dead, embalmed body here! It's not a body at all!"

Rita pointed to the side of the elderly man's face. I peered and saw some sort of crease or seam under the jawline. It had come loose beneath one ear, and a flap of skin, if it was skin, was turned down there, exposing smooth white bone, if it was bone.

"Check it out," said Rita, and used her thumb to push up an eyelid and show us a startlingly realistic fake eye set in a grimy socket. Then she pinched the loose flap of skin between her thumb and forefinger and pulled. It came off easily, exposing a bony tri-lobed bulb with openings

that couldn't have been for eyes or any other familiar
organ. Where the jaw ought to have been was a complicated prosthetic jaw complete with upper and lower rows
of teeth and a fake tongue.

Nobody spoke for at least half a minute.

Latham looked at Rita and then at Taylor, whose frown
deepened when he saw me. I said, "What," and then,
"Why did, why would someone bury this," and couldn't
think of a suitable noun. I had to settle for gesturing.

"Prosthetics," Rita said. "The whole thing's goddamn
prosthetics. *Feel* it," and first Taylor, then Latham, and
finally I knelt beside the coffin. I touched the right cheek.
It felt gritty but . . . I pulled my hand away quickly.

Rita looked about wildly and said, "Now what is that
stuff?"

Latham said, "It feels like," and stopped and shook her
head perplexedly.

"Fleshlike," murmured Taylor, barely audibly.

Rita nodded vehemently. "So what kind of stuff *is* it,
Bob?"

"I don't know. Some plastic, I don't know."

"This grave was dug and filled in nineteen hundred,"
Rita said, "and no one touched it until it was opened today. I know because Gil and I opened it ourselves, and
we'd've known if it'd been disturbed. This thing was *in*
the ground ever since it was *put* in the ground, back when
nobody, *nobody*, could make plastic like this."

"Rita," Latham said, "just calm down and—"

"Calm down? Gertie, nobody can make goddamn plastic like this *now!*"

Everybody was quiet again for a time. I looked around
a circle of red sweaty faces. Taylor said to Rita, in a
strangled voice, "What's under the clothes?"

Rita carefully opened the coat and the shirt, exposing
a dirty but otherwise normal-looking human torso. It was
an old man's torso, flabby, loose-skinned, fish-belly white.
Wiry hair grew in tufts around the nipples and furred the
skin. Rita touched the belly gingerly, pinched up a fold,

and, wide-eyed, peeled it right off like skin off a hard-boiled egg. The inner surface had many small fittings and trailed strands of wire as fine as spiderweb. Within the exposed cavity, where a ribcage ought to have been, was a structure like a curved piece of painted iron lawn furniture.

Someone muttered, "What in the hell—" Maybe it was me, though I am not a swearing man.

Rita started to touch the structure, but her hand trembled, and she pulled it back. She looked around, gray-faced, and said, "Too weird for me, Bob. Just too goddamn weird. I'm sorry."

Taylor touched the bulb carefully, then the chest structure.

"Doctor," I said, "what're we looking at?"

"Well, obviously, some kind of articulated skeleton, but—"

"Is it, is this more—what, some birth defect, bone disease, what?" I was panting now, my heart was bursting out of my chest.

Taylor worried his lower lip with his teeth. "No disease in the world twists ribs into latticework. Whatever this thing is, it looks like it was supposed to grow this way. I don't even think it's bone. It feels almost like . . . I don't know. Coral."

"Coral?"

"Something."

"Jesus, Jesus Christ," and I pushed myself up. Latham looked after me and asked if I was all right; I barely heard her. The roaring in my head was louder now, and I staggered away, ran as only lame men run, disjointedly, agonizedly, until I found myself standing shaking before my grandparents' common headstone. I sat down on the ground between their graves to let my breathing slow and my heart stop racing, stared at the stone, tried to draw some comfort, some something, from the inscription, *Beloved in memory, Ralph Riddle, Mary Riddle*. All I could think of, however, was furry pale plastic skin draped from

Rita's fingers, the bony white bulb inside the headpiece, the false tongue in the false mouth.

"Are you all right, Mister Riddle?"

I started. Gertrude Latham had followed me and was hovering concernedly.

"Just an anxiety attack." I punctuated the remark with a bark of mirthless laughter. "I'll be back in a moment." She choked on a reply to that, so I said it for her. "You think I shouldn't go back?"

She all but wrung her hands.

"If you people are playing practical jokes—"

"We would never, ever, play jokes!"

"Somebody's up to something here! If this is some kind of, of stunt, you, Taylor, the historical commission, none of you will ever see the end of trouble. I can promise you that."

"What do you think we'd possibly gain from a *stunt?*" she demanded hotly.

"Money, publicity, I don't know."

"There's no *money* in archeology, Mister Riddle," she said, biting off the words. "Certainly not in this kind of archeology! You think we do this to get rich, to be on television?"

I was about to snap back, but then I saw that she was really angry, too, as angry as I was, maybe angrier. I got a hold on myself and said, in as reasonable a voice as I could manage, "What *is* that thing?"

"It's not a joke!"

"Well, it's something, and it doesn't belong. If it's not a joke and not a box full of junk—and it sure isn't human, or any animal, vegetable, mineral I've ever seen or heard about—"

"I'm sure there's a logical explanation," she said, obviously not convinced herself. "We'll be able to find out more when we get the . . . remains to the lab."

"Yeah? And how long will that take?"

"We'll have to get all kinds of permission. It's going to be very complicated. Anything you could tell us about this Doctor Sweeny could be very important."

"Doc Sweeny," I said, and had to pause to clear my throat loudly. My voice was lined with wet sand. "Doc Sweeny was the only doctor here for thirty years. My great-grandmother was at his funeral. She told me once the whole valley showed up to pay last respects. I don't know any more than what she told me and what's on his stone. He came here after the War Between the States. He died at the turn of the century."

She didn't say anything for several seconds. Then: "Where did he come *from?*"

"How would I know? Who knows if he ever said?"

"All right," she said, "then why did he come here?"

"Everybody's got to go somewhere."

"But why *here?* We're not talking about your standard-issue nineteenth-century doctor. We're talking about . . . God, I don't *know* what we're talking about. A guy with plastic skin, latticework for ribs. A skull like, like—"

She couldn't find the right word, if there was a right word, and the sentence hung unfinished in the air between us until I said, "A skull like *something*. And a face like nothing. Those bones back there are the bones of a—"

"A Martian, for all anybody knows." She was embarrassed to have said that, and I was embarrassed to have heard her say it. I couldn't look at her again for several seconds, until I heard her suck in her breath like a sob and say, "Whatever he was, nobody caught on to him in thirty years. Thirty years! What was he doing here all the time?"

"Driving around the countryside in his buggy. Dispensing solicitude, advice, and placebos."

"No, what was he *really* doing? Gardner's small, isolated, even backward."

I could only nod. The roads hadn't been paved until the 1920s. There hadn't been plumbing and electricity in all the homes until the 1950s.

"There's no money to be made here," she went on, "and never has been."

I nodded again.

"So why," she began, and hesitated.

"Maybe he was stranded. Maybe the place just suited him."

She appeared to mull that over for a moment, then nodded. "Who'd've bothered, who'd've been able, to check anybody's background in a place like this in eighteen seventy? Why else except that a doctor, someone claiming to be a doctor and willing to settle here, would've seemed like a godsend? He could've given them anything he wanted to give them and called it medicine."

I heard the roaring in my head again. I thought of my grandmother, breaking snap beans and humming, *Are you washed in the blood?* I murmured, "Or candy."

"What?"

The roaring in my head rose in pitch and blended into the incessant twirring of the cicadae. I thought suddenly that I knew the words to that song—it was a song of the need to obey the biological imperative; *Keep your genetic material in circulation*, the chorus went—and I suddenly felt cold and feverish at the same time.

I said, "What if," and then on second thought knew I could never go on and say what if Doc Sweeny had come to small, isolated, manageable Gardner from God knew where and become one of its citizens in order to become one *with* its citizens and had been accepted by them though the flesh of their children ever after twisted itself into knots trying to reject the alien matter he somehow had bequeathed to them, and those children, those who survived, had gone out into the world to pass along that same alien stuff to their children in turn, and—

So I said no more, only lurched past Gertrude Latham, and if she called after me, I didn't hear her. I wanted to be away from her and away from here, in my car, speeding homeward with the radio turned up and wind roaring past the open window. The waters could not close over Gardner soon enough to suit me. I didn't stop moving until I was through the cemetery gate, and then only because I put my bad foot in a shallow hole hidden in the grass and went down on one knee. The stab of pain in my leg and hip was so intense that I believed for a moment I was going to black out. Gasping, I dug my fingers into the earth, gripped it desperately. Maybe I was going to be sick anyway.

THE GOLDEN KEEPER

Ian R. MacLeod

"The Golden Keeper" appeared in the October/November 1997 issue of Asimov's, *with an illustration by Steve Cavallo. British writer Ian R. MacLeod was one of the hottest new writers of the nineties, and, as we enter a new century, his work continues to grow in power and deepen in maturity. MacLeod published a slew of strong stories in* Asimov's, *as well as in markets such as* Interzone, Weird Tales, Amazing, *and* The Magazine of Fantasy and Science Fiction. *Several of these stories made the cut for one or another of the various "Best of the Year" anthologies; in 1990, in fact, he appeared in three different Best of the Year anthologies with three different stories, certainly a rare distinction. His first novel,* The Great Wheel, *was published in 1997, followed by a major collection of his short work,* Voyages By Starlight. *His monumental novella "The Summer Isles," an Asimov's story, was on the final ballot for both the Hugo Award and the Nebula Award, and won the World Fantasy Award. MacLeod lives with his wife and young daughter in the West Midlands of England.*

Here he takes us back to Ancient Rome, to a distant outpost of the Empire where some very strange things are going on, for a vivid, compelling, and scary look at the wisdom of leaving well-enough alone . . .

My grandmother once told me that she witnessed the last ritual murder to occur in Rome. A young Vestal who had broken her vows was forced to watch the flogging to death of her lover before she was buried alive.

I was only a child then, living in the high house that has been my family's since the days of the Republic. Of course, I was curious. A few days later, I walked along Vicus Iugarius to the Forum. But what I found in the corner of the great square where my grandmother claimed to have stood hugging the folds of her nurse's cloak were sightseers harangued by barking orators as they thronged amid the stalls of moneylenders, flower-vendors and trinket sellers. On that day, even the Temple of the Vestals resembled a building site, with fresh marble decorations being chiseled as a statue to a Head Vestal was prepared for erection.

Still, in my innocence, I pressed my ear to the paving, imagining that I might still hear the Vestal woman's pleading screams as the newly turned soil filled her mouth above all the passing roar, perhaps even the flack of leather against her lover's flesh. I only found out many years later that unchaste Vestals were in fact immured within niches of the temple and left with a small supply of bread and water, although that still seems a strange kind of mercy.

Knowing the time that has passed since such practices took place, I wonder now if the tale is not one that my grandmother herself heard in her own youth, and passed down to me as if it were her own memory. But I remain sure that she intended it as some sort of lesson; which is why the tale returns to me now, when the sweeter ones with which she comforted my nights are forgotten. For I know now that even gods themselves may crumble with the dust of those who had served them. It even seems to me that the sacred fire of the Vestals will one day go out, and that the grand monuments and porphyry busts that our Emperors erect to themselves and their patron deities in the Forum will become nothing but tumbled blocks of masonry, the meaning of which men in some lost future time will argue over.

Here, in this new posting after my long journey up the Nile, I am surrounded by dead gods, old stone, dispossessed memories. I made detours at Heliopolis and at Memphis and again at Thebes to see some of the so-called splendors about which Herodotus and many others have written. Perhaps seven hundred years ago the efforts of these decadent and barbarous people to maintain the remnants of their history were more successful. For the most part, all I found were lopsided blocks of stone more like mountains than any work of man, broken pot shards, giant sand-buried heads and a few soot-stained tunnels that roared with files as you entered them, and reeked of ordure and piss. The guides were generally stooped, wall-eyed, jabbering on about Isis and Osiris as if they imagined that such things were still the fashion in Rome. Frankly, I regret paying them. I should have made my passage down the Nile with more speed, the sooner that my year's work here might be ended.

The Colossi at Memnon were the only monuments that in any way lived up to their promise. I visited them at dawn by raft just as the spring floods were abating, and they truly rose huge from the shining marsh. As is the custom, I pressed my ear to the graffitied stone to hear the marvel of its groaning. The other sightseers I was with professed disappointment, yet I must record that I heard— or at least thought I heard—something. A sound that came not so much from the enormous statues themselves as from the earth beneath them. The sound of an agonized wind. Shrill, high-pitched, echoing with the blood howl of some distant, terrible memory.

Let me describe myself to you now in what I intend will long remain the privacy of this journal. Let me imagine that those loose scraps of papyrus will be gazed at on some distant day by civilized eyes—and then understood, for I know that I make a poor scribe despite the efforts of my teachers.

I am Lucius Fabius Maximus. I was born thirty-three years ago in that high house in Rome. I have trained, reluctantly and at the bidding of my father, as an accountant in the class of Germanicus, and have since practiced with even greater reluctance in the Province of Sicily—and, it must be said in these days of dubious currencies, to little financial gain. On my father's recent death and with the slates of my family house falling, and our beloved villa above the sea at Naples becoming a ruin, I have been forced to volunteer for service overseas.

I must say that the thought of Egypt appealed to me, and I was surprised and flattered when, at the bidding of my patron Servilius Rufus, the Procurator agreed that I should go there instead of some damp bandit-raided fort in Gaul. I had imagined lush wheat fields, lakes filled with flamingos and tall reeds, bright flowers, sporting hippopotami, and tombs and temples filled with sacred treasure. But instead I have been posted here, up beyond Gebel Barkal and the cataracts, beyond the boundaries of our Empire. At the very rim of the world.

The sun here is a hot brand against your shoulder, and soon withers anything that attempts to grow. Yet even the lands of the delta that I passed through on my journey were less appealing to my sight than they had been in my mind. Upper Egypt may still be the grain basket of our Empire, yet it is also muddy, filled with insects, ugly savages, the stench of cattle. At least I can take comfort from the fact that, unlike my immediate predecessor, I have at least not come this far simply to be stricken by fever and sweat out the waters of my life. But I am sure that the bed in my quarters still stinks of him. I must ask, once again, to have it changed.

My dwelling here is a villa of sorts at Cul Holman, a place that once attempted to become a town. It lies at the neck of a large valley, where the paths and gullies from the hills that form the last rampart against the desert finally join. I am responsible here for the counting houses, the weighing houses, fifty or so scribes, and upward of five hundred slaves. I am assisted in these duties by Taracus, a captain of the VII Cohort in command of two centurions who, whilst of pure blood, has never actually seen Rome. Otherwise, I must rely on Konchab, my slave foreman, and Alathn, my chief scribe. In my household, I also have Henrika, my treasured personal slave, a cook and perhaps a half score of slaves of both sexes; all of them local, and none in their prime.

The land here, east of the river, is heaped over itself in a way that gives the impression, as one first approaches, of soiled linen. The inclines are riddled with deep gorges, sudden drops, the caves of old workings set high on the face of sun-bloodied cliffs. You know even as you stumble across some new vista from the base of a dried-up rill that you will never find it again without the help of guides. Elsewhere, there are many deep pits and heaps of rubble; the remains of earlier delvings for the gold that also brings me here. In this confusing maze, the sun himself often becomes unanchored within the sky. Not only do shadows shift and change so rapidly that a valley may become a ridge as you approach it, but a standing, beckoning figure may turn to a pillar of stone, then a blackened demon, then a man again, before vanishing entirely. The colors are so varied as the hours of the day change—and then again under the moon—that even now I cannot say with any certainty what the true shade of this rock through which the slaves burrow is.

I have a lump of the stuff beside me now on this desk as I write these words. Held close to the lamp, the fresh-broken side has a gleam almost of fish scales. It contains, I imagine, some ore which perhaps contributes to whatever subterranean process it is that produces the gold.

At midday, these hills become molten. Now, close to midnight and the time when I make my final inspection

of the counting houses and the breaking rooms, they have
the appearance not of hills at all, but of piled bones. They
look cold, yet the heat still swarms against my flesh
through these open shutters in gritty waves.

This truly is a terrible place.

I had guests at my dinner tonight. The wine came from
my private purse and was brought from the vineyards of
Heptanomia. The food I also prided myself in choosing,
and was dealt with reasonably well by the cook. There
were dates and figs. Capons stuffed with rice flavored with
caraway. Fish baked in the aromatic leaves. A side of pig
done in a charcoal bed. Fresh if somewhat gritty corn
bread. A round of green-veined cheese. Roasted wild duck
garnished with lemon. Soured cream with herbs. Decently
flavored honey cakes. Nuts and hot pomegranate.

For company, alas, I had to make do with my assistants
Taracus, Konchab and Alathn, and also Kaliphus, the local pagarch, with his robes and his rings, his weak attempts to assume the manners of Rome, his disgusting
habit, as he talks, of physically touching you. Those who
abuse him, it is said, are speared alive on the giant reeds
that grow in the silted canals around his palace.

Such is the balance of power here that none who were
gathered this night could fully trust the other—nor yet act
independently. Taracus knows that, despite his legion-
naires, he relies on Kaliphus to collect the taxes that pay
his and their salaries, whilst the wealth of Kaliphus and
his fellow Egypto-Greeks would be nothing without the
might of Rome. As local slave master, Konchab relies
upon them both for the threat of force and the provision
of his slaves: whilst Alathn, who supervises the counting
and weighing, seeks their security in the tricky business
of monitoring the traffic of the rock that will eventually
yield gold. I, whilst supposedly in overall command, hold
a post that is changed yearly so that its occupant may gain
no upper hand. Thus, even in this empty place, are the

calculations of power that assure the everlasting greatness of Rome.

The wind, for once, rose less strongly than usual, and at first we were able to eat with the shutters open and the doors drawn wide to the courtyard, where the pool had been cleared of its slime and refilled from the cisterns of a nearby slave village. My servants, well-briefed for once, laid out scented vials to keep the insects at bay, and the lanterns were well-filled with oil. The tapestries that I had had hung to disguise the peeling decay of these walls drifted and flowed, bringing life to scenes of cool forests, white pavilions, gods and animals. I would not have chosen my companions, yet for a while I could almost imagine that I was back amid the pines of Rome.

Alathn, the chief scribe, showed his lack of breeding by raising a matter of work; some small discrepancy in the records of the sweepings of the counting house floors. Almost a dwarf, foul-breathed and toothless, with his shoulders hunched sideways, Alathn has an obsessive proficiency with numbers, and seemingly no interest in the wealth they record. Taracus suggested that such problems were easily enough dealt with by the application of the brand or the bastinado by his soldiers.

The local pagarch Kaliphus at least provided me the favor of listening to my opinions when I tried to improve the conversation. I was speaking of gods by the fourth course when the hot night wind began to rise, and the doors and shutters were closed that they might cease their banging. I opined that there were so many gods now, so many faiths, that no sane man should be expected to honor them.

"Perhaps," Kaliphus said in his high, poorly accented voice, "the universe truly is filled with many conflicting deities. Not simply those of Olympus, but also Baal-Hadad and the new- and old-style Jehovah and Ahura Mazda and Isis. Perhaps they all—and many others whom we have forgotten about or not yet learned to fear— exist in their different realms. . . ." He smiled. "Would that not explain the chaos and conflict in this world? The fact that we are trapped between them in their fight for dominion . . . ?"

Taracus, of course, disagreed. He is a plain soldier who doubtless makes his tribute to the Jupiter and dabbles his finger in a bowl of blood before he orders the slaughter of some local tribe. Yet I, who choose to worship no gods and view the world as a mere interaction of the elements, somehow found Kaliphus's ideas persuasive.

"Romans such as you, Lucius Fabius," Kaliphus continued, "have always portrayed your Gods in madness and conflict, and have added ever more—even your own Emperors—to their list."

Full by now with the wine, we all ended up bidding the servants help us from the table to inspect the villa's wooden cupboard-shrine, as if it might offer some proof. I confess that, in my days here, I had not even looked at the thing. Clearly old, and yet cheaply made, the dry leather hinges creaked with neglect as we opened them. Yet I admit I felt a small twinge of anticipation; the vague hope that a devout predecessor might have left some tribute of value behind. In that, I was disappointed. Yet, as the five of us breathed in the oddly sour air that seemed to emanate from inside, we all seemed to forget for a moment what argument it was that this inspection was supposed to settle.

The contents of the shrine were ordinary enough. A small statuette of a dancing boy, with his head broken off. A blue glass bowl that held the sticky residue of some kind of offering. A dried-up piece of salt-cake, a few mundane prayers, on wax tablets, and a five-pointed star of greenish soapstone. The latter was new to me, and clearly of some age, chipped and worn, marked with odd dots and signs, yet well-made, almost warm. As I held it in my hand, Kaliphus backed away and seemed to mutter something, making an odd protective sign. I cannot imagine that the thing has any real value, but I will take it with me when I return to Rome.

As we reclined back on our couches, and on the pretext of continuing the discussion, I asked Kaliphus if he knew of any remains in this area from the great Egyptian dynasties. He replied that there was nothing more than a few carvings in dangerous and otherwise empty caves, and pillars and blocks that were more probably the work of the wind.

"After all," he shrugged, "these hills have been empty in all the time of man. No one would ever come here but for the gold."

There is little else to record of my evening. Now that the guests have left, I am glad of my solitude again. Even civilized company always leaves me feeling thus. Sometimes, a panic rises in me as I lie at a well-stocked table and realize that I am surrounded by the flesh of other bodies.

Still, the occasion went passably, and in Kaliphus I must seek an ally. "You have done a splendid job tonight, Fabius Maximus," he said to me as his entourage rode up. "And with such servants—so old, I couldn't help noticing. Yet in a man there are also other needs . . ." Here, he made an unfamiliar yet disgustingly obvious gesture. "Perhaps I will send to the markets at Pathgris for you, and see what can be obtained."

I took the offer without comment.

Now, the night draws long. The servants are abed. A few of Konchab's dogs are howling, and the wind howls and screams with them. But for the lantern-lights of a few sleepy sentries, all of Cul Holman lies dark beneath me. Whilst I still have energy to hold back sleep, I must make my final inspections.

This afternoon, I mounted and rode alone but for Konchab to inspect the mines. In truth, I needed to escape Cul Holman after being required by the ever-punctilious Alathn to confirm that a few precious scraps of papyrus, ink, and a writing implement were missing from one of the scribe rooms, and to authorize the required punishment. Knowing that the four scribes in question had been chosen as an example rather than for any responsibility, I settled for the bastinado rather than the brand. I had never seen it used before, and had wrongly imagined that wounds to the soles of the feet, whilst scarring, would be less damaging than a hot iron applied to the face.

The mines are easy to find from the donkey tracks leading into the hills, the heaped dirt, and the sound, long before you reach a final turn, of hammering and shouting. Here, under the merciless sun, beneath the distant and skull-like gaze of the many worked-out pits and caves that pock-mark the hills beyond, near-naked slaves burrow and hammer. After I had inspected the grey-colored lumps that constitute the produce of these mines, Konchab drew me further up an arid slope and showed me a place where the hill had been swept away in the blackening wind to reveal a floor of rock that cannot have seen the sun in all recorded time.

Konchab is muscled, tanned, a mixed product of all the local breeds. He shaves his head in the manner of the natives and goes bare-chested most of the time. I had never imagined that he was burdened with much thought. Yet here he showed me an incredible thing. For on this bare rock there were markings, as if living remains had been worked into the stone. Some were strange to me, yet others were unmistakably in the likeness of seaweed and fanning arms of coral. Here, certainly, were the bones of an odd-looking fish. I noticed also the coiled shell of a giant snail, and a large creature somewhat between a squid and a woodlouse. Stranger still were the large triangular marks that bore all the appearance of footprints. I am no scholar, yet here seems to be evidence that this high arid land once lay, unimaginably long ago, deep beneath the sea. Either that, or I witnessed some folly of the gods that I profess not to believe in.

Now, as I write these words, the vision seems fanciful. I almost doubt my eyes, which feel tired, eroded as if from inside by the heat and the sand. As I rode back from my inspection, the sun seemed to shift and dance about the bottomless sky, haloed within a ring of swarming darkness. Such was my weariness that, looking up as I rode amid pillars of rock too high to be climbed, I was sure that I saw a figure, wind-wrapped in ragged black clothing, looking down at me. I once even thought to see its face beneath the hood as it turned toward me, yet revealed only the harsh flash of the reflected sun.

Back at Cul Holman, the late afternoon sky was yet hotter and darker, and there was word that one of the slave-scribes had already died from the effects of the bastinado. I wandered amid the block-buildings and the heaps of discarded rubble, and watched as the donkeys bore down their loaded panniers from the mines, guarded as always by Taracus's soldiers and Konchab's chained and growling dogs. There is much weighing and counting in the making of gold. There are scribes at the mouths of the pits and caves, and again here at Cul Holman, where all is checked and weighed even as the donkeys shed their panniers. At each process of the shifting and breaking, and forever closely supervised by Alathn, records are made and re-made. The penalty for any serious discrepancy is death—and the reward for those who report a culprit is freedom if a slave, or money for a freeman. As you, my reader, may imagine, false reporting is a greater problem than theft.

At the end of it all, in the final counting house sheds and after days of weighing, discarding, sifting, and breaking, the gritty rubble that remains still has none of the appearance of gold. Alathn tells me that this stuff, which is weighed and recorded yet again by two independent scribes, contains about one fiftieth of its weight in pure gold. Sometimes, of course, a small nugget is found, or a few glimmering grains may be glimpsed at this final stage, but for the most part it would be hard for any observer to understand what we were producing. It is certainly not as I expected before I came here. The final sifting of the residue requires much water—an element that is even scarcer here in these mountains than the gold—and takes place many leagues' journey down beside the Nile in the beds and pans at Tarsil. I am reminded once again of how cleverly our Empire divides its power.

At nights here, I find myself dreaming of gold. Of beaten gold, caskets of gold, jeweled hinges made marvelous to contain yet more golden soft intricate nuggets. And my grandmother sits once again beside me on her drawn-up stool. She tells of Catechuan, who walked to the moon on its path across the ocean, and of Midas, whose touch transformed everything to gold. Hearing her voice, I feel the softness of gold against my teeth, its warm pure smoothness beneath my hands. I breathe a mist of gold and slip though gold-clad shafts into secret treasured lands where the stars shine differently and gold flows in shining rivers and its dust forms the glowing sand.

When my ship from Ostia first arrived at Alexandria on my way here, I spent the days wandering the streets and markets, seeing the sights, visiting the disappointingly decrepit lighthouse and library. Famously, the city is a greater hotbed for new sects, seers, prophets, and charlatans than even Jerusalem. Yet as a man who prides himself on his rationality, my interest lay in the oft-repeated claim that gold can be created from the combining of other elements. There was talk of a creature named Zosimus, almost fabled, so it seemed, and certainly shy of the public attention that most other so-called scientists and seers craved. Yet finally I tracked him down, or at least someone who claimed to be him, on the late afternoon of the last day before I set out on the long final leg of this journey.

Led by a guide, and clutching a knife beneath my toga, I plunged deeper and deeper into the dubious back streets that writhe around the low hills in the east of Alexandria. The rats, or whatever creatures scurried at the corner of my eyes, grew bigger, and the few people I glimpsed in dark doorways and alleys were even less well-favored than those I had grown used to. Although some way from

the port, a predominantly fishy smell combined with all
the usual reeks of humanity and decay. Finally, when I
was thinking of running even though I had no idea of
where to run to, I was led through a curtained doorway.

Here, my memory becomes vague. I suspect that the
air was drugged by the smoke that writhed upward from
the many glowing chalices hanging from the low ceiling.
The man who called himself Zosimus was bulge-eyed, his
skin beneath his voluminous shifting robes not so much
black as blackened. He talked in a strange droning voice,
the meaning of which seems to depart even as I think of
it now. Suffice to say that I feared an ambush and did not
detain myself long in his hovel. For once, I truly did thank
the gods when my hurrying feet drew me back toward
familiar squares.

Kaliphus has, just as he had undertaken, obliged me with
a gift.

For these last few days, I have been possessed of two
fresh slaves. She is named Alya. He is Dahib. They are
young, fit, and, as far as I am ever able to tell these things,
well-favored. They may be brother and sister, or in some
other way related.

You, my reader, will not know that I am repulsed by
the intimate pleasures of the flesh, and have been so all
my life. These two creatures are thus of no use to me in
the erotic ways that Kaliphus doubtless intended. The boy
Dahib, in fact, has the habits of an animal. After Henrika's
efforts to teach him a few rudiments of house-craft failed,
I had Konchab take him to work with the other able-
bodied creatures up in the mines. Alya, though, I have
kept for myself. She has a grace of manner, and speaks a
comprehensible version of the Roman tongue. She has
cleaned and re-ordered my private rooms, and bears flowers with thick purple petals each evening from some hidden place. Their scent brings some coolness to the hours
of the night.

In taking Dahib to join one of his mining gangs, Konchab muttered that he and Alya were of a tribe of nomads from the desert beyond these hills, recently captured and thus far too close to their home and their freedom to be trusted. In truth, as I gaze at Alya as she stoops and works with her braided hair, her pure blue eyes, the sense that she brings of somewhere else, I truly wonder how she would have reacted if I had been a man of baser appetites.

Bad news comes to me this midday from my patron Servilius Rufus in Rome. Now that the accounts of my father's wealth have been finalized and the full extent of penury can no longer be hidden, the creditors of my family are demanding full settlement.

For now, I can do no more than make vague but tantalizing promises about the fresh wealth that I had hoped to return with from here. It pains me to realize that I will have to sell off the villa and vineyard near Naples on my return—if I can find a buyer. It pains me yet more to know that even that will not be enough.

For all this, I have not been idle on the matter of discovering some valuable ancient relic since I raised the matter over dinner with Kaliphus. Some of the caves in which I have wandered with the slave guides bear traces of being not mine-delvings, but narrow tombs. I have excavated a line of them that look down over the spoil heaps of Cul Holman. Sometimes these narrow pits contain versions of Egyptian hieroglyphs and I have also discovered a number of the star-shaped soapstones, dot-marked and with a central indentation, much like the one in the shrine. They are clearly ancient, yet of no seeming value or purpose. Otherwise, I have found nothing but dust and, once, and disastrously for one of the slaves, a nest of poisonous snakes.

What, I can't help wondering, happened to all the supposedly great wealth of the Pharaohs? If the tales are to be believed, they buried their princes and kings in sarcophagi made of solid gold, which were decorated in turn with incredible jewels, and then laid in vast gilded subterranean vaults filled with amazing riches, the better that they might enjoy the next world without losing all the fruits of this. In Memphis, Giza, and Thebes, I can well understand that nothing is left now after all the ages of digging and banditry. But here at Cul Holman, at the very place where much of the gold must once have been mined, might there still not be some forgotten remnant? All I ask for, truly, is one still-sealed door, a mere antechamber—a single relic, if the relics were truly as great as is rumored.

Yet even as I write this, hope fails me. I know what the digging of gold is like here. I know how little comes from all the efforts of Rome. To entomb a man, to gild a room, to form statues and vases and make vast ceremonial necklaces—all of this would take more gold than could ever have come from these hills even when the seams were richer, or from any other place on earth.

Often in the night, it now seems that my grandmother is beside me, telling tales that fill my sleep. Her familiar voice murmurs once again of King Midas; of how, once Bacchus released him from his gift, he came to hate all wealth and splendor and dwelt in the country as a worshipper of Pan. I smile at the thought of those cool forests and the quivering piping of the reeds, then half-awaken in the hot stirring darkness of Cul Holman and the stink of this bed. Yet it almost seems as if a dark figure within a robe's brown shifting folds is still with me, and that there is a shrill piping, weird and unhuman—ungodly, even—as the wind screams in these hills.

Dreaming thus as I am each night, and with the grim prospect I face when I return to Rome, I find myself thinking much of the past, and of my father. After all the years when he deceived and squandered and borrowed against what I had fondly imagined was my own rightful wealth, I can see him as little more than a bloated monster. And what caprice was it that made him choose my calling in, of all possible professions, accountancy? I could, after all, have been a lawyer—a soldier, even—perhaps a legate. But instead, I am cursed to study these figures that speak of a richness I can never touch, trapped in a calling that, it seems now, has brought me by some unremitting logic to this terrible place.

My father had me summoned to him once when I was nine or ten years old. It was the morning of a summer's day in our Naples villa when a pale sweet haze hung over the headlands. It was not a time of day, from the little I knew of my father's habits, that he was likely to be up, and thus I was all the more surprised that he wanted to see me. Even in its decline, I still think of that villa as a place of shifting light, of the scent of orange groves mingled with sea air. Yet my father's quarters were shuttered, curtained, still lamp-lit. I doubt if he even realized it was morning.

Everyone said that my father had grown in the years since my mother had died in giving me birth, but I saw the man so little that I had come to imagine he was some kind of giant. But he was little taller in stature than I, and had the same elongated chin, the same face that seems mournful even when it is smiling, the same large brown eyes, the same long nose. Every time I look in a mirror, I still see my father welling up before me. But my father's face was framed in fat, puffed out as if by some internal pressure and patched by white and red blotches that drifted and changed like the clouds.

This world, he told me in a voice that was both high-pitched and rumbling, is a place of secrets. There is little you can expect to trust, although in youth you may strive to do so. But when you reach my age, you will realize that your actions are merely the performance of a ritual designed to appease powers of which you will never have any understanding. We are all, in everything we do in our lives, the acolytes and priests of nothingness.

Such was the sum total of the knowledge that my father chose to pass on to me. He had been raised in the bad years and spiraling prices of Gallienus's worthless coinage, when the wealth of my family must largely have disappeared. Yet somehow he managed to borrow and confuse and keep at bay the creditors who now assail me. No wonder, surrounded by a charade of wealth that he used to fool all those around him, that he took a dark view of the world. Nor that he finally ended his life by casting himself down the well in the villa's courtyard. Perhaps the only surprise is that the vast bulk of his body fitted.

On that morning that he summoned me, my father bade me eat with him. I had to watch the fruits and breads and cheeses disappear into his mouth, washed down by the wine that the pampered servants on whom he also sated his other needs brought to him. He bid me eat from the heaped plates, although I could barely pick at the stuff. When I hoped the process had come to an end, but more feared a gap between courses, he asked me if I would like to see some gold. Grateful for any diversion, I agreed.

He stood up from his couch with difficulty, and lumbered over to one of the many tall stone vessels that were half-set into the carpeted paving. He lifted the lid of one, and reached in. Looming over me with a small casket of scented wood, he turned the catch to open it and bid me look inside. It contained several leaves of a shining material, so thin that I feared they would disintegrate if I breathed too strongly. Closing the box, keeping it close to the huge folds of his belly, my father shuffled back toward his couch, and called the servants to bring yet more food—strawberries, for it was the time of year when the villa gardens filled with their scent.

The fruit were laid before us on a plate of bronze. My father reached into the scented wooden box and lifted out one of the fragments of leaf. He wrapped a strawberry in it, placed it in his mouth and chewed with his mouth set apart in a grin, flakes of metal dissolving with the pink fruit and threads of saliva. Then he selected another strawberry and folded it within the delicate leaf. His fingers as he held the thing out and commanded me to eat were coated in the remains of all the other things he had eaten, and his nails were coarse. I had never known it was so difficult to take something within my lips and swallow.

Thus, between us, my father and I got through a dozen leaves and a large plate of strawberries. The metal was almost tasteless, and grazed my teeth before it folded and dissolved within my mouth. At the end of the process, my father belched. When, with a single gesture of his hand, he waved both me and the foul air that he had made away, and I ran down from the villa into vineyards, to lie gasping for air amid the droning insects and the lacy shadows of the hot sun. A little time later, I found myself bent double in the corner of the field as all that I had been forced to eat came back out of me. There was no sign, within the usual traces of the vomit, of anything resembling gold, and I was weak and feverish for days. To this day, I hate the taste of strawberries.

Enough, enough. How the wind howls and shrieks here at night! I must raise myself now and make my final inspections of the counting houses before the guards change. And hope for better dreams.

To the palace of Kaliphus this day, to return the favor of his visit to Cul Holman.

A longer journey than I imagined, but at least it took me out of these hills. Closer to the true waters of the Nile, there is at least some vegetation. Indeed, here are grown many of the crops that keep us. Once, the ditches and canals must have been filled with each spring inundation. But most now are dry or impossibly silted, and the villages are poor, stinking places.

Kaliphus's palace lies at the center of what I suppose must once have been called a town. I was reminded of my wanderings in Alexandria as my entourage was forced to dismount to make our way through the narrow, disordered streets. Here, it almost seemed, were the same ill-made faces, the same filthy textures of shadow, the same darkly draped and shifting figures. The same fishy stink.

Rising out of these hovels, Kaliphus's palace was larger than I'd imagined, and constructed in the main of stone. When I inspected the halls and columned entrances, I realized that most of it had been pillaged from ancient sites. The slabs were broken, lopsided, worked into different colors and ages, with all the usual hieroglyphs, the scarabs and the birds. Within the palace, beneath the bright but crudely dyed tapestries and rugs, I even glimpsed walls made of fine and more clearly blocklike sections, with markings that reminded me of the soapstone in my villa's wooden alter.

Most of my conversation with Kaliphus was devoted to the tribute the boatmen of Rasind are demanding, or was too trivial to record. The food was poorer than that which I had given him, and ill-flavored with alien spices, but I finally thanked him over ale for the gift of the slaves.

Kaliphus explained that Alya and Dahib were members of a desert tribe who had been captured in some minor war, and thus brought to the markets at Pathgris. The remainder of her family still served in his palace.

"But there is some sport, is there not, in breaking a new horse?" he said when I mentioned Konchab's doubts about such slaves. "And anyway, you have nothing to fear as long as I keep the rest of the family here. You need do no more than tell me of any, ah, refusal . . ."

Sick at heart, I nodded.

"Their kind make *interesting* slaves," he added. "Simply because they do not believe they are slaves. It is like keeping a wild bird, touching the fluttering brightness of its feathers, teaching it not to damage itself. Watching it sing . . ."

The chief scribe Alathn was waiting for me beside the counting houses when I finally got back this evening to Cul Holman. He was more than usually agitated, concerned about some tedious discrepancy in the accounts. Once again, it was the records of the sweepings of the counting house floors. Unlike most such things here, these are not kept in duplicate, and can only be checked approximately against the amounts that are inevitably lost as the refined dust is ladled in and out of the great scales.

Watching the weighing process as I often do, or visiting the counting houses in my nightly wanderings, I am reminded of the tale of the dogheaded Egyptian god Anubis, who once enjoyed a minor cult in Rome. He was often portrayed weighing the souls of the dead on similar scales. About Alathn, of course, there is no such poetry. He argues that, whilst the recorded weight of the sweepings of the floors has actually increased in the time since I have arrived here, the amount of gold that is eventually extracted from this mixture of desert dust, hair, footscrapings and an occasional fallen grain has dropped noticeably. I did my best to dismiss him with promises that I would take command of the matter myself. He refused, though, my direct request that he hand over the relevant scrolls on the excuse that they were not fully completed.

The man is odious. I know I cannot trust him.

Today, and the days before that, I have devoted myself to the pursuit of the relics that, since my visit to the palace of Kaliphus, I am once again certain must reside somewhere in these hills. Konchab has grudgingly released four of his better and younger slaves on the pretext of looking for new gold seams—but of course, if any such were found, they would belong not to me, but to the Empire.

It is dark, troublesome work. I do not fully trust the slaves to explore the many pits and caves as fully as they might, and I have sometimes had to delve beneath the ground myself. Inside the few sealed caves I have been able to find, the air still has the odd, faintly sweet smell of antiquity. Undisturbed for untold centuries, there comes a whispering, a faint muttering and crackling of echoing movement as the entombed bodies crumble to dust in the new air. Pushing on, coughing through this ancient decay, I am often forced to use the smaller of the tar-wrapped bodies as brands to light my way. Yet it is all to no avail. The only relics I have been able to find are a few more of the greenish star-shaped soap-stones. I have now, in total, twenty-three of the things, which I keep in a pile beside my trunk in this room.

Once in my explorations, moving forward too hastily toward the back of a cave, the ground began to give beneath me, and my makeshift brand was extinguished. In a darkness of dust and bones, my mouth begin to fill. Luckily, I was soon dragged out and carried coughing into the harsh light outside the cave.

I cannot imagine a worse way to die.

Last night, I dreamed once again that my grandmother was sitting beside me. Each time, the tales she speaks of change and unfold. I am no longer sure whether I am witnessing a memory, a portent, or merely fantasy.

When I look straight at her, she appears black, wizened as an old date; even her eyes are a blood-threaded brown, giving way to the darkness of immense pupils. Her words are often hard to follow, they seem to fade in and out of my hearing and buzz like the rattle of a loose shutter or the droning of a trapped insect. The meaning also ebbs and flows. Sometimes it could be the Roman tongue, at others the mutterings of some crude local dialect, then again it becomes something else stranger and darker that sounds more in my head than in the hissing air.

When I look away at the hangings on the walls, I see stars and dots and cuneiform signs that may be decoration or some kind of lettering. And my grandmother seems to shift and change at the edges of my sight. It is almost as if she is folding in upon herself. Her limbs slide together like a bird preening its feathers, then her whole body diminishes and yet regrows within strange angles. It is, as her voice rises and falls and slips in and out of my comprehension, as if I am looking at her from some other place entirely.

Now, she speaks to me of the old Greek gods, and I

witness their sport in ancient Thessaly where there was once a blue lake surrounded by mountains as high as the sky. In this luxuriant country of the dead, over which dark Pheraia reigned and the dead rose from cracks in the ground to flood the plains, Apollo himself was forced to slave for a Great Year, which is the time it takes for all the stars in the heavens to return to their original positions.

But here, my grandmother begins to tell of things of which my waking mind knows she had no knowledge. A Great Year, she tells me, lasts for twenty-six thousand of our earth years. And she speaks of how, before the Greeks, the Pharaohs also studied the stars. They, too, marked the slow progress of the Great Year, and little doubted that their dynasties would live through it. Indeed, such was the certainty of the Pharaohs that when their astronomers discovered a small miscalculation in the earth's own short year, it was decreed that they wait some fifteen hundred years to make their amendment until the seasons had returned to their rightful place.

Yet even before the Pharaohs and their eventual fading, there were other powers, and even creatures that bore no resemblance to men. My grandmother speaks of bearded Assyrians who rode their chariots and built temples toward the skies. And yet before them there were lost kingdoms, now long-forgotten, who carried the last wisdom of another distant age when the Old Ones came down from the stars on incredible wings, fleeing some impossible darkness. The Old Ones, too, built cities gaudy and vast that are now lost beneath the oceans, although they thrived and prospered for many ages before man. But the darkness they finally fled was inescapable, for it lay outside even the vastest turnings of the universe and time. Mind-wrenching beasts that the Old Ones themselves had once tamed broke loose from their bounds, and for a numberless age, all space was riven by the incomprehensible horror of Azathoth and her minions. . . .

Although by now I have little comprehension of what

the buzzing voice of my dream-grandmother means, those last words seem to strike some special nerve, and I look up at her, pleading that she end this tale. At this point, my eyes did seem to open, and I was returned to Cul Holman, the distant howling of dogs and the screeching wind that caused the hangings of the room to sway. But my grandmother leaned closer over me and opened her mouth once again, as if to resume her tale. Nothing came out but a foul rushing blackness, and I saw, as it gaped wide above me like the maw of a great snake, that the mouth of the thing my grandmother had become had filled with stars.

I could not sleep the rest of the night. My throat was dry from the dust of those hidden graves, and from the screaming horror of my dreams. I summoned the slave girl Alya to bring me wine and keep me company, and I commanded as I drank that she tell me whatever tales she knew of daylight and some better place and age.

Alya's tribe, it seems, are traders, people such as those who follow the salt road to Tripoli. They are proud and loyal, and move with horses and creatures named camels that in all my time here I have only glimpsed from afar. To them, the desert is like some ocean upon which they drift and fight and trade, in the way a mariner plies the seas. Like mariners, they love their chosen element, and know its dangers and moods as few who ever lived.

She spoke of frost in the desert at midnight, of the pure white blindness of midday, and the slow-turning roof of the stars. Sand can be hard and harsh, or smooth as silk, soft as water. The dunes may move overnight—drown you as you sleep like the rising of a storm-wave, or remain unchanged for centuries. Each wind carries a different taste, each day a different shade and substance to the horizon. There are deserts of sand, deserts of bare rock, deserts of smooth or jagged stones, deserts of ancient forests where dead trees stand in leafless perfection, sand-smoothed and polished to a different beauty, rising on their roots as if ready to walk in search of water. There are mountains and lowlands. Dream cities of spires, temples, colonnades and glorious fountains shimmering above the plains.

Alya and her people have always known of the Nile. There was once even a time when they were the true dwellers beside her shores, and when the desert was still a green wilderness of cedar and pine, and meadows and waterfalls scented even these hills. It was her people, Alya claims, who built the first great works that the Pharaohs were later to claim as their own. Amongst these, and although she can never have glimpsed them, she numbers the pyramids at Giza, some sand-buried work she calls the Great Sphinx, and the temples of Seti at Abydos. They were made, she says, with magics that are now lost to mankind.

By the time of the reign of the Thirty-One Dynasties many centuries after, her people had long been nomads. They traded and learned the new languages, and watched through the slow ages as other great civilizations rose and fell. They saw the coming of the Assyrians and the Minoans and the Greeks and the Phoenicians and the Romans, they wandered amid the ploughed and salted ruins of Carthage. When they learned that their own great relics had been appropriated and restored as tombs of the Pharaohs, they wondered how anyone could credit them as simply the works of man. But all of this her people accepted without regret—even the reworking into new forms of their treasures of gold. . . .

I was half-sleepy by then, and the fears of the night had departed me now that Cul Holman's few scrawny cocks were crowing. But at the last words Alya spoke, I was fully awake in a moment, although I did my best to hide my eagerness.

"These ruins that you speak of," I said to her. "Surely they must exist in other places than the Lower Nile if the civilization you speak of was as great as you claim?"

She nodded at that, although there was suspicion in her eyes. It was as if, sensing that I was near to sleeping, she had been spinning her words to herself more than to me, and now regretted what she had spoken.

"In my own small way, I am something of a scholar," I said. "I would be interested if you could tell me where you think such ruins might still be, or perhaps even show. . . ."

She stiffened again, and stared long at the ground.

"Of course," I prompted, "someone in a position such as mine would have ways of expressing their gratitude."

"You must give me freedom," she said, looking back up at me with a sudden boldness that was not of a slave. "Freedom to myself and to Dahib, and also to my people who still suffer in Kaliphus's stinking hive."

I was taken aback; that someone of her kind should attempt to negotiate with me! Yet there was something about her talk of ancient gold and magic that rang true. Almost as if she had spoken not of the past, but of that which my dreams were already striving to foretell.

"If you do what you offer," I said, "on my honor as a man of Rome, I agree to give you what you ask."

"Then," she said, blinking the light from her eyes as the first flash of the sun rising through these shutters cast the rest of her into deeper gloom, "I will show you."

A day of wonders and disappointments.

Yes, there are tombs and ruins beyond the age of the Pharaohs within the far reaches of these hills—Alya has shown them to me—but they are wind-riddled, empty, almost unimaginably desolate. Yet there are other, deeper twists within this whole story.

On the assumption that Alya could ride, I had arranged for two sturdy ponies, but she assured me that they would be of little use on the route that we would be taking, to where these hills make their final rampart against the desert. Normally, I would never have set out on such a journey on foot, least of all in the dubious company of a single female slave—but you, my dear and honored reader, will understand by now my need for discretion and secrecy.

And Alya was in no doubt about the instructions I had left with Taracus as to what should be done to Dahib and the rest of her people should I fail to return.

The heat was already rising, forming a haze over Cul Holman like some evil storm cloud. Following Alya's quick heels into the shadow of the cliff and then along a hidden vale, I was glad to be away.

It was a long journey, keeping to secret routes. I know now where the places are that Alya collects her strange, dark-scented flowers. They grow like crystal in hidden profusion from the very rocks, in what seems like the total absence of water. Sometimes, in the distance, we heard the shouts and hammerings of the mines, yet along the narrow gullies which she led me, we never glimpsed them, nor yet were seen. As the sun finally rose above the shadowed rock walls, I knew that she had already led me far.

I remembered, as I paused to take the food and drink Alya had carried with her, that Konchab had warned me about these deep clefts that lay in places beyond the mines. We had already stepped over the antique bones of many unwary goats and jackals, and as we rested and the hot afternoon wind began to rise, the air pressing through the narrow walls began to whistle and scream.

The sound grew louder as we moved on, filling my ears, making speech almost impossible. These hills are burrowed and threaded as if with the airways of some vast musical instrument that I can still hear echoing across Cul Holman as I write these words. As we clambered our way through twists and turns and the wind's wild shrieking grew yet louder and the maze more complex, I began to doubt whether Alya had any real idea of where we were going. What could *she* possibly know, anyway? Just some memory of the fables of her ancestors.

It was then, leaning against the rock to catch my breath, that I saw just how incredibly smooth the surface of these gullies had become. It was almost as if, through some unimaginable process, they had actually been constructed.

I lifted a fallen flint and experimentally struck it against the smooth wall. The stone eventually shattered, leaving no mark whatever. Alya watched and twisted her hands as if, in this empty, shrieking place, she was somehow made anxious by the noise.

The gullies became still better formed as we moved on—and more elaborate, drawn in twists and turns as if by the pen of some insane architect. And with each turn, the harsh piping of the wind grew louder. There was still greater evidence, here, of the bodies of fallen animals, some so recent that they seethed with flies, and others piled into ancient heaps that Alya and I had to climb over. I was surprised at this, as I had always imagined these hills to contain little life. And would so many full-grown animals be as foolhardy as to lose their footing in this way? Unless, that is, they had been brought here, and then purposefully thrown in as some kind of tribute. Forcing myself to inspect one or two of the cleaner corpses, I saw that their skulls were often missing, the vertebrae torn almost as if they had been bitten off, and sometimes coated with the remnants of a blackish-green sticky substance that I was not able, and would not have wanted, to have named.

Above us now, the rocks piled in a greater impression of order, of huge squared blocks suggestive of buildings. Yet the wind-driven heat of afternoon was now so intense that they had only a loose sense of substance, like cities seen in a dream. I saw also, or thought I saw, a black-robed figure. I could only reason with myself that it appeared too often, in too many places at impossible angles of accessibility, to be human, or real. And I saw now as we finally began to climb upward from the gullies, that there were fallen pillars, walls truly made of giant blocks of stone, wind-rotted remains of shapes that might once have been statues.

We came then, as evening was settling, to the sloped walls of a fastness that rose high against the cliffs at the far edge of the mountains. It was a long climb to ascend the huge blocks of which it was constructed, and Alya often paused and waited for me, offering a hand, which in my weariness I was then forced to take. I had already resigned myself to the fact that we would have to make our way back to Cul Holman under the moon and stars, or else camp in some remote shelter. But despite this, despite the shortness of my breath, I was truly excited.

We stood in the last of the dusk at what seemed like the final edge of the world. Beyond these mountains and the great crumbling walls of the edifice over which we had climbed, reddened with the last of the sun to the color of drying blood, lay the shifting blue-grey immensity of the desert. Here it was possible, as I rubbed my scraped and bruised limbs, to believe the writings of such as Eratosthenes and Ptolemy—that the world is a globe floating in vast emptiness, and that we are all but ants upon it.

But the sight that drew me more was the single great block-pillared entrance set into the cliff-face above. With the light already passing, I was anxious to find my way inside before full darkness fell. But when we had scrambled up the last stone courses and stepped inside the vast portico, the sun, suffused in the whirlings and dust clouds of some far-distant storm, cast long rays of a thick grey light that were somehow regathered on the facings of granite. It was as if this was the precise moment that we were expected to enter.

Yet, after the initial thrill of discovery, my feelings became those of disappointment. I was slow, as we stepped into the glowing shadows of that great squared archway and saw a vast and well-made passage stretching ahead set with the dark outlines of many entrances and openings, to appreciate the most obvious fact of all. Alya made a sign that was like the one that Kaliphus had made beside the shrine at my villa, muttering to me that this place was filled with old magics, and that on no account should anything be taken. But, although clearly intact, this edifice was also open; unsealed, difficult to access, but certainly not hidden. It had long been emptied of all treasures.

Looking up at the roof, I saw the smoke tracks of lanterns, whilst in places the smooth faces of the walls were chipped and scrawled with crude Egyptian hieroglyphs. The protective eye of Horus was much repeated, although here it was gazing inward on both sides of the tunnel, instead of looking just to the left. There were even signs, marks in the dust that lay on the floor of the dragging and trailing of some pointed object, of recent habitation.

As we moved in and the light of the entrance began to fade, I put a spark to the torch that Alya had brought with us. Yet, despite the dark that had fallen outside, the place never grew entirely black. Within the tunnels and shafts, strangely shaped rooms and turns and alcoves, many narrow slits had been hewn, through some art that escapes me, rising far up through the stone to open out on the mountainside. Even now, they admitted enough of the moon and stars to give some light—and often the impression, as some new vista was revealed, of glowing heaps of precious objects, twisting amorphous forms or beckoning shadows that, as we grew closer, always turned out to be nothing but faint stirrings of air and dust.

It was clear to me from the fearful, watchful way that Alya looked about her, and her wariness as we turned each new corner, that the knowledge that had brought us this far had departed her. In fact, I doubted even then that this was truly the work of her ancestors. Yet at the same time, I observed her reverence as she touched the strange dots and carvings that began to appear on the walls, and the way she pursed her lips as if she, an illiterate, were attempting to read them.

I had, whilst I was there, the strong impression that the place was a vast and empty tomb, but now I wonder if there was not some other purpose. From the faint, malignant odor that pervaded the place, I expected at each turn to reach a mass of poorly mummified bodies or the bloody mess of some ancient sacrificial table. Yet the smell ebbed and flowed with the wind's piping, which somehow penetrated the very furthest depths I was able to reach.

The only sign of recent human habitation was, in its way, fortunate. Just as the flames were starting to fade on my torch and I knew that I would have to turn back, I stumbled upon a larger and more roughly made brand that some other recent wanderer had dropped. It was only some passages later, when I was forced to put light to the thing, that I realized that the weight around the bottom, which I had imagined to be a handle, was in fact a human hand, severed at the wrist, and coated in the same ichor that I had noticed about the bones of the fallen animals in the gullies.

I gave a cry, then prized the thing off and flung it away. But the whole incident was too much for Alya. She turned and ran, sobbing, back the way we had come. I watched her go without attempting to call her back, but hoping for my own sake that the moonlight fanning from the narrow slits would be enough to guide her back to the surface, and that there she would wait for me. The severed hand, I noticed, shriveled and writhed through the process of some long-withheld contraction, moving briefly across the stone before finally collapsing in a twisted heap.

Fear is a strange thing. You, my reader, may well have imagined that it was with me at that moment as I stood alone in the depths of this strange, ancient palace, yet in truth, only now in reflection does a chill begin to gather, a sense of unease, almost as if a part of me was still there in that vast empty palace, forever lost and wandering.

Sadly, there is little else of interest in my explorations to relate. It occurs to me, though, that I should record some other of my impressions. In the absence of gold, perhaps I could keep at least a few of my creditors at bay by writing some fatuous history or novel about the place.

The tunnels are complex. I have almost the impression of an inwardly constructed fortress based around some central keep or core. The sudden turns, the many small alcoves and rooms into which a soldier or a priest might turn to lose or outwit an assailant, bear witness to that fact. The other point that would argue toward this are the

shafts. There were many within the tunnels—and not of
the narrow type that I have already described for the pur-
poses of letting in light and air. These were wide and
immensely deep, with narrow walkways at their sides,
thankfully still sound, around which I was forced to make
my way. The air that came up from these pits was shock-
ingly foul. Much like the shallower versions of such shafts
that I witnessed in the tombs at Thebes, I imagine that
they were traps for the unwanted visitor. Either that, or
they were used as the gullies were for the casting down
of sacrifices.

But I remain, I confess, confused as to the essential
purpose of these shafts. Now, weary as I am this night, it
even strikes me that they were some vertical equivalent
of the horizontal tunnels that I passed along, although
their sides were so smooth, the depths so deep, that I
cannot imagine what other use they could have been put
to.

As to the passages themselves, I should record that the
dots and carvings grew more intricate as I pressed further,
although most were strange to me. I stopped, though, at
a few places where somewhat newer slabs had been affixed to the walls, although these too were ancient, and
many had fallen aside or cracked and crumbled. On these
there was an almost Egyptian style of marking, although
much changed. There were carved scenes too, that might
once have been colorful when the gilt and the paint still
held to them. I saw men and women with eyes much like
Alya's, gathering corn, drawing water, going about life's
unchanging tasks.

In other places, I saw what I can only take to be scenes
from the construction of the great pyramids. Once again,
many people were shown going about these tasks. There
were supervisors too, and in places what I took to be the
draped and oddly shifting forms of human figures—perhaps some kind of priesthood. I had passed several such
slabs before I noticed another shape. Before that, I had
taken it to be the destructive hacking of ancient graffiti.

But the form recurred—if form it can be called—representing, I supposed, some feared chaotic deity whom the priests were supposed to keep at bay. Now, though, another explanation occurs to me. Certainly, if I am to turn my discoveries into a novel rather than a history, I would now say that the amorphous thing that the priests surrounded was the representation of an actual being.

Alya had spoken of the magics that her people had used to build the great pyramids and the other monoliths. Perhaps the truth is that they used this hideous shifting creature—for I can scarcely imagine that there is room in this universe for more than one—in the great labor of breaking and shifting the stones. I can well imagine that its escape from the priest's control would have brought the downfall of a civilization, persistent rumors of ancient magic, and the many myths of some destructive flood or holocaust. It all makes a type of sense, although it strikes me now that night at Cul Holman is not the best place to dwell upon it.

Finally, I turned back within the tunnels, hoping that I would be able to find my way back out again. In fact, the choices were surprisingly easy. The foul shrieking wind that rose up, I was by now almost sure, from the pits themselves, seemed to push and lead me as I worked my way around them. When my borrowed brand finally died, I found that I was already near to the surface, and that the narrow upward shafts admitted threads of dawn. Thus my mood was calm as I walked back toward the square-set portals overlooking the desert. In this new brightness, I could almost glimpse the protective shadows of those long-dead priests standing guard around me, leading me on, murmuring prayers of protection.

In the last of the side-rooms into which I peered, drawn by a stronger glow of light, I saw a wider space than I had anticipated; a roof borne up by great squared pillars. The light shafts here were numerous, and angled in such a way that they crossed and threaded at a point near the hall's—or temple's, I might now call it—center, and threw its far reaches into flowing drifts of shadow. There, caught in the web of light, hung a central core that was ill-defined in shape. It was an illusion that I had become used to in my explorations, but still I felt drawn to cross the surprising vastness of the hall on the chance that I might at last have stumbled across some valuable relic.

As I drew close to the web of light, the ball of shadow it contained began to shrink, but, for once, it did not disappear entirely when I reached it. Lying as if recently discarded upon the floor, I found a lump of stone, black, multi-faceted, like some complex kind of dice. I have the thing beside me on the table now, and would record how many sides it has, if I were able to count them exactly. It is heavy for its size, and rubbed at my thigh in the pouch where I carried it. Even now, my flesh aches at that point, as if it were burned. The thing is too large to hide under the loose tiles beneath my bed where I hoard these notes and what little other wealth I have acquired here. To keep it from the prying eyes of my servants, I will bundle it up in my trunk that lies beside my valueless heap of starstones. If I spin it sufficiently well into the tale I plan to write, who knows? I may even be able to sell it.

What else is there to record?—little other than that Alya was indeed waiting for me beside the great blocks of the entrance way, sitting with her hands clasped around her knees and shivering even though she was in the full warmth of the rising sun. That same sun then led us back here to Cul Holman without confusion, although the way was long and weary, and it was the edge of another evening when we finally came into taste, sight, and hearing of its dust clouds and hammerings.

Alya called to me as I made to enter my private quarters.

"Lucius Fabius," she said, raising her voice above the mad barking of Konchab's dogs which had begun with our arrival. I started in surprise and turned back to her, that she dared to use my given names. "I call on you now to fulfill the bargain we made."

I, of course, asked her what bargain she meant, and reminded her that I had expected her to lead me to hidden riches and gold. How, otherwise, could I buy the freedom of her entire family from Kaliphus—or even that of her and Dahib? At that, she looked at me. But she had the sense not to argue.

"At least, Lucius Fabius," she said, casting off the goat-skin and pack she had been carrying. "I ask you that you at least release Dahib from his work in the pits at Dylath, before he dies of it."

To that, I agreed. Dahib will start menial work at the counting houses this morrow-morn.

And now: I must to bed. I am far too weary to proceed with my usual late-night inspection.

They say that the seasons change but little in this place, and then only about the Nile. Yet, as what might otherwise be called autumn passes and we face the beginnings of winter, I am sure that Cul Holman has grown hotter. The sun blazes. Sour heat breathes from the rocks at night. I have the slaves bring water and fan me as I lie abed or try to set about my labors. My body sweats as I toss and turn.

I confess that I am grown irritable. Only yesterday, for no other reason than that he stumbled amid the rocks where he was working and I thus had to walk around him, I ordered the flogging of a slave. And news has reached me of the ill-fortune of my patron Servilius Rufus, and of the bewildering demands of my father's bankers, creditors, and clients.

Everything is bad, and I am too weary to give the details. At least, though, I am now past a half year in this dreadful place. Were the days not still so many, and the prospects of my return to Rome so grim, I could almost begin to count them.

In my dreams, I find that I am still often wandering the strange catacombs to which Alya took me, which in turn become once more the stinking streets of Alexandria under leaden skies, which unfailingly lead, if I cannot awaken myself, toward the dark-draped room of the villa in Naples in which I slept as a child, and where something that is no longer my grandmother awaits me. And even when I cannot hear her words amid the swarming dimness, the shrieking of these mountains that somehow penetrates even the deepest of my dreams, I know that it is always speaking of gold.

Gold, which has traits far beyond the pliancy, glamour, and incorruptibility that men so innocently crave. Gold, which claims ascendancy in a rubric of elements vaster than anything Aristotle conceived, and lies close to the point beyond which this universe must dissolve. Gold, which gives onto other places, other times. A million unfolding doors. Gibbous lines of insanity.

At the worst moment, it seems that I am falling, pushed down and through and under by a stifling weight. Strong hands then reach up to rescue me, and I am lifted into the light of some vast place amid the strangest of buildings. There are angles and shapes that my eyes can hardly comprehend, a sky that has a texture and a color that can never have been of this earth. And I am surrounded by vast, ugly star-headed creatures, and I know that I am lost—unimaginably so.

Yet still I reach toward them.

Now that I am a little better, and although the weakness of the fever that I suffered is still upon me, I can look back on this last entry—and the odder suppositions with which I laced my record of my trip beyond the mountains—with a clearer perspective.

Perhaps the malady that killed my predecessor at last caught up with me. It could have been the foul vapors of those catacombs. Whatever, I am still sane and alive. After the terrible depths of the fever, I must do my best to be grateful. A full month has now passed since my last record, and already, my replacement will be setting out from Rome. For that, also, I must be grateful. Konchab and Taracus have proved themselves more than capable of running these mines without me, and even the miserly Alathn seems happy once again with the regularity of his accounts. I suspect they all welcomed the resumption of their independence. Alya, at the worst of my fever, closed and re-closed the shutters that flew open in the shrieking madness of the wind. Even Kaliphus has been to see me, and left fresh fruit and rose water, and a suggestion that I have the pile of starstones immediately disposed of—which hints well that they might have some small value.

I saw a dark, wind-flapping figure standing high on a rock above the pits at Dylath when I finally roused myself to make an inspection with Konchab this morning. Some of Taracus's soldiers happened to be about, and I ordered that they attempt to capture whatever it was that I was seeing. Soon, I was face to face with an elderly shepherd, quivering with fear, stinking in his filthy robes. Such was my relief that I laughed and I bid him released back to his starving flock.

All would be better but for the return to Rome, and with it the final loss of the wealth of my family. Childless, and with no desire to correct that situation, my only sister enfeebled by her long ugly face and no prospect of a dowry, it almost seems that I must now contemplate the end of my family's once-dignified name.

The days now drag interminably. There is the ordering of the new slaves, and much bargaining for tributes and fees with money I do not even control. Yet I throw myself into this work with a new passion, and do my best to demonstrate to Alathn the breadth of my expensively acquired education by ploughing through Cul Holman's intricate accounts.

In the dust, in the very air here, hang fragments of gold. I sometimes think I see their glimmering when the sun falls in some new way, or shining on the limbs of the slaves as they emerge from the pits as if transformed into intricate gilded machines. In truth, I must have breathed in a little of the stuff along with all this foul air, so that it now infuses the humors of my body.

This last night, I was assailed by yet another foul dream. In it, I found that once more I lay beside the changing and sliding shape that was once my grandmother, although now I fear her form. In a ghastly, buzzing voice, it speaks to me only of darkness and atrocities. Times when the star-headed Old Ones had to flee their great cities from a timeless wind that flooded beyond the stars. As the tapestries billow around us and the wind shrieks, I sense the near-presence of shambling amorphous entities.

"There was once and is and always will be the three-lobed burning eye," the creature begins. "It was named Nyarlathotep, by one who dared so to name it, and briefly called himself the Golden Keeper. But these are only sounds, and he was but the seed. . . ." At that, she cackled. Within a vast maw, teeth gleamed. "What it truly feasts upon is terror and debasement. It needs no meaning. It lurks forever beyond all comprehension, writhing at the back of everything. . . ."

Behind the beating curtains and the thinning walls of the room that I must share with whatever my grandmother has become, I sense the scratching and sliding of something massive, bearing before it an insane stench. I know, then, that were I to even glimpse it, my mind would dissolve. But still I sense that this is all part of some ghastly ritual. That, somehow, I am being prepared.

I awoke, slimed with sweat, to the howl of the wind and the persistent barking of Konchab's dogs. Even then, the curtains of the room still seemed to sway and flutter, and I sensed the fading of some terrible disturbance, and a crouching weight lay upon my head. All of this, as you my trusted reader may well imagine, left me in a poor mood for the meeting that Alathn had requested this morning.

As he talked at his usual tedious length about the intricate principles and procedures of his work, I glanced at

Konchab and Taracus, my two other companions, and
sensed that they were already pondering other duties. Perhaps, I mused, this ugly dwarf was always thus—and
nothing will ever come of the discrepancies of which he
speaks.

"Gold," Alathn said, in what I hoped was his conclusion, "has a greater weight than stone or all other metals.
It tends to sink and gather. Of course, this is the very
principle upon which it is collected amid the pans, pools,
and washing fleeces at Tarsil."

Here, as if this was all of some especial relevance, he
licked his thin lips and glanced boldly at me.

"For this same reason," he continued, "there have been
surprisingly rich finds made amid the sweepings of the
counting house floors. Many small grains and even nuggets are thus recovered. And within this last year, the
weight of these sweepings have gone up noticeably. Yet
we have recovered barely any of the expected gold they
can be expected to yield."

At this point, I had opened my mouth to say that the
records of such gathering would only be found by the
washing beds in Tarsil. But Alathn then laid his hand
upon the pale tube of a freshly copied papyrus, and I
could guess what it was. I should have admonished him
that he had ordered scribe-work done at Tarsil without my
authority, but my mind was blurred.

"In truth," he went on after he had explained all that
these new figures meant, "I fear we have all taken too
small a care of this particular matter. It needs, after all,
little more than for a weighing pan to be nudged, or a
sleeve to be brushed across the top of a loaded pannier.
And each night, the sweepings are guarded by one . . ."
Here Taracus bridled, although Alathn didn't actually say
sleepy. ". . . centurion. We are faced, I fear, with a small
plot to deprive Rome of its rightful wealth. A minor conspiracy . . ."

I have, my trusted reader, no reason to lie to you—for
the small bag containing what pitiful amount of gold I

have been able to collect by the means that Alathn so carefully outlined lies hidden beneath the same paving bed as I keep these scraps of my writing. On the evidence of either, I would be condemned. Of course, the grains amount to a fraction of what I would need to regain the good name of my family. But if I were to shed my identity, to move cheaply into some minor but decently furnished place ... you, knowing all that you know, will understand that it is the least I can do; to permit myself a small, hopeful dream after all the nightmares that have assailed me.

From there, the meeting proceeded along a predictable path. Alathn confessed that he could name no specific culprit, as is usually the case in these matters. But whilst he spoke, he fixed his gaze shamelessly upon me. As my junior and lesser, of impure and polluted blood, he knows that he cannot make the accusation that he longs to make alone. Of course, if Konchab and Taracus were also to take his view, things would be different. But their manner remained unchanged. If they suspected me also, they made the wise decision not to risk their careers over such a matter.

Logic thus compelled me to agree with Taracus when he suggested that, as this fraud follows on from a long trail of minor stupidities and disobediences, the time had come to make a proper example. With new slaves recently arrived and our quotas in all other respects well up, it would be an appropriate gesture. I mentioned, of course, the brand, the bastinado. But it was clear by then that stronger measures were required.

"It is sometimes necessary," Taracus opined, "just as a gardener must prune and weed to ensure the best blooms, that a number of slaves must be put to death if the whole body of them are to thrive."

I nodded, thinking of my beloved villa in Naples, and wondering what this brutal man had ever even known of the dewy sun-washed fragrance of a proper garden.

"I would suggest, Fabius Lucius," he continued, "that

ten is a simple number that brooks no argument, to be chosen equally from amid the counting house slaves. Of course, the manner of their death must also be an example, something that will stick well in their primitive minds. Mere spearing . . ."

Through all of this part of the discussion, Alathn remained silent. But I knew that he kept his eyes fixed on me. I understood his feeble tactic well enough: he imagined that I, a Roman, would weaken like his own retarded race at the prospect that was now laid before me. Of the suffering of others for a crime of which he knew I was guilty. But if this truly was his trap, I passed over it easily. Death amongst slaves is as natural as it is to the beasts of the farm—especially here at Cul Holman. If it were not the sweepings of the counting house floors that brought about these executions, it would soon be some other matter.

Thus determined, I took the lead, and the discussion proceeded apace. We agreed that, as crucifixion uses too much rare and valuable wood required for pit-props and hammers, the slaves should be immured; buried alive within some of the many openings in the ravaged hills that overlook Cul Holman, and left to die there.

As is my duty this following morning, I stood witness as the slaves were selected. They were then chained before they were dragged up the hillside, closely supervised near the precipices in case they should attempt to end their lives in an easier way. I stayed within the camp and watched as the figures dwindled in the hot grey light, thinking once again how we are mere ants upon the face of this world, and how little anything that we do matters.

The stone masons, still visible at the narrow pits that had been chosen, soon began their work, and the ring of struck stone and the cries of the slaves came distantly on the hot shrieking wind, to mingle with the moans and weepings of those who watched. Little enough work was done at Cul Holman this day despite the lashes of Konchab and his supervisors, and the threat that he would loose his already wildly excited dogs from their pens. Occasionally, for the greater good it fosters within our Empire, such prices must be paid.

I write now in the early part of the night, and all of Cul Holman seems strangely dark, strangely agitated. More than ever, the wind howls. The dogs will not quieten. But for that, I suspect I would also be able to hear the sleepless wailing of the slaves. Although those selected have been immured without the added mockery of food and water, it will still be necessary for the narrow pits in which they lie to be guarded for several days. Their deaths will not be quick—crushed together in the hot infinite darkness, flesh against flesh against unyielding stone, barely able to breathe, unable to move. But then who knows what finally kills any man, beyond thirst, hunger and lack of hope?

I write again after an unwarranted interruption. Without my calling or seeking Henrika's permission, the slave girl Alya has come to my quarters. Sensing some presence in the room as I finished writing my previous words, I turned and saw her standing in the doorway. For a moment, I confess I almost felt a flood of relief that it was her and not something else, until irritation took over. Still, the girl has nerve. For that I must credit her.

"I have come to plead with you, Fabius Lucius," she said.

"Well and good," I said, remembering that we had bargained before, and wondering if there was perhaps still some knowledge that she held back from me. "What is it that you want?"

"Dahib."

"Dahib?" I repeated, puzzled, before I remembered. "Indeed. He was brought here with you, and I recall that I was generous enough to have him relieved from his duties in the pits . . . and moved to sweeping the counting house floors."

She gestured wildly then, and I saw as she stepped

closer into the flickering and tonight oddly dim light that her eyes and face were shining with tears. "He's buried—dying."

I nodded, wondering that I hadn't recognized him in the process of selection. But then, all slaves soon look alike when they labor here. "Understand, Alya, that the choice wasn't mine."

"What can I give you," she interrupted, "to free him?"

I shrugged, easily keeping my composure. "I am a rich man already. But then I am also a collector. That place that you showed me. Is there perhaps another—somewhere that has *not* been emptied?"

She stepped back from me then, almost as if in horror, and shook her head. For a moment, her eyes traveled wildly about the room, like those of some trapped animal. I saw them widen and she gave a gasp as they settled on my grey-green collection of starstones piled in the room's far corner. And I noted that, tonight, a special light seemed to be within the stones; like the phosphorescence that lies at the edge of the tide.

"Otherwise," I continued, "there is nothing I can do. You must understand that I am not some flesh-hungry beast like Kaliphus. I—"

But that was an end to our bargaining. At that point, Alya turned and fled. I have since summoned Henrika and a half dozen centurions, but she has gone from the villa, and seemingly also Cul Holman. I suspect that in her folly she will try to climb the cliffs where Dahib is immured. But she will find the way guarded.

Before Henrika and the soldiers left me again to what I had hoped on this disturbed night would be my slumbers, I asked for him to bring more lamps, and to add oil to all the existing ones. Even then, I asked him if he also noticed an odd effect, doubtless from some coming storm, in the way that the light seemed to hang in close spheres around the flame without passing further. He agreed, of course, but I do not think that the truth had penetrated his pagan senses.

A dark closeness now lies upon all of Cul Holman. Konchab's dogs are barking wildly, but for once the winds have ceased. The air hangs still, infused with this preternatural blackness, and there is a prickly sense of waiting that I associate with thunderstorms. Yet the only rumble comes from the beat of my heart.

Just this moment, as I reached toward the iron ink pot to replenish my nib, a greenish spark flew out from my hand. I have heard from mariners of just such an effect in storms; and also of the crawling of the skin, the rising of the hair, the suffocating sense of expectancy, although I have previously witnessed only the flash of clouds over the rain-swathed bay of Naples and the green hills of Rome.

No wind, and yet something within me seems to be blown wildly as if by a mad silent gale. In this itchy uncertainty, with the need always to look behind my back at the starstones and the lamps that withhold their suffocated light in the thick mass of darkness, there is clearly no prospect of sleep. This night, indeed, seems to me quite unlike any other, and yet ordained, much in the way that my presence here was—and, before that, the death of my father.

Much, it now seems to me, comes back to that. Now that we know each other well, trusted reader, and we seemingly have this night to share together, I will record a tale that will otherwise reach no eyes. Let me tell how, when I returned to Rome from the tedium of my duties as accountant in Sicily, little enriched and much in need of solace, I was greeted in the street outside my family's high house by the sight of wagons and carts. Too weary to take notice, I pushed my way through, only to find myself restrained and led toward a small group that included my sister and a few of our more elderly servants, all of whom were sobbing.

Understand, reader, that until that moment I had imagined that the drudgery of my work as an accountant was but a preparation for my true responsibilities as head of my family. Such things, I had reasoned, were not uncommon. Even as I learnt of the repossession of the furnishing of my house and the sale of my best slaves, I did not assume this indicated the loss of my family's wealth—but simple bad management of finances by my increasingly degenerate father.

Yet I was in a foul mood after I had made what arrangements I could from my own meager purse, and rode in haste toward Naples. In other moments, such a journey would have given the chance for cooler reflection. But anger only seemed to grow within me; and a sense of destiny.

As I dismounted at nightfall four days later and my feet clattered on loose mosaic through the villa's moldering halls, I remembered the time when I had been summoned to eat leaf-gilded strawberries. And as my face was brushed by cobwebs and rotting hangings, I remembered also the sickness that had come upon me afterward—when gold is prized by apothecaries, and taken by those who can afford it for its powers of goodness and healing. It was then, even before I reached my father's presence, that the first worm of doubt began to slide within me. How, for so long, could I have ignored this decay, when it could all be put down to the simplest of explanations?

The few servants that my father still kept about him were drunkenly abed, or had absconded entirely. Yet I knew as I threw open the last doors into that windowless inner chamber that he would be waiting for me.

He lay as always upon his great couch on the dais, and the place was filled with the sweet stench of rancid oil and perfume. He had grown yet more in the year since I had last seen him. His flesh shone coldly with sweat, and his vast stomach tumbled out in a slippery mass from his dank robes. His tiny eyes regarded me from his swollen face, whilst his chin sloped down, white-mottled and immense like a toad's.

"So now you come to me," he said in that voice that was broken into two pieces—both high and low.

"I *came,*" I began, "before it is too late—"

But here his wild, chilling laughter interrupted me.

"My son," he shrieked, "it was too late long ago! It was too late before you were born!"

"We need money," I said. "Money to pay off the creditors who have ransacked our house in Rome. We need gold."

"Ah, *gold* . . ." His body quivered again at the word, as if he were about to recommence laughing. But—as far as I could tell—his face remained grave. Looking up at him, I felt as impotent as a child. "Go, then," he whispered, leaning forward with a sound of sickly sliding, "go and look for your gold. . . ."

Moving slowly around the dais, at first fearing some joke, I crossed to the line of great jars inset into the paving that he had opened for me long ago, and lifted the lid of the first, and placed my hand deep inside. It was empty. As was the next, and the next. As they all were. Dragging down rotting hangings, kicking over chests and boxes, I found nothing but dust and leaves. Admittedly there were a few coins; worthless radiati and fake aurei that I could bite through with my teeth.

Twisting his head this way and that, my father watched as I moved behind him, his tiny hands quivering at the ends of his immense arms. He made a breathless eager panting that soon became a high-pitched giggling, then a growling belch of laugher. His shining face grew livid.

In my anger, I raised one of the caskets and threw it toward him, but it seemed to slow in the thick dark air and broke on the paving in shards of thin wood and metal. He bellowed at that as though the laughter would break him, greasy beads of tears and sweat flowing down his face, and I realized then that he had long anticipated this moment, like the maturing of a sour wine.

I shouted at him that he was a degenerate, a disgrace to all the honor of Rome. At the mention of honor, his laughter only increased.

This, then, was the state to which I had been dragged—

to face a future of meaningless penury. And I was filled by a new and even greater anger. I was a high-born Roman, yet my life seemed to have passed from my control. Understand, now, reader, how much against my nature it was to climb the dais to my father's couch and strike him. Anyway, my efforts were useless, and only increased his laughter—it was like punching rotten dough. I had my small dagger about me, and I ploughed that into him, too, rending his clothes, slicing his thighs, his belly, his chest. But the blade cut nothing but white layers of fat, and did not even cause him to bleed. Enveloped in his stench, I seemed to be falling into him, the shrieking pit of his mouth, the quivering wounds I had opened.

At some point in all of this, the weight of our struggles caused the couch beneath us to break with a tearing of wood and the sparkling scatter of cheap glass beads and fake ornaments. My father began to slide from it—and I with him, although thankfully we separated as I tumbled from the steps of the dais, or I fear that I would have been crushed, suffocated, drowned.

As it was, I climbed to my feet, and looked down at him as he lay sprawled, my greasy dagger still in my hand. He was but a spill of flesh; scarcely human, more like some rotting sea-leviathan. Yet from the discordant whistle of his breathing, I knew that he was still alive.

He had fallen almost entirely upon one great carpet. Experimentally, I lifted a corner and tried to drag it. His weight was immense, but a power was upon me. Somehow, I hauled my father though the doorway and along the corridors which I had come, and thence out into the open courtyard that contains the villa's well. There is no lip, and the aperture, once I had removed the iron grating, is wide and square. And deep also, so that I could never catch the glimmer of water when I peered down it as a child, nor be sure, when I cast a surreptitious stone, that the faint splash I finally heard wasn't simply the chattering of birdsong in the near woods. Yet for all of that, I almost doubted that my father would fit into the well. His gross limbs sprawled out as I heaved him off the carpet, snagging on the topmost stones even as the rest of him slid into it. I was forced, like a midwife in reverse, to work and push at his slick flesh until the last part of him gave way. Even then, he was slow in his descent down the dank sides of mossy stone. There was even a moment, looking down, when I was sure I saw the pale glint of movement as he began to climb back out. But then there was a great sound of ripping and sliding, and a gust of foul air as the last of his body's resistance gave way. That night, I truly did hear a thickly echoing splash as my father's body finally struck water.

I dragged the carpet back to his quarters, and left the place otherwise as it was, in disarray, and with the well's iron grating removed. In what remained of the darkness, and unseen by all but the creatures of the night, I rode off toward the hills.

That, my reader, almost marks the end of this bitter little story. I dwelt the next night at a roadside inn, and spoke loudly of how I was heading toward Naples from Rome. I arrived once again at the villa the next noon, to find much commotion. A day-woman's efforts to draw water had already revealed my father's presence, and local workmen were already laboring to extract him.

Too swollen to be recovered whole, my father was being hauled up in pieces. It was easy enough for me to display shock and surprise; and secretly to note as the glistening lumps of his body rose out on ropes how well the evidence of our struggles had been obliterated. As to the chaos of empty jars and broken caskets, I was able to offer an explanation that was all too easily borne out by a subsequent inspection of the family accounts: driven by penury and the thought of the loss of our family's great name, my father had chosen to kill himself. Would, I thought in darker moments as I pondered my future, that he had followed the tradition of older time in such matters, and also killed me.

Once the initial labors and inquiries had finished and a

show had been made of grieving, it seemed wise to seek
a posting in some distant place before my creditors began
to regather—which, by a long route, brings me back here
to Cul Holman, to this night where the darkness still
hangs, and there is a windless creaking tension. From
somewhere, I sense a faint smell of burning, and my body
seems to

What was that?

I saw a scorpion scuttle across the floor beside me, and
then another. Several moths and gaudy insects have flown
out from the window into the darkness instead of, as is
their nature, toward the light. A rustling stream of cock-
roaches have made their way toward some crack in the
wall that I do not remember seeing. And now there is
silence. At last, even Konchab's dogs have ceased their
barking. In this stillness, the earth seems to hold her
breath. From somewhere comes the smell of burning.
Looking behind me for a poorly trimmed lamp, I see that
all the flames hang still as amber beads—and give as little
light. Yet upon the starstones, there lies an intricate pattern of fine silver lines. Oddest of all, clear and almost
reassuring amid this blackness, a grey stream of smoke is
rising from the sides of my trunk.

I must.

There marks a fitting end to that night's journal, and to
the much that has happened since. I assure you, dear
reader, that I am still alive and well. Indeed, I am well
and wealthier than I could ever have expected.

I should have realized that the dense silence and other
strange portents at Cul Holman signaled more than a mere
storm. Indeed, I am somewhat angered that Konchab, Taracus, and Alathn, with their greater knowledge of this
place, did not see fit to warn me. But they also professed
innocence at the greatness of what was to occur, and I am
currently in a mood to forgive them.

If, as Virgil contends, earthquakes truly are the rest-
lessness of giants sleeping deep beneath the earth, then

what has occurred here must have been caused by the greatest of them all. I can smile now at my unreasoning fear as the world shook loose from her anchors, as the walls that sheltered me moved and the villa's roof rattled in a rain of tiles, whilst from the darkness beyond came a massive groaning and rumbling that deafened the ears and sickened the belly. A strange glow seemed to rise. The stifled flames of the lamps suddenly spat great tongues of spark. Veins of fire ran along the walls and floor—even through my hands as I looked down at them. After all the portents and horrors I have been subjected to, I truly believed that the universe was coming apart, to be replaced by—I know not what.

But, in echoes and groans, the rumbling slowly died, and then, for the first time that night, fading as if already from some long way off, came the piping and whistling of the wind, to be replaced as it, in turn, died, by the screams of the slaves, and the hiss and clatter of settling dust and masonry.

Dawn came then, as if the sun finally had shaken loose from the earth in the process, and never more grateful was I to see his light. I emerged, as did many others, into a broken and rearranged world. I can see now the dark silhouettes amid the drifting mist—but this journal is not the place to record the damage, and the work of reconstruction that has gone on in these recent days. I am preparing, in fact, a report that I propose to submit to the Senate upon my return to Rome, which will doubtless be copied into other libraries should you wish to refer to it.

For the purpose of this, my truer journal, let me say that the very crudeness of Cul Holman—the low stone dwellings, widely scattered—meant there was none of the vast loss of life that there might have been from an earthquake in a more civilized place. Still, there were numerous injuries amongst freemen and slaves—and in the buildings and workings of their trades.

It was only when I made my first inspection into the hills beyond this valley this morning that I realized the true enormity of what has taken place. Clouded by the risen dust, the light itself had changed, yet had a clarity it had lacked before. The hills seemed more solid. New fissures of rock had reared up, peaks had fallen, cliff-faces had broken.

Truly, the earthquake was the author of strange events, which would have been put down in more primitive times to the work of gods. One of the counting house sheds seems to have been bodily moved; more amazing still, a small quantity of gold was found lying upon the scales when all the wreckage was removed. I myself have seen, in the dust around this villa, evidence of incredible stirrings that I could have taken to be dragging clawmarks were I a man of lesser knowledge. And, as far as it is possible to tell amid the new face of the hills that overlook us, the imprisoned slaves were shaken out from their graves by the movement of the earth, and thus released. Of them—and of Alya—there is no sign, although the soldiers who had been stationed to guard them, and also Konchab's dogs (although I, for one, am glad to be rid of their ceaseless howling) were found strangely beheaded, their torn necks coated in a foul greenish-black ichor, which I can only presume rose up from some deep portion of the earth.

At some point in the afternoon after the earthquake, weary of issuing instructions and the cries of the wounded, deprived of an entire night's sleep, I went back to this room in the villa that the servants had made some small effort to tidy, and laid myself clothed upon the bed.

I scarcely knew that I was asleep, yet it seemed to me that I saw once again, as if from afar, the vast, strangely angled cities of which I have sometimes found myself dreaming. They are built from huge blocks of stone set and faced with shining gems, and in truth I felt a sadness to know that what I saw lay so impossibly far in the past that all but the faintest remnant has faded. For I recognized that they were made in the manner of the ruins to which Alya had taken me; and not by man, who was not

even upon the face of the earth at this far time, but by
great beings, star-headed and with many strange limbs,
who moved on the pads of three triangular feet. Despite
their ugliness, I felt a sense of kin; for I saw that, in their
own alien way, they were wise and purposeful. These, I
thought, are the Old Ones, whose wisdom trickled down
through the eons in enough measure for Alya's ancestors
to use it in the building, puny to them, yet still vast by
our human standards, of the great pyramids. My sense of
distance was redoubled by the knowledge that these creatures would ultimately be obliterated by a mad darkness.
But here, it seemed to me as they moved within their
towering cities, they were at their prime. The whole earth
was theirs, from the highest mountains to the deepest
trenches of the sea. And they looked upon the hellish creatures, whom they bid do their work using only the power
of their minds, with contempt. They ruled everything.
They knew no doubt.

Such, then, was the vision that was presented to me—
and I, a Roman, at last witnessed a race with whom I
could converse as an equal, had these creatures but
mouths and eyes and ears. I watched, charmed more than
repelled, as the Old Ones went about the incomprehensible business of their lives beneath the strangely colored
skies of a lost ancient earth. I saw on shining walls the
dot-markings with which I have become familiar, and
heard, or thought I heard, a sweeter version of the piping
that carried so often on the wind. I saw, also, many of the
starstones, less worn but otherwise exactly like those I
have collected, and glowing with fine inscriptions. These,
I noted, were passed between the creatures by their odd
appendages, and I soon reached the conclusion that they
were a coinage of sorts. But here the matter does not end,
for I also saw several of the creatures bearing black, multi-
sided stones like that which I found in the edifice at the
edge of the mountains. They would place these at the
center of a starstone, causing a strange transformation to
take place. The starstone changed color, and the veins

within it ceased to glow as it took on all the appearance
of gold.

Reader, as you may imagine, I awoke with a start then.
In the thin light of dusk, I hastened to my trunk, remembering as I opened it the smoke that I had seen coming
from it on the previous night. Indeed, the whole contents
were charred and soot-stained. As I reached through the
ash of my ruined clothing and closed my hand around the
many-sided black stone, the ground once more gave a
faint growl. Masonry crackled, and again the slaves of Cul
Holman began to weep and wail. But the tremor proved
to be nothing—a mere settling back of the earth.

I gazed at the black stone, and picked up also one of
the starstones, turning them both over. It seemed quite
impossible that one thing thus angled should mate with
the curved indent in the middle of the other, as I had seen
in my vision. But the two artifacts fitted well when I tried
them; so well that I could not separate them when they
were joined. In fact, the lines within the starstone began
to glow, and it became so hot that I dropped it to the
floor. Within a moment, too quick to notice, the starstone
changed color. It gained a smooth golden luster and—for
I discovered that both objects were immediately cold, and
could be separated easily—had increased greatly in
weight. Then I placed the black-faceted stone within the
center of another starstone, bringing about the same transformation.

Here, reader, you may imagine that I proceeded to
transform all the starstones into what I could only con-
clude was gold. In fact, I performed the process only three
times; and for the third, by way of an experiment, I used
the most scratched and damaged of the stones, with two
of its arms broken, although that also changed. But gold
is a tricky substance to possess, especially here, and at
that moment I still doubted the sense of what I was seeing.
It was enough. Before light next day, when all was quiet,
I summoned a smithy to one of the makeshift workshops.
To allay my remaining doubts, I bid him work one of the

changed starstones in ways that only the most precious of
all metals can be. Despite the man's protests, the stone
was easily cut and beaten into twenty fat coin-like discs
of roughly equal size. They are warm to the touch as I
hold them now, and feel smooth upon the tongue, creamy
yet with a faintly salty flavor; much as I imagine those
who indulge such matters find the flesh of a loved one.
Gold truly is the most human of metals, yet it also brings
us closest to the gods. As for the smithy, I have had him
beaten on the pretext of some minor offense. If he sur-
vives, his tale will be taken as mere raving.

I have less than a quarter of my given time left here at
Cul Holman, and I am torn between a desire to return to
Rome, and to remain for longer, gathering starstones. This
afternoon, beginning my search, I went out to where the
further mines are being reestablished, and sought the gullies along which the slave girl Alya had led me. But I
could not find any, and I surmise that they were closed
up by the great movements of the earth. That would also
explain why the wind sounds differently now—although
it blows as hot and fierce as ever. Gone is the weird piping: gone, too, I imagine, are those vast ruins to which
Alya took me—or so buried as to be lost forever. For it
became apparent as I wandered deeper into these hills that
the greatest disturbance took place in the far reaches. If
there truly are such things as Virgil's sleeping giants, it
is there that the greatest of them all must lie.

Long have I neglected these writings, and now that I begin
again, it is upon a proper roll of papyrus, with better ink,
and in a better place. Indeed, I have often toyed with the
idea of destroying all that I have written, in view of the
hazard it would present were it to fall into greedier hands.

You find me where all of this began; which was not
Rome or even Cul Holman, it now seems to me, but at
my beloved villa in Naples. Of course, I still think of Cul
Holman. Yet the place seems darker than it does even
within the wilder ramblings of my writings, and its mem-

ory tugs me in strange and uncomfortable ways.

Much of the remaining time since I deserted you there, patient reader, I spent in the pursuit of starstones. I confess I remained aloof from the harsh duties of reviving Cul Holman's fortunes. I kept myself to myself, and ate and walked alone, and glanced but occasionally over my shoulder at the black figure that even here still sometimes seems to follow me. But at the end of it all, I found nothing—not one more stone. Any that remained must have been buried in the sliding and twisting of those hills.

Apart from this seemingly odd pursuit, I did nothing to arouse suspicion at Cul Holman, and changed no more of the stones to their true metal. Nor, save in one instance, did I use them for currency; the idea for which seemed to stay with me oddly. For I confess I went to Kaliphus's palace to purchase the freedom of Alya's family. Kaliphus was his usual self, inquiring about Cul Holman's fate in the earthquake as if his spies had not already informed him. Still, he seemed almost reluctant to accept the excessive amount of gold I offered for the freedom of his slaves—though I had credited him as a man of business, if little else.

Eventually, even as he made the sign I had seen him make before, he took the six heavy discs I offered. And he accepted my explanation that they were but a little of the personal wealth I had brought with me from Rome. In fact, there was an odd gravity about our transaction, as if the exchange were necessary as one small notation in a complex scroll of accounts where some greater total was to be balanced.

As is the way with such arrangements, I left Cul Holman and began my long return journey down the Nile aboard the same craft that had borne my successor there. We barely had time to exchange greetings, and still less for me to pass on the little I have learned about mining for gold. Konchab and Taracus will soon also go to other duties—even Alathn, if he is wise, will seek a re-posting before he runs the fatal risk of becoming indispensable.

The slaves and freemen, of course, will come and go. They live, they die, they breed. Soon, all that happened at Cul Holman in my time there will be but a rumor.

The great papyrus raft that bore me upon the spring flood of the Nile was readied to depart in the blue of evening. Henrika had come with me upon this journey— sadly, he paled and died soon after of a fever—but otherwise I traveled alone. I felt a curious calm as I watched my trunks and belongings being hauled onto the shadowed deck. I had made no attempt to hide my collection of unchanged starstones, and the gold was bound as a thick weight around my chest and belly beneath the folds of my toga. I would also have carried the black-faceted stone upon me, were it not that it caused my flesh to burn and ache. The workmen and mariners seemed mere shadows to me. I felt sure that I was protected.

We pulled out into the black waters as the stars began to shine, and a cool wind, so unlike that which I had long become used to, began to fill the vast red sail. All about me, glowing in the light of a huge rising moon, lay the plains and hills and pillared ruins of upper Egypt, and beyond that the beckoning edge of the desert, and the sense that pervades everything there that the present is but the trembling surface from which the currents of the bottomless past will always rise. I stayed on deck as the ropes wheezed and the sail crackled stiffly and we moved further into the smooth flow in which the whole world seemed upturned in reflection. The air was filled with a strange wailing, and when I looked to the shore, I saw that many of the dark-robed natives had gathered in lines and were making this wavering cry at the passage of my boat. And beyond the palm trees and the villages and the fresh-flooded ditches, where moon and starlight silvered the last edges of the hills before they faded into the desert, I thought I saw also a cluster of other figures. It seemed to me that they were mounted, leading those strange humped creatures called camels, and that they raised their arms in salute before turning toward the desert. Thus, so

I imagine, I saw the passing of Alya, Dahib, and her tribe.

I broke my journey as before at Alexandria whilst passage to Ostia was arranged, and wandered the same streets. Despite the turn in my fortunes, I was curious to renew my brief acquaintance with the alchemist or charlatan known as Zosimus, for it seemed to me now that the walls of his dark room had been adorned with similar shapes and figures to those I had seen elsewhere. But my pursuit along the odd twists and turns of those shadowed and stinking alleys was fruitless, and I was ever afraid, as I looked behind me, that I was being pursued by some bandit. I also sought enlightenment in the moldering library; for it seemed that I recalled a glimpse of star-shapes and strange drawings on forgotten scrolls. There again, I was disappointed—if disappointment is the right word.

Here in my Naples villa, much work has been done in daylight, although time is wasted by the laborers' refusal to dwell here, and I find it hard, even at inflated prices, to obtain and keep any decent quality of slave. Rumor of my wealth, of course, has spread as quickly as these things always do, and now I fear that I am probably the dupe of shoddy dealings. In view of my father's penury, the gossip is that I returned from the far reaches of Empire with a cache of hidden gold, and the story is near enough the truth for it to be fruitless for me to attempt to deny it. There is also a malicious whisper that I stole gold from the mines I was supervising, and I have had to endure a visit from the Emperor's auditors on the strength of it, although there was hardly any charge worth answering. Still, some shadow seems to hang over me, and I have found it harder than I might have imagined to clear my family's name.

Even with the starstones, all is not quite as I had hoped. Although I regretted that I had not found more than the twenty-three I had with me, I had calculated that they would represent a wealth which is more than the equivalent of Cul Holman's produce in a whole year. It was with the joy of a pleasant task long delayed that, at last alone in the privacy of my father's old quarters, I set about transforming them all to gold. All went well to begin with, until I set to work on what would have been in total the tenth starstone. When the black-faceted stone would not even fit the indentation, I imagined some fault in the mechanism and moved onto the next. Yet I tried them all, and in each case it was the same. Thus, I must make do with a total of merely nine golden starstones, more than four of which I have already been forced to exhaust in repaying my father's debts, of which I fear, much like the cracks and strange defects that the builders find here, there are still more to be uncovered. Of course, I would have readily accepted such an outcome when I first set out toward Egypt—by most normal standards I am wealthy—but the feeling remains at the back of my mind that I have somehow been cheated in a bargain I never intended to make.

At first, I made a great show of new riches to my neighbors, patrons, and acquaintances at great feasts at my refurbished high house in Rome. But I found poorer solace in their company than I had even in that of Alathn, Konchab, Taracus, and even Kaliphus. Often, I would gaze down the table at the odd geometries of plates and arms and bodies, breathing the jagged scent of all the food and the flowers that I had ordered, and wonder at the meaningless drone of their voices, and if this truly was eloquence, elegance, civilization.

Here in Naples after the first work on this villa had been done, I summoned my sister and a fair scattering of other guests, including men whom I deemed would make eager suitors now that our family's wealth was no longer in doubt. In truth, though, when I saw her face, sad and long and flat, it seemed to me that the poor creature had grown more sullen than ever. The occasion went as all the others had done, which is to say pointlessly and expensively, as I lay at table and watched the people move and unfold like shadows and tried to catch the buzzing of their words. Like the other occasions, I knew that it would end early, with poor excuses, uneasy laughter, glances back from my departing guests. My sister, almost as bored with it all as I was, must have wandered off between one of the many courses, for suddenly the air from the un-improved passages beyond this villa's newly lighted hall was torn by a blood-chilling shriek. To this day, I do not know what she imagined she saw upon the dais where my father had once sat, and it seems unlikely, in the gibbering incontinent state in which I found her and that to this day she remains in, that she will ever be able to explain what fancy has riven her mind. She dwells now in a place where, if you pay enough, her kind are looked after. There, she is changed and fed like an infant, and her hands are kept bound and bandaged to thwart the attempts she has made to take out her eyes.

Still, I am proud of the way that work has proceeded at this villa, even if it seems I am to be the last in my family's line unless I take the step of adopting an heir. In the daytime, when the sun is brightest and there is less need for the lamps that I otherwise keep about me, I wel-come the sounds and sights of people working, even if the refurbishing of this villa has been a matter of much argument and debate.

These last few days, in fact, following a protracted ar-gument between myself and a foreman about a new win-dow, all work has ceased. It was plain to me that his joinery was out of true, and that whole aspects of the room were finished shoddily at odd degrees. The man and his assistants still had the temerity to claim that all was as it should be; he even produced a rule and set it against the wood and plaster to prove his point, although the thing was clearly as crooked as he was. Thus, and with all my slaves and servants recently gone, I find myself alone.

Naples itself and this coast and countryside have de-clined in the time since my childhood. An ominous black pall hangs over Vesuvius. The air often stinks. The mar-kets are full of cheap goods and sour produce; once fine streets have become rows of hovels and the harbor reeks of dead fish, I sometimes fear that all our Empire may be declining. There are risings of peasants and shepherds in Gaul, usurpations in Britain, German invasions along the Danube and Rhine. There is even talk that Rome may one day cease to be the capital of our Empire—although, despite the strange things I have heard of and seen, that is one outcome I will never believe.

Alone as I find myself in this villa with you, my reader, my last and trusted friend, it might be imagined that I am prey to robbers. Yet only two nights ago, after the leaving of my last few servants, a body was found not far away in the woods. It belonged to a notorious thief, and was roughly beheaded and coated in a foul slime. So it seems to me, my reader, that in some way, I am still protected, although as I wander the deep lanes whilst Vesuvius growls and rumbles and black flakes of its soot drift like snow upon the air, the people shun me and call in their children at my approach, and close the shutters of their homes.

It is near now to the height of another summer. I go out but little anyway, as the lanes are intolerably filled with the sharp stench of strawberries. In truth, now that I could afford to eat and drink whatever trifles I please to, I find that my taste in food has become bland. My previous cook, before he left, made me many loaves of unrisen cornbread which, stale though they are, I had been eating, and, since they ran out, have made do with the dough he left uncooked in his hurry to leave. Even on such poor rations, I fear that I may be gaining some of my father's girth.

Each night, I light as many lanterns as I can—and try to restrain myself from drinking their oil. In the few times that sleep comes upon me, I wish that it had not, for I find myself within the presence of the thing that was once my grandmother again, although it seems to me now that she was always thus—a black assortment of angles—and that the things of which she speaks in that buzzing voice are all that she has ever told me. For I know now, although I would give much of my gold not to, of Nyarlathotep, of Great Cthulhu, and Shub-Niggurath, the black goat of the woods—of beings beyond all darkness.

Last night, I tried to break the spell by speaking back to her.

"What do you want?" I asked—then added a half-remembered phrase that came back to me. "Are you the Golden Keeper?"

She chuckled at that, and the sound thinned and faded into a thousand echoes. "What I keep is not gold. And it is not my task to keep it."

"What can I do?"

"Nothing."

"There must be something—"

"—I give that you may give," she says before her voice trails off into inhuman buzzing. Then she lifts something from within the twisting folds of her robes, although it takes a long time for it to emerge, and her arms are like the tearing and stretching of something ancient and rotten. But I recognize it when she holds it out for me. For the thing is black. Multifaceted.

"Here," she says, and, although the stone is already mine, I reach out to take it.

It shifts within my hand as it begins—segment on unfolding segment, as if from the workings of a hidden mechanism—to open. Something smooth and living slides out from it across my fingers. A shining worm of sorts, mucus-coated and somehow larger than the stone within which it was contained. It is truly ghastly to look at, and I watch in horror as it begins to burrow into my hand.

I opened my eyes then, and the room was filled with a sound that I imagined for a moment was nothing more than my own screaming. I stumbled out from my bed, drawn and repulsed by a mad endless piping as Odysseus must once have been by the sirens who lured sailors to the rocks on these very shores. I stumbled naked along dark swirling corridors, no longer knowing what I was escaping or seeking, until I found myself standing out in the well courtyard beneath a sky lit and blackened by Vesuvius's fitful glow. It seemed to me that the piping here was strong enough to burst my ears, and that I knew at once where it came from. Still possessed by the logic of a dream, I drew back the grating of the well.

Perhaps I truly was dreaming, for there can be no rational meaning to what I saw when I looked down. For a moment, the well seemed truly bottomless, filled with stars. Then there came a liquid click, and a sense of something rising. If I could describe the thing at all, I would say that it was made of bubbling, shifting matter. As to its true shape, it had none—or many; for as it rose toward me with impossible speed, piping and shrieking, I imagined that it re-made itself into a mockery of many forms. I saw dog-headed Anubis, I saw Medusa, bearded Jove, a horned bull, and the livid, bloated face of my father. Then, I stumbled back, swooning in the terrible blast of air. And I remained that way for much of night, crouched shivering by the well as Vesuvius smoked and shook and glowing flakes of ash burned at my flesh, almost urging the thing that I had glimpsed to finish its ascent. Yet nothing happened, and as dawn grew, the piping slowly faded.

I am no longer sure what happened last night; and how much of what I saw was due to some fevered condition, or the effects of sleepwalking. This day, since I could summon no workmen to do the task for me, I have busied myself with laying the grate back over the well, and weighing it down with stone blocks and what pieces of furniture I could manage to drag unaided into the courtyard. It was harsh work, made more difficult by the problems I found in negotiating their shapes around the incredibly odd angles and openings of corridors and doors.

As I look out now, near to sunset as Vesuvius rumbles threateningly and brings early darkness across half the sky, it seems to me that the familiar and beloved landscape of my childhood memories formed by the intersections of sea and hills shifts and breaks like panes of ice upon a lake. But for the fact that they were moving, I would take the figures I can see crossing a distant field to be the limbs of twisted, blackened trees. And earlier, as I rested from the task of dragging a large and recently purchased mirror out into the well courtyard, I saw another odd effect. Leaning against the wall for support as the corridor ahead of me seemed to twist downward, I looked at myself in the polished brass. The mirror's inner surface flared out, and my face, admittedly broader and paler now, became not so much that of my father, as of that terrible distortion of him which I saw coming up from the well. And then began the maddening piping that has been with me ever since.

Now that the sun has set on this dense and windless night, and with the mouth of the well surely covered by enough weight to muffle any sound, the piping grows louder still. Entwined within it is the muttering of some mad incantation that I recognize now comes from my own throat. I hear it speak of the Great Gate of the Stars, and of the living seed that is and always was the Golden Keeper.

The shrieking now is incredibly loud—triumphant, even, as the ground shakes beneath me and the walls begin to shift. Perhaps, after all the years of threats and mutterings since the time of Herculaneum and Pompeii, Vesuvius is preparing to erupt. No doubt, if that is all this is, the women will be wailing, offering the blood of lambs on the hot smoking slopes above their dwellings. But to me, it all seems far closer than that. Closer even than the well or even the sliding walls of this room. I feel a stronger presence, as if the very ground beneath me were about to crack.

My head swirls so much with this chaos, dearest reader, that I fear you and I must soon part, for I can barely write these words. Stopping my ears does nothing but increase the terrible sound, this sense of something within me rising. I would also bind my eyes, were it not for what I see in the greater dark, which is now so vivid that I can scarcely bear to blink. I would but speak to you now, reader, but each breath is agony, and with the parting of my lips the piping grows yet wilder and guttural words spill out. I tried to call upon Vesta, protector of households, that strong and humble symbol of goodness and light. But the sound came out as mad shrieking, and I could barely close my jaw as my chin was jerked back and my throat widened on a stream of darkness and foul air. Even now, with my chin tightly bound and my mouth filled with the gold discs and papyrus that are all I now have about me, the sound grows in power.

I will wait for what this night brings me, and distract myself meanwhile by ordering these scraps of my writing before they are spoiled by the dark fluid that now bubbles from my lips. Perhaps my father was right, and I will never understand the meaning of the rituals I have been performing, nor yet the purpose of the Golden Keeper. Perhaps our lives really are without purpose. But, in that, at least, I fear that I may yet prove him wrong. Meanwhile go in peace, reader, and know that I am Fabius Lucius Maximus, a trained accountant of high Roman blood who has done service to the Empire in both Egypt and Sicily. Truly, I am a murderer also, and I fear that I have treated many of those I came across harshly. But all I ever wished for was decency and comfort. I trust that, after all we have shared, you will understand all of this, gentle reader, and strive not to condemn me.

All stories originally appeared in *Asimov's Science Fiction*.

Asimov's Science Fiction is published by Dell Magazines, a division of Crosstown Publications.

Explore *Asimov's Science Fiction* on the World Wide Web at
http://www.asimovs.com